PRAISE FOR MOLLY HARPER'S WITTY PARANORMAL NOVELS

"Harper writes characters you
can't help but fall in love with."
—*RT Book Reviews*

The Nice Girls series

"Makes me laugh and laugh."
—*USA Today*

The Naked Werewolf series

"Comedic entertainment at its best."
—*Single Titles*

A WITCH'S HANDBOOK OF KISSES AND CURSES
RT Book Reviews **TOP PICK!**

"Harper serves up plenty of hilarity. . . . Fans will be thrilled by this return to the hysterical world of Jane and crew."

—*Publishers Weekly*

"With her distinct, captivating style, Harper hits it out of the park. . . . This reviewer has come to depend on the clever wit and heart that comes with Harper's books, and I'm happy to report that the last page was turned with a contented sigh."

—*RT Book Reviews* (4½ stars)

THE CARE AND FEEDING OF STRAY VAMPIRES
RT Book Reviews **TOP PICK!**

"A perfect combination of smarts and entertainment with a dash of romance. . . . Harper has found a place at the top of my 'must buy' list."

—*RT Book Reviews* (4½ stars)

"Harper's feel-good novel is great beach reading, filled with clever humor, snark, silliness, and endearing protagonists."

—*Booklist*

NICE GIRLS DON'T BITE THEIR NEIGHBORS

"Harper serves up a terrific fourth dose of vamp camp. . . . The stellar supporting characters, laugh-out-loud moments, and outrageous plot twists will leave readers absolutely satisfied."

—*Publishers Weekly* (starred review)

"Molly Harper is the queen of side-splitting quips. . . . Hilariously original with imaginative adventures and one-of-a-kind characters."

—*Single Titles*

THE ART OF SEDUCING A NAKED WEREWOLF

"Harper's gift for character building and crafting a smart, exciting story is showcased well."

—*RT Book Reviews* (4 stars)

"The characters are appealing and the plot is intriguingly original."

—*Single Titles*

HOW TO FLIRT WITH A NAKED WEREWOLF
RT Book Reviews TOP PICK!

"A rollicking, sweet novel that made me laugh aloud. . . . Mo's wise-cracking, hilarious voice makes this novel such a pleasure to read."

—*New York Times* bestselling author Eloisa James

"A light, fun, easy read, perfect for lazy days."

—*New York Journal of Books*

BOOKS BY MOLLY HARPER

In the land of Half-Moon Hollow

Nice Girls Don't Have Fangs
Nice Girls Don't Date Dead Men
Nice Girls Don't Live Forever
Nice Girls Don't Bite Their Neighbors
Driving Mr. Dead
The Care and Feeding of Stray Vampires
A Witch's Handbook of Kisses and Curses
"Undead Sublet" in *The Undead in My Bed*

The Naked Werewolf series

How to Flirt with a Naked Werewolf
The Art of Seducing a Naked Werewolf
How to Run with a Naked Werewolf

The Bluegrass series

My Bluegrass Baby
Rhythm and Bluegrass

Also

And One Last Thing . . .

Available from Pocket Books

Better Homes and Hauntings

MOLLY HARPER

Pocket Books

New York London Toronto Sydney New Delhi

Pocket Books
A Division of Simon & Schuster, Inc.
1230 Avenue of the Americas
New York, NY 10020

Copyright © 2014 by Molly Harper White

First Pocket Books paperback edition July 2014

For information about special discounts for bulk purchases, please contact Simon & Schuster Special Sales at 1-866-506-1949 or business@simonandschuster.com.

The Simon & Schuster Speakers Bureau can bring authors to your live event. For more information or to book an event, contact the Simon & Schuster Speakers Bureau at 1-866-248-3049 or visit our website at www.simonspeakers.com.

Interior design by Yvonne Chan
Cover photograph and design by Patrick Kang

Manufactured in the United States of America

10 9 8 7 6 5 4 3 2 1

ISBN 978-1-4767-0600-9
ISBN 978-1-4767-0603-0 (ebook)

*For Melissa Boldry, Brenda Metzger, Iris Garrott,
and youth librarians everywhere who maintain
the paranormal nonfiction sections and keep
kids like me entertained and inspired*

Acknowledgments

THANK YOU, as always, to my ever-patient agent, Stephany Evans. And to my lovely, possum-obsessed editor, Abby Zidle: thanks for letting me try something different. There were so many revisions to this manuscript, and you both stuck by me, without saying "I told you so" once. That alone puts you in the running for publication sainthood.

Thank you to my mother, Judy Harper, who let me watch an inordinate amount of *Scooby-Doo* as a child, which led to my lifelong obsession with haunted houses. And to all of the school librarians who put up with me repeatedly checking out the nonfiction "Mysteries of the Paranormal" type books over the years: I was not a normal little girl. Thanks for never holding it against me.

To my critique partner/life-support system, Jeanette Battista: thank you for all of your time, patience, and honesty. Ruthless, ruthless honesty. To Liliana Hart, Heather Osborn, Nicole Peeler, and Jaye Wells, my beloved S-Sisters: you all inspire me, so you only have yourselves to blame.

Ignoring the Frantically Waving Red Flags

BEWARE ALL ENTERPRISES that start with the purchase of Crocs.

Nina Linden glared down at the bright orange clogs protecting her from slipping on the deck of the S.S. *Sine Waves* and, for the third time that morning, cursed her assistant's poor choice in boating shoes. Too wrapped up in the details of the Whitney project for shopping, Nina had told Carrie she needed something safe to wear when ferrying back and forth between Narragansett, Rhode Island, and Whitney Island, something that wouldn't be ruined by traipsing through the gardens she was responsible for resuscitating. Nina should have been more specific. She should have said, *No foam-rubber shoes in radioactive colors that make me walk like a hobbled duck.*

But considering that she was barely able to pay Carrie—who was a competent and loyal assistant in all areas save fashion sense—Nina knew she shouldn't complain. The shoes, while unfortunate, were not what she needed to focus on right now. She needed to pull herself out of her negative funk. This was the start of a new phase in her life. Demeter Designs would be a going concern. Hell, it would be a sought-after service among the ridiculously rich. All she had to do was survive the next three months.

Nina leaned her forehead against the sun-warmed teak railing of the perfectly lovely yacht used to ferry the renovation staff back and forth to Whitney Island, a small spit of land twenty miles southeast of Newport.

Nina had been through so much worse than seasickness in the past year. Near-bankruptcy. Identity theft. Stolen garden tools. This was going to be an adventure, she promised herself. She'd played it too safe with Rick, and it had cost her. She needed this time away. She needed to clear her head.

The other passengers seemed nice enough. They'd all boarded the Whitney yacht at the same time, and of course, Nina had immediately managed to whack the GQ cover model running the boat in the shin with her rolling suitcase. Instead of getting annoyed, he'd simply offered her a brilliant white smile and taken her bag in addition to his own.

The other woman on board, a sweet-faced blonde who might have doubled for a fairy-tale princess if not for her Jessica Rabbit figure, was clearly at home on the rocking, creaking vessel. The minute she'd stowed her bags, she'd slipped on her sunglasses, slipped off her shoes, and begun sunning herself on the deck on top of the tiny cabin. For a moment, Nina thought she was the girlfriend of their benefactor, but then she realized how unlikely it was that social-media magnate Deacon Whitney would have let his girlfriend make the crossing with "the help." Nina wasn't exactly sure what the other woman's role was to be in this . . . mission of theirs.

Twenty-eight and so upwardly mobile he practically had his own galaxy, Mr. Whitney was the sole programmer/creator of EyeDee, a social-networking site with nearly one billion users that had changed the face of online interactions. Users could "EyeContact" anyone from former high school classmates to childhood friends to—heaven forbid—their parents and share every waking moment of their lives. Whitney had launched the site just after graduating from New York University, eventually parlaying a public offering of his company's stock into one of the largest personal fortunes in the United States. He was now using that fortune to restore his family's dilapidated Gilded Age mansion to its former glory, using the team now assembled on the yacht.

Nina knew she should walk over and say hello to the others. They were going to be working and living together on the Crane's Nest property over the next few months, until the renovations were finished. But at the moment, she could only concentrate on keeping her breakfast down.

The boat hit a particularly rough wake, pitching Nina back against the cabin. She moaned, bending at the knees and propping her arms against her thighs.

A smooth, tanned hand appeared at the corner of Nina's vision, bearing brightly wrapped candies. She startled, drawing up to her full height, and swayed. The other hand steadied her at the elbow. "Whoa, there," he said, a laughing lilt to his soothing tone.

"Sorry about that." Nina groaned, squinting up at the owner of the outstretched hand.

"Seasick, huh?" he said, eyeing her sympathetically over the rims of his mirrored aviators.

"Ever since I was a kid," she said, glaring at the water glittering in the distance. "I ruined every family fishing trip. My brother always told me it would help to keep my eye on the horizon. But I think my brother is a dirty liar."

"Try these," he said, pressing a few foil-wrapped candies into her clammy palm. "Ginger drops. They'll help your stomach. And as far as the horizon goes, I think it's better to concentrate on more immediate surroundings."

Unwrapping the candy, Nina followed his line of sight to the blonde's long, tanned legs and rolled her eyes. Of course, he was eyeing the pretty blonde. He was practically a work of preppy art himself. Perfectly mussed sandy hair, bright blue-green eyes twinkling out over the aforementioned aviators. Pressed khakis, a light purple madras under a navy sport coat. He was fit and tan and managed to pull off the "lavender shirt" thing without seeming effeminate.

Well, not *terribly* effeminate. Definitely metrosexual.

Watching his eyes trace the line of the blonde's ankles, Nina subconsciously rubbed a hand over the bridge of her nose, which tended to burn if she wasn't religious with the sunscreen—the price of being a redhead. Typical, she thought wryly: the blonde got ogled, and she got treated like a kid sister.

The man's lips quirked a bit when he realized Nina had caught him looking. "Jake Rumson," he said, offering his hand. "Amateur yachtsman and chief architect who's supposed to be undoing the mess we're getting into."

"Nina," she said. "Linden."

"Like the tree," he said, smiling. "You're with Demeter Designs."

"Like the tree, exactly," she said, a genuine grin breaking through her uneasy expression. She tamped it down quickly. "Not everybody catches that."

"I cheated," Jake whispered, the smooth façade melting a bit to reveal a naughty-schoolboy smile. "I got a look at Whit's staff list ahead of time. You're the landscape architect, and you're named after a tree, and *bam*, instant mnemonic device."

"Do you use little tricks like that often?" she asked.

"You're reducing my famous charm to parlor tricks? That's harsh," Jake teased, elbowing her in the ribs.

Months before, this sort of casual contact, particularly from a man she didn't know, would have made Nina edgy and uncomfortable. She was proud that she'd progressed enough that her only response was a faint blush.

"Well, what do you know about Cindy Ellis, over there?" he asked. "She owns the Cinderella Cleaning Service."

"Never heard of her." Nina lifted her brow. "She's a maid?" Whitney's extensive service contract hadn't mentioned anything about providing maid service.

"Not exactly. Ms. Ellis—as she insists I call her—runs a sort of maid-slash-organizational-guru service. She cleans and installs those crazy storage systems in some of the swankiest family-owned estates in Rhode Island. Families who own places like that are always circulating collections of antique furnishings, Christmas decorations, that sort of thing. Ms. Ellis can organize, store, and reset those furnishings on a seasonal system that even the dumbest millionaire could figure out."

"Are you saying we're working for a dumb millionaire?" Nina asked, the corners of her lush mouth tilting up.

Jake snorted, grinning at her over the rims of his aviators. "First of all, Whit's a billionaire. And second, it wasn't his idea to hire her. The Crane's Nest has been virtually looted by various generations of Whitneys over the years, but there are bound to be a few valuables tucked away where the relatives' enterprising little paws couldn't reach. The family is demanding that Whit catalogue every item of historical or monetary value and save it so that they can do battle over them later."

Nina frowned. "But it's Mr. Whitney's house."

"House, yes. Furnishings, no. And Whit's too decent of a guy to follow my advice, which involved letters from attorneys and a lot of four-letter words."

Nina giggled but covered it with a cough. Despite his slick exterior, Nina believed she was going to like Jake—or at least, his ability to make her forget how miserable she was for a moment. If nothing else, he was sharing insider information about their mysterious employer, a precious commodity in this harebrained scheme she'd signed on for—living full-time on the job site for an open-ended period of time with people she barely knew.

Mr. Whitney had informed Nina during her interview that he wanted to be each contractor's full-time first priority until the job was completed, that he wanted to reduce opportunities for the contractors to be distracted by other clients' demands. But according to two contractors Nina had overheard in Whitney's waiting room, his chief concern was the fact that there had already been several false starts to the renovations. He'd previously lost contractors and workers to "frayed nerves," courtesy of angry thumping footsteps on the stairway between the second and third floors, strange shifting shadows that darted around at the corners of one's eyes, the overwhelming sense that someone was watching. The upstairs bedrooms smelled of rose water when no one had sprayed perfume there in decades. And of course, there was the sound of weeping that came from the widow's walk. Keeping the restorers from returning home every night was supposed to prevent them from losing their nerve to come back to the island in the morning. Not to mention that it would save them the lengthy water commute.

Nina cleared her throat, trying to find an innocuous reason for the staff to be sequestered. "Would Mr. Whitney's shaky relationship with his extended family have anything to do with our being hidden away on the island for the summer? I know I wouldn't want to take the chance that one of us could be persuaded to sneak stuff back to the mainland."

"No, but that's just one more pro for the list," Jake said brightly, offering her his most charming grin. "Whit wants to finish the project as quickly as possible, and the best way to do that is to have your full attention and have the team stay within shouting distance in case there are problems."

Nina arched a sleek red brow. "That sounded like a well-rehearsed statement."

Jake's smile stayed resolutely in place, as if he hadn't heard her.

Nina asked, "Why do you call him 'Whit'?"

Jake leaned against the cabin, copying her posture. "Our moms were close friends at college, so we've known each other since we were in diapers. Even when we were kids, you could tell he had something the rest of us didn't, that spark of genius that meant he was either going to be a CEO or a supervillain. And in a very conservative prep school that valued conformity and had the resources to guarantee a certain 'aesthetic standard,' a scrawny, six-foot-three freshman who loved comics and D and D stood out. I had an easier time of it, but 'Deke the Geek' was bullied like it was his job. Instead of getting all bitter about it, he was still the most decent person I knew. Hell, when my parents refused to believe that a Rumson could have something as pedestrian as ADHD—despite an official diagnosis from people who actually went to medical school—it was Whit who figured out tricks to help me focus and study. I probably wouldn't have graduated from high school, much less college, without his helping me. So I helped him avoid being tossed into Dumpsters whenever possible and came up with a nickname that didn't remind him of the assholes we called classmates."

Yes, Nina was going to like Jake Rumson— potentially douchey prep vibe and all.

"You OK there?" Cindy asked, sliding off her perch to fetch Nina a bottle of water from a pretty polished metal cooler. She eyed Jake suspiciously.

"Barely containing my vomit," Nina said with a sigh. Cindy's brow furrowed. "Is . . . that 'OK' for you?"

"It's normal for me," Nina said, extending her hand for a shake. "Nina Linden."

"Cindy Ellis. Nice to meet you," she said, giving Jake one last warning look before ducking back around the corner of the cabin and into the galley.

"Somebody's got a friend already," Jake singsonged, wriggling his eyebrows at her.

"She just feels bad for me."

Jake shook his head. "Nope, I have a sense for this sort of thing, Nina Linden, and you are a lady who draws people to her, like moths to a sassy but vulnerable flame. I'll bet Deacon will fall all over himself when he sees you. I should warn you. He makes random *Star Wars* references when he's nervous. So expect a lot of Lando Calrissian jokes."

"Yes, who could resist the pasty-green girl who looks like she's on the verge of puking?" Nina pushed her windblown mess of thick auburn hair out of her face.

"Some guys are into the *Exorcist* look," he said, shrugging.

She let out an indignant grunt—half laugh, half gasp—and slapped at his shoulder.

"See? You're feeling better already," Jake said. "Hitting me with the force of a toddler must have required some energy— Ow!" He yelped as she whacked him again, with significantly more strength. He chuckled as a bit of color crept back into her cheeks. "You'll be all right." He nodded to the horizon line again. "And here is your first introduction to the lady herself."

Once the playground where the indecently rich escaped the heat and "vapors" of the big cities each summer, Newport was now a respectable tourist destination. The upper class still retreated to their private clubs and the middle class toured monuments to excess built by families such as the Vanderbilts and the Astors. During the so-called Gilded Age, mansions like the Breakers and Miramar set new standards in architectural extravagance, while the ever-so-*riche* matrons fought for dominance of the social scene. At the tail end of this era, Gerald Whitney had chosen to separate himself even further by building his home on his own private island.

Long before the Whitneys were a wealthy family, Gerald Whitney's great-great-great-grandfather Loudon was a simple sailor who ferried people around the bays surrounding Rhode Island. Eventually, those little bays and inlets became very important to the Revolutionary War effort. Loudon volunteered his services and his growing fleet of boats to get the Colonial troops where they were most needed, all along the seaboard. His assistance was instrumental in winning some of those first early skirmishes. Loudon invested more and more into the boats as time went by and continued to allow the Colonials to use them. He was rewarded handsomely and made friends among the earliest politicians. He made a particular friend of the governor of Rhode Island when he managed to get the governor's son to a doctor after he was wounded in battle. The governor showed his appreciation by rewarding him in the way of the old country, with land grants. Of course, at the time, the island was virtually useless. Who would want to live on a tiny spit of land twenty miles off the mainland? But old Mr. Whitney thanked the governor profusely and held on to it. Gerald Whitney was the first to make any use of it.

As for the house itself, the Crane's Nest rose out of the water like a drowned debutante, her fine lines eroded and obscured, tangling into the overgrown green expanse of Whitney Island. Nina could see evidence of what had once been an exacting geometric landscaping plan leading up to a rounded porte cochere, hiding the massive front doors in its dark, cavernous maw. The gardens were long past feral, with dry, withered grass strangling the remains of statuary and rosebushes. The façade consisted of three levels, a loggia flanked by two-story wings leading into the main structure. Rows of windows stared back at her with the blank sheen of dolls' eyes. A ring of tall chimneys crowned a flat slate roof, echoing the pattern of blunt cornices extending from the porte cochere.

Despite the warm, sunny afternoon, there was an air of melancholy to the house, and not just in the overall state of disrepair and decay. The patina of age and grime over the battered gray limestone seemed like a black mark on the house's soul, a warning to passersby to move along. Contentment and happiness were not to be found in the Crane's Nest.

The photos that had been provided for Nina's bid hadn't prepared her for the sheer size of the building. It felt as if the house could tumble down the sloping yard and swallow their little boat at any moment. All the more reason for Nina to want to disembark as quickly as possible.

As they drew near shore, Jake ducked behind the helm and started making adjustments to the boat's trajectory, calling out an occasional request to Cindy to pull a line or tighten a sail. With Nina out of commission and no other sailors aboard, Cindy's reluctant, untrained help was the best Jake could get. The boat jolted with a splash and made a slow turn, causing Nina to groan.

She couldn't help but feel as if they were intruding, their arrival disrupting the house's slumber. The Crane's Nest had stood for nearly one hundred years, untouched and uninhabited. And now Nina felt as if she'd wandered into a church full of people to ask directions, only to realize she'd interrupted a wake.

Nina felt Cindy approach from her right, staring up at the decrepit mansion.

"Just a little cottage built for two," Cindy mused, sliding her cat's-eye sunglasses up through her thick mane of curls. "Complete with twelve bedrooms, a formal dining room, and an evil spirit in the basement that wants to eat your soul, if the urban-legend Web sites I read are to be believed. I mean, who wouldn't want this gem for their weekend place?"

"I don't think the Whitneys were known for their subtlety," Nina said, trying to focus on anything but the quivering tumble of her stomach.

"You realize that as the blonde, I'm probably going to be picked off first," Cindy muttered.

"Picked off?" Nina asked.

"Did you not hear me mention the soul-eating ghoul in the basement?" Cindy teased. "In the movies, the blonde always gets killed first, to establish the rules on Certain Death Island, such as 'Don't wander off on your own to go to the bathroom' and 'It's not a great idea to wear a negligee to investigate spooky noises armed only with a flickering candle.'"

"But you could be a postmodern blonde," Nina suggested. "You could be Buffy or Naomi Watts in *The Ring*. They were always the last girls standing."

"Oh, we're going to get along just fine, hon," Cindy told her, patting her shoulder. "You get extra cool points for any Jossverse reference."

"Well, that's a relief." Squinting in the glaring afternoon light, Nina traced the line of the roof with her eyes, admiring the wrought-iron railing that enclosed the widow's walk. There was potential for a terrace garden there, from what she'd seen in the pictures. She was trying to estimate the roof's square footage when a dark feminine figure stepped up to the wrought-iron boundary. Nina gasped. A cold wave of nausea washed through her as the dark shape seemed to stare down at the approaching boat. For a moment, Nina thought she could make out the lines of an old-fashioned gown, a slim waist, dark twists of long hair blowing in the wind. But there was no detail to the face or form, only shadow. Nina shivered and braced herself against the bow, taking deep breaths. When she looked up at the roof again, the figure was gone.

"Is it always this quiet?" Cindy asked, surveying the island with a worried expression.

"Yes," Jake called from behind the wheel. "The Crane's Nest is the only home on the island. So, no crazy neighbors or barking dogs to keep you up at night. Don't worry, though. We'll make some noise soon enough," he told her. Cindy's delft-blue eyes narrowed at the suggestion, and Jake's cheeks flushed. "I meant with construction equipment and workers! Hammering, nailing . . . oh, good God, there is no recovery from this, is there?"

He looked to Nina for help, but the sudden deceleration of the boat plus the possible hallucinations of shadowy figures had finally tipped the scales in her battle with nausea. She was currently bent over the rail, saying good-bye to her breakfast.

Cindy rushed over to Nina, whipped a blue bandanna from her pocket, soaked it with Nina's water bottle, and held it to the back of the ailing redhead's neck. She looked to Jake, who surveyed the scene with a horrified expression. "What did you do?" she hissed at him.

"I didn't do that to her. Poor inner ear dynamics did that to her."

"Well, you must have done something! I know I've wanted to throw up since boarding this boat with you."

"Me? What did I do?"

Cindy exclaimed, "You're you. That's all it takes!"

Oddly hurt, Jake turned on his heel and devoted his attention to running the boat. "Well, it can only get better from here."

Orientation for Residents of Spooky Island

EACH OF THEM handled the stress of officially landing on Whitney Island in a different way. Cindy was organizing the pile of luggage and boxes stacked near the defunct fountain just short of the sparsely graveled drive. Nina sat on a stone bench with her head between her knees. Jake was wandering around the lawn, trying to find cell-phone reception, although Nina suspected he was just trying to distract himself from staring up at the house. Every time he looked up at the huge structure, a *What have I gotten myself into / I want my mommy* expression fell across his boyishly handsome face.

Nina had no desire to look at the house, either. Had she imagined the dark figure on the roof? Had the atmosphere, combined with the house's reputation, created some sort of surreal illusion? She wasn't one for flights of fancy . . . but it had seemed so real. Mr. Whitney said that they would be the only people present on the island full-time, but maybe he'd hired cooking staff or had his own administrative staff from his office there to make way for the renovators. Did administrative personnel wear old-fashioned gowns with tiny wasp waists?

Every local knew the story of the Crane's Nest and the tragic death of its mistress. Nina had grown up on the outskirts of Newport, and it was an urban legend among the local kids. Townies like Nina, who spent summers on the less picturesque stretches of beach trying to avoid summer people, grew up hearing tales of the wailing ghost of Catherine Whitney wandering the halls of the Crane's Nest, searching for her killer, her lost treasure, a hidden illegitimate baby . . . the details tended to change depending on who was telling the story. It was a common dare among the high school set to sail to Whitney Island and spend the night at the house. Very few kids managed to make it as far as the island's dock without getting spooked and speeding back to the mainland. This led to a rumor that the island was cursed, that no boat would moor on it. Nina had lived in Newport for most of her life, and this was the first time she'd ever laid eyes on the place.

So it was only natural that her fertile imagination, after she'd grown up on these stories, would bring the tortured ghost of Catherine Whitney to life. Right?

Nina rubbed her hands over her face. She had to get a grip. The Crane's Nest job would be the crown jewel of her portfolio. Impressing Deacon Whitney would help her gain entrée into the eastern seaboard's most exclusive circles and the rich potential clients therein. She would build her business. She would rebuild her life and her credit rating from the ground up. She would stop imagining scary shadow people on the roof.

"Feeling better now that you're on solid ground?" Jake asked, pressing a cold soda can into her hand.

She accepted it gratefully and guzzled the better part of the bubbly elixir before answering. "Much, thanks," she said, glancing over shoulder again toward the still-uninhabited roof. "I swear, I'm not this high-maintenance on dry land."

"Hey, you're the first girl to throw up on that boat for reasons unrelated to alcohol. That sets you in a class all your own," Jake assured her.

"That's not particularly flattering," she mused. "Jake, you said we were the only people on the island. Surely, Mr. Whitney sent a prep team ahead of us to clean the staff quarters or stock the kitchen."

Jake shrugged. "Cindy's crew came out to clean up the dorms for us. And the catering staff from Whit's office stocked the kitchen. But they haven't been here since yesterday. Why do you ask?"

Nina chuckled weakly, sorry now that she'd said anything. "It's just silly. I thought I saw someone on the roof, right before I got sick."

Jake smiled at her, but there was a hitch to the expression, a hesitation that made Nina curious. "We're the only ones here, I promise. There's nobody else. What you saw? It was probably just a trick of light."

Nina observed that tricks of light rarely wore hoop-skirts, but she thought better of saying that out loud. Before she could come up with a more suitable response, a chopping noise in the distance caught their

attention. A tiny black dot in the sky grew closer and
closer, the sound of propeller blades beating a regular rhythm against the wind. The unmarked helicopter landed about forty yards to their left, flattening a
patch of perfectly nice purple gypsy flowers into the
dirt. Nina winced at the sight. She doubted the delicate
stems would recover from that.

Oblivious to Nina's botanical distress, Jake helped her
to her feet. "That's Whit!" he shouted over the noise,
that happy grin brightening his face again.

The helicopter landed nimbly on the shaggy, but
level, patch of grass. A slim, long-legged man in jeans
and a blue Oxford shirt emerged from the helicopter.
He slapped the helicopter door twice, prompting the
pilot to take off. As the wind whipped his Oxford aside,
Nina caught a glimpse of Captain America's shield underneath.

Deacon Whitney ran a billion-dollar company, and
he still wore comic-book-hero T-shirts. That was sort
of adorable.

As the helicopter and its hair-wrecking winds disappeared into the horizon, she did her best to straighten
her mussed clothes and look presentable. She took one
last breath-freshening sip of her soda and stepped forward to greet the man who would save her financial
future.

Deacon Whitney was all long, lean limbs and angular
lines, with high, sharp cheekbones and a jawline most
matinee idols would sell their mothers for. But his hair
was a shaggy, curling mess of light brown and combined
with his rumpled business-casual clothes to complete
the disgraced-aristocrat look. Much as he had when

they'd first met at his corporate offices, Deacon gave Nina the immediate impression of being uncomfortable with his surroundings. He'd covered it quickly enough, with no-nonsense eye contact and firm handshakes all around, but Nina recognized the look of someone who was stressed and burdened. She'd seen it in the mirror every morning for months.

Despite the kindred twinge she felt for another neurotic, she was determined to stay as far away as possible from Deacon Whitney. She'd had more than her fair share of men whose money made the world go 'round. Nina had no interest in falling prey to that brand of man again, even if it came wrapped up in a yummy geek-chic package.

Jake stepped close and whispered something in Deacon's ear. Deacon frowned and glanced at Nina. Suddenly self-conscious, she combed her fingers through her hair. "Excuse me for just a second," Deacon said.

Leaving the ladies to their own devices, Deacon and Jake wandered down the lawn a bit, deep in discussion. Deacon seemed unhappy, glancing over at Nina and then at the house, shaking his head. Jake shrugged and, judging from the smirk on his face, had just made some completely inappropriate comment. Deacon rolled his eyes skyward, as if asking heaven why he'd been saddled with this man as his friend. Deacon's expression of exasperation was too well-practiced. And Jake was too good at blithely ignoring it.

Jake poked Deacon's shoulder, making Deacon roll his eyes again. So Jake nudged a second time, shoving him toward Cindy and Nina. Deacon reluctantly joined the group.

"Jake just reminded me that 'nice, nondouchebag employers' greet people by name and make some effort to be sociable," Deacon said, blushing slightly. "So hello, I'm Deacon Whitney, owner of this very large pile of bricks. Please excuse the dramatic entrance, but I've never been fond of boats."

Nina would have liked to have known about the nonboat option. But perhaps there was no nonboat option for nonbillionaires.

"I chose each of you, not because you're the biggest names in your fields but because you presented the most original ideas, and I was excited to see what you would do with the place."

"Not me," Jake interjected cheerfully. "I was chosen because of *nepotism*."

Deacon sighed and continued on as if Jake hadn't spoken. "So, thank you for joining me here this summer and giving me your full time and attention during what I'm sure is your busy season. I promise the project will be worth your while. If you have any questions or concerns, don't be afraid to come to me or Jake, here. And if you will follow me, we can get settled into the staff quarters."

Nina had expected Whitney to take them toward the main house, where they would bunk in abandoned guest rooms. But he led the group down an overgrown pebbled path around the main house to a series of low-slung bungalow structures flanking the coach house and the stables.

"The original mistress of the house, Catherine Whitney, ordered the architect to build separate staff residences," Cindy whispered as they trudged past the jagged remains of the greenhouses. "Even though the other cutthroat—but ever so elegant—Gilded Age ladies kept their servants close in case they had some urgent need for warm milk at midnight."

"So why did Catherine have them built so far away?" Nina whispered back.

"Catherine wanted the servants to feel that they had a home with privacy and peace, to foster a neighborly camaraderie among the staff. She figured happier servants made for a happier household. She came from a family with just one servant, and in that kind of household, the servant was just like part of the family. I guess she was a bit more sympathetic to the plight of people living 'belowstairs.'" Cindy lowered her voice even further. "Also, a less savory suggestion has been made that Mr. Whitney hadn't wanted the servants to hear what he did to his wife at night."

"I grew up around here, and this is the first time I'm hearing any of this," Nina said quietly. She looked over her shoulder to see Deacon watching her while Jake chattered about imported tile. Just as her brain managed to communicate the *Smile like a normal person!* message to her face, he looked away, to the tablet Jake was shoving in his face.

"A friend of mine oversees the special-collections room at the local public library," Cindy said, a little dimple winking at the corner of her mouth. "She may have let me borrow some newspaper and microfiche materials not available to the general public. Plus, there are a few interesting history books on Newport's mansions if you know where to look."

So the bombshell was a closet bookworm, Nina

mused. She didn't know whether that made Cindy less intimidating or more so. But since they were going to be neighbors for the foreseeable future, Nina was determined to find this unexpected aspect of Cindy's personality charming and useful.

CYNTHIA ELLIS HAD been born to a proud family of restaurateurs. Her late father had owned one of the most famous clam shacks in Rhode Island, Jimmy's. She'd worked there every summer and every school afternoon that her dad would allow, with his admonishment that studies always came first. She'd loved the hustle and bustle of the dining room, chatting with the regulars as she served up fresh clam fritters and lobster rolls. She'd loved the routine of it all, even if that routine was occasionally interrupted by the odd "handsy" summer renter—who would be promptly treated to either a smack of her tray or harsher justice from a nearby regular, none of whom tolerated rudeness toward the waitresses.

With the passing of her mother, Cindy had become the lady of her house at an early age. She'd learned to enjoy bringing order to the chaos, whether it was Jimmy's dining room or the junk drawer in their house, which received a thorough weekly sorting. Although he'd known he would miss her, Jim Ellis had looked forward to the day she left for college and her chore list was reduced to classwork and turning down dates with unworthy boys.

But just as Cindy was graduating from high school, her dad had developed a cough he just couldn't shake. When the cough turned out to be late-stage lung cancer, Cindy had deferred college so she could see her father through chemotherapy and make sure the restaurant stayed open, even if the medical bills left them far past bankrupt. By the time he passed, Cindy had been working full-time for three years. College had seemed like a moot point. While she'd loved the restaurant, it was a painful reminder of what she'd lost, and she'd been happy to sell it off to a waitress who expressed interest and had the cash. She'd used the money left over from settling her dad's debts to start the Cinderella Cleaning Service.

She'd started cleaning inns and B&Bs, working her way up the food chain. Her big break had come when Martha Stark's rotten teenage son threw a wild party, wrecking several luxurious rooms of her mansion on Cove Road while Martha was out of town for the weekend. Normally, Martha would have deferred to her own housekeeper for such a (regular) occurrence. But Martha was due to host her anniversary party in just a few days, and poor Esther couldn't handle the cleanup *and* the party prep.

Cindy thought her father would be proud of what she'd built, her own operation, with her own staff and the pleasure of assessing each challenge as it came along to determine how she could use it as a way to grow. Even if those problems currently included a slightly eccentric boss, an annoying male coworker, and what appeared to be an enormous *Scooby-Doo* set just waiting to launch spooks at her.

Nina seemed to be intentionally lagging behind to put a bit more space between the men and Cindy and herself. Cindy allowed the delay. Everything about Nina

Linden read *nervous and fragile*, and Cindy doubted it had much to do with lingering seasickness. Oh, sure, Nina was beautiful, in that earthy, natural, *the only makeup I wear is ChapStick* kind of way. But between the dark circles under her eyes and the way she held her arms around her middle, as if she was trying to hold herself together, the lady was clearly exhausted. She acted as if she was about to file a restraining order against her shadow. And since the two of them would be sharing space for the immediate future, Cindy just couldn't have that.

"Was there something you wanted to ask me, sweetie?" she inquired. "Something about the dorms? They're safe, I promise."

"No, that's not it," Nina said. "I was just wondering, did you read anything about Catherine's . . ."

Cindy made an indelicate choking noise as she mimed being strangled. Nina frowned but nodded.

"About as much as you probably heard around the campfire when we were kids," Cindy whispered. "A much-celebrated society wife flees her older husband's palatial, recently completed summer retreat in 1900, only to be found the next morning floating in the bay not two hundred yards from her front door. She had suspicious bruises around her throat. There were a lot of whispers about the Whitneys' marriage before the murder, and Mrs. Whitney's spending so much time with the handsome young architect who designed their house didn't help matters. The husband, Gerald, was immediately suspected and put through the indignity of being questioned by the police, but they either couldn't or wouldn't charge him with her murder.

Gerald never recovered from the ordeal. The loss of his entire fortune in a series of bad investments sent him into a downward spiral, health-wise. He died in 1903, and their children, Josephine and Junior, were sent to live with relatives. With the debts, the estate was a legal mess. The house was left fully furnished, clothes in closets, objets d'art still on the shelves, everything. The family never managed to recover their reputation or fortune. The house was abandoned, fell into disrepair, and here we are."

Nina stared at her, hazel eyes wide. "Jake was right about you."

Cindy's own eyes narrowed at Jake, who had been frequently checking over his shoulder to make sure the girls were keeping up. "What did Rumson say about me?"

"That you were good at organizing," Nina said. "That summary of the Whitneys' sordid past was succinct and factoid-packed."

Cindy blushed. "Oh, well, I like to keep things tidy."

"I can't believe they never proved Gerald Whitney did it," Nina said. "It's so sad that a death like that went unpunished."

Cindy had no problem believing it. Growing up as one of the "less advantaged" residents of Newport, she'd lived around the comfortably rich for as long as she could remember. From the time she was a preteen, she'd seen the seedier side of that glittering world. As a maid, she'd cleaned up unspeakable messes. She'd dodged the sons' (and husbands') roaming hands. Rich people had a habit of trying to get away with more than the average person, because they thought they could buy their way out of the consequences. She liked to believe that Deacon Whitney was different, from what she'd seen so far, but she reserved the right to revert to her original opinion.

"Well, it's not like they had *CSI* back then," Cindy quietly said as Deacon unlocked the massive oak door for the men's dormitory. "No fingerprints, DNA, trace evidence, or anything like that. There were no witnesses to Catherine running away. She just—*poof*—disappeared one afternoon when the staff was busy dealing with a brush fire that had started on the south end of the property. There were dresses missing from her closet, and jewelry, and a skip missing from the family dock. Who would have thought she never really made it off the island?"

Nina shuddered, rubbing her hands over her arms as if she'd caught a chill. "That's so sad."

"Ladies?" Jake suddenly called from inside the dorm. "If you keep lollygagging, you're going to miss the tour."

"Sorry," Nina said. "We were just trying to figure out where to start tomorrow."

"We'll begin at the beginning and figure everything else out," Jake said, giving Cindy a lingering look before seeming to recall himself. He turned his attention to Nina, leading her through the main door, which opened into a large sitting area with a long distressed-oak table. "Now, come on. The construction crew has been able to put a little work into the dorms. So our immediate future isn't quite as grim as you'd think."

Several broken chairs had been moved into a corner marked with a sign, "Save for restorer?" Through the main sitting area, Cindy was pleased to see that her crew had left behind a clean kitchen, complete with a new stove, a kitchenette set, and a refrigerator. Jake was explaining that he'd had electrical wiring installed to supply the appliances and lights, but because all of the island's power was currently supplied by generators, they might experience occasional shortages. When the main house was wired, an electrical crew would install the equivalent of a miniature power plant to make the Crane's Nest self-sustaining.

Cindy was grateful that she wouldn't be reading by Coleman lantern for the next few months. As they walked down the long hall of bedrooms, Jake pointed out that the original architect, Jack Donovan, had designed a series of vents in the ceiling, allowing warm air to rise out of the room and keeping the occupants cooler in the summer months.

Each of them would have an individual room. Jake's construction crew had done basic renovations to three of the rooms, patching up holes in the plaster, painting, and giving the floors a thorough cleaning. Deacon had taken the butler's room, the largest in the building and the only one with a private sitting room. But in what Cindy considered a remarkable show of fairness by their employer, all of the "new" rooms were decorated with the same pale wood furniture and polished metal fixtures. Jake's room also included a drafting table. And Cindy imagined the queen-size beds were an accommodation for the sheer length of Deacon's six-foot-*good-God-how-tall*-is-*this-guy?* frame.

Cindy glanced over to see Nina staring up at the

wainscoting and crown molding, a frown tugging at her full pink lips. "Honey, no brow deserves that much of a furrow. What's up?"

Nina seemed to jerk herself out of her contemplative mood, blinking owlishly at Cindy and saying, "Oh, I was just thinking, it seems so bizarre that the architect would devote those decorative touches to a utilitarian building that guests of the Crane's Nest would never see."

"I'm trying to think of it as living in a college dorm, so it feels a little bit less bizarre." Cindy looped her arm through Nina's and led her down the hall toward the sitting room. A shaft of bright afternoon light filtered through the cloudy round window set high in the far wall. "Not that I've ever been to college, but I've cleaned plenty of dorms. Ugh." Cindy shuddered, shaking her golden curls against the sunlight. "Word to the wise, honey. Choose night-shift jobs carefully."

"I'll keep it in mind," Nina assured her. "Of course, if any of us chose jobs carefully, I'm not sure we would be here."

"Yep." Cindy grinned at her. "Cooler and cooler all the time."

They found the ladies' dormitory, which was a mirror image of the men's building, save for the larger bedrooms. The Crane's Nest required more maids than footmen and valets, so the younger women slept four to a room in the same iron bedframes. The recently updated kitchen shared a door with the men's dorm, so the mostly female cooking staff could provide for both sides during their off hours. Nina guessed that the multitude of locks on the ladies' side of the shared door had been employed overnight to protect the servants from temptation.

As they explored their new living space, Nina announced, "I'm going to cash in on some of those cool points and ask you a blunt, intrusive question."

"Ooh, a sudden shift in demeanor when I least expected it, you little rebel." Cindy giggled, slinging her bag over her shoulder. "Hit me with it."

Nina started dragging her luggage into her assigned room. "Why are you being somewhat hostile to Jake?"

Cindy tilted her head, gave Nina a long once-over, and made a mental note not to be fooled by the invisible and occasionally inaccurate "Fragile" stamp on Nina's forehead. This was a girl who knew how to sift through bullshit. Cindy hesitated before finally muttering, "We dated a few years ago."

Nina considered that for a moment. "Yeah, that would be awkward, being forced to live in close quarters with an ex for months at a time. Then again, my most significant relationship only lasted three months, and he ended up immediately leaving for an expedition to South America to research the potential medicinal properties of exotic monkey orchids. And I'm not sure that the continent of space between us made his assertions that I 'wasn't exciting enough for him' any less awful. Seriously, I *bored* a research botanist, a guy who catalogued exotic plant pollen as a hobby. A continent was not enough."

When she looked up, Cindy was grinning at her. "Well, I just learned a whole bunch about you."

"I tend to ramble when I'm nervous. So was it a bad breakup?" Nina patted Cindy's shoulder, making sympathetic *tsk*ing noises, but Cindy shook her head and mumbled something unintelligible. "What?"

"I said, there *was* no breakup."

"Then I am confused."

Cindy sighed. "I was at a party with a friend. My friend knew his friend, so we were left to talk while they caught up. I was all prepared to say no when he asked for my number. I mean, you know what those guys are like. Townie girls like us, it's like open season during the summer. But he was just so sweet and cute, and before I knew it, I was agreeing to dinner. We went out on two dates. And then he just never called again."

"So he got you into bed and then dropped you?" Nina's opinion of Jake was rapidly declining. "That's awful."

"No, he never lifted the lid on the cookie jar. The cookie jar remained intact."

"So the dates were bad?"

"No! They were practically perfect!" she exclaimed, blue eyes flashing. "He took me to a nice restaurant on the water one night. The next date was an outdoor concert. He was charming. He opened doors. He complimented my shoes. The conversation sparkled. I mean, I never use that word, but it did. I was like Audrey freaking Hepburn to his Cary freaking Grant. He gave me a cute little kiss on the nose to say good night on the first date. He pushed just a little bit more on the second but was still a gentleman. And then nothing. I never heard from him again. By the time I stopped waiting for his calls, summer was over, and it was time for him to go back to school. And I had other things going on, and it was just *over* before it even started."

"I take it there was some pining?"

"I'm not going to pretend he was the great love of my life or anything. I didn't hear church bells ringing when I ran into him again at Mr. Whitney's offices. Heck, I really didn't think about him that often in the years after. I had a lot of other stuff going on. But it did sting like hell when I introduced myself and there was not an iota of recognition on his end. I mean, how many Cindy Ellises are there out in the world? And more important, who's going to forget all this?" She gestured to her hourglass figure.

"And so modest, too," Nina observed dryly.

"Hey, I'll do false modesty about a lot of things but not the cookie jar."

"OK, so that brings me to the question, why haven't you told him?"

"Would you want to admit that you were so attractive and fascinating that a guy completely erased you from his memory banks?"

"Good point. But I don't know if feeding your ego a steady diet of righteous indignation is healthy."

Cindy frowned, crossing her arms over her considerable chest. "No, but it feels a lot better than seeing him staring at me and trying to figure out what sort of dud I must have been if he can't remember me."

"So you're just going to let him keep digging himself further into a hole with every conversation?"

"Yeah, that's the plan."

"Can we make it into a drinking game?" Nina asked, an inappropriate edge of excitement creeping into her voice. "Every time he makes a reference to not knowing you very well, we take a shot. If he asks you out on a 'first date,' we take *two* shots."

Cindy stared at her, eyebrows quirked. "You've got a dark, snarky center hidden under that wounded-baby-deer vibe, don't you, sweetie?"

"It's coming back to me, slowly but surely."

World Finance and the
Fine Art of Cookie Bribery

CONTRARY TO POPULAR belief—meaning Cindy's belief—Jake wasn't a womanizer. If anything, he was a serial monogamist. He had a long string of girlfriends whose inability to get him to settle down stretched back to his dorm days. Over the years since what Deacon's cousin, Dotty, called his "free-for-all" dating period in college, he'd definitely developed a type. It wasn't so much about build or hair color as a mind-set. He leaned toward driven women, women who liked to spend as much time at the office as he did. Because in general, those women were going to time their "long-term commitment goals" carefully after they built up their careers, and he didn't feel pressured about proposing after three months.

It wasn't that he didn't want to settle down; he just

wasn't ready yet. He liked his life. He liked trying new restaurants every night. He liked being able to drop everything and go skiing or diving for the weekend with Deacon. Or forcing Deacon to leave his office at water-gunpoint and *making* him go skiing or diving. Committed girlfriends, the women who were in it for the long haul, had objections to that sort of thing.

But Cindy. The minute he saw her, he felt as if he'd run out of oxygen. It wasn't just the fact that she was outrageously, undeniably beautiful. He'd been around a lot of beautiful women, and they'd never affected him like this.

Cindy was unspoiled, unpretentious. He loved the way she didn't try to cover up her feelings, even when it meant turning that acid tongue on him. He loved that she actually *ate* in front of him during the group's shared meals. She drank beer. She cursed. She walked around in dusty shirts with smudges on her face. She wasn't trying to impress him. She wasn't trying to cover up any flaws. She just *was*. And he knew he could trust her. If she was this rude to his face, she couldn't possibly do or say anything worse behind his back. The same couldn't be said about some of his ex-girlfriends, who were so accomplished at masking their emotions (through finishing school or Botox) that he couldn't guess what was going on in their heads. There was Sophie, whom he'd caught going through his banking statements when she'd asked to use his bathroom. Or Caroline, whom he'd overheard telling her mother that Jake was "boring as hell but a suitable escort for parties." And then Elizabeth, who had done a full financial and background check on him before orchestrating a meeting at her friend's Labor Day party—and then didn't understand why Jake found that unsettling.

But Cindy kept rejecting him. He didn't understand it. He'd asked her to join him for a beer and watch the sun set over the bay. She'd said no. He'd asked if he could take her off-island for dinner at his favorite Italian place. She'd said no. He'd snagged a few blooms from the plants Nina was having brought over for her garden plans—prompting sweet, quiet little Nina to threaten him with one of those mini-rake things—and left a pretty bouquet on Cindy's nightstand. He'd found it later in the trash can in the communal kitchen.

He knew she wasn't playing coy when she rejected him. She truly, honestly had no interest in him. It was baffling. Most women liked him. Most *people* liked him. He was a likable guy. But Cindy seemed to have had some sort of grudge from the moment they met. Maybe it was a money issue? Could it be that she had a natural aversion to wealthy people after years of cleaning up their messes? That seemed as unfair as people in his circles discriminating against people without money. It wasn't his fault that his family had been well-off from the time they strolled off the *Mayflower*. He knew it had kept him from some of the fundamental experiences growing up, such as mowing his parents' lawn, having an embarrassing summer job, or driving a secondhand beater truck. But while it took care of most basic problems—food, shelter, education—it created others. Social competition, discontent, the pressure to keep up with the Joneses. His parents had provided for his basic needs but had never figured out how to connect with the son whose parenting they'd primarily left to nannies and various coaches. Then again, he knew how *lack* of money had affected Deacon and Dotty, and he was thankful that he'd never had to worry about that. He was even more thankful that the distinction had never caused problems between him and the people he considered family.

But none of this was helpful at the moment, because Cindy was standing in front of him in the second-best guest room, furiously tapping the toe of her sneaker against the floor. "Just what do you think you're doing, telling my crew that they're not *allowed* to work in the guest rooms? I have a schedule to keep, Mr. Rumson. And that schedule includes clearing out those rooms before that wall gets knocked out."

Jake scowled at Cindy, despite the fact that she looked downright delightful in her royal-blue "Cinderella Cleaning Service" T-shirt with a matching slipper-printed bandanna wrapped around her head. "What are you talking about? We're not knocking any walls down in the guest rooms."

Cindy pulled a sheaf of papers from her blue, color-coordinated clipboard and showed it to him. She pointed to the big red "APPROVED" stamp at the top of a diagram showing several different shelf units. "I sent Mr. Whitney a proposal for some extra storage rooms to maximize the displays for his collections. He approved of the plans last week."

"Well, I appreciate Whit's input. But considering that I'm the architect, how about I decide which walls we knock down?"

Cindy's blue eyes narrowed. "Or you could listen to what the client wants instead of insisting that you're right just because you have a certain job title."

"I'm not insisting I'm right because of a job title, I'm insisting I'm right because I'm actually right!" he exclaimed.

Cindy growled. "I can't even talk to you when you're like this!"

"Like what?"

"All arrogant and jackassy."

" 'Jackassy' isn't even a word," he retorted.

Cindy snagged a container of grout cleaner and turned on him with murder in her eyes. Now that Jake thought about it, his correcting the way she insulted him might be the reason Cindy didn't want to go out with him.

THE SUN BEAT down on Nina's shoulders, a pleasant burn that soaked into her skin and chased away the pervasive chill that had plagued her since she'd stepped onto Whitney Island. Perched on her knees, clearing gnarled weeds from the base of the water fountain, with the sound of the waves in the distance and the sun on her back, Nina felt she could breathe deeply for the first time in months.

As intimidating as it was to be so isolated, it also gave Nina a measure of freedom. She was too far from the mainland for her creditors to reach her. Rick and his cronies couldn't influence what happened to her here. She could finally relax and enjoy getting her hands dirty again.

The six-man day crew she'd hired had arrived at

first light to start clearing away the overgrowth. They'd ferried over that morning with the construction crew, who were swarming the interior of the main house like little worker bees. The construction team was headed by Anthony LaRossa, a sweet old bear of a man who smelled like peppermint candies and Old Spice and had big, fluffy gray eyebrows that came down over his eyes when he spoke.

Anthony had barely recovered from triple-bypass surgery the year before and was therefore the only key member of the staff who was allowed to stay off-island, so he could be near his cardiologist. With his loud, booming laugh and heartfelt promises to direct his crew's footsteps away from her flower beds, Nina was sure Anthony was going to be her favorite coworker. Or, at minimum, he would be the least crazy.

To be fair, she'd seen more of Anthony than she had of the other island residents all day. Although he'd promised a meeting with "Team Crane" over breakfast, Mr. Whitney had received some sort of important business call around seven that morning and hadn't been seen since. Jake was holed up in the main house's library, reviewing blueprints. Cindy had been called away by her crew with questions about furniture for the guest rooms.

Nina's first night as a resident of Whitney Island had not been a momentous one. Dinner had been a stilted, uncomfortable affair, with the team seated around the long dining table in the men's dorm, scarfing down takeout Japanese food that Jake had ferried across from the mainland in a cooler. Jake had tried valiantly to get a conversation going, bringing up Deacon's love for a particular sashimi bar in Boston near EyeDee's corporate headquarters and funny stories from Jake's family's travels to Kyoto when he was a teenager. But Cindy had glumly picked at her food—when she wasn't narrowing her eyes at Jake in suspicion.

And Nina had studiously kept her head bent over her plate, unable to make eye contact with Deacon, who was staring at her as if she was some sort of puzzle he was trying to unlock. Maybe he didn't like people who threw up on his fancy boat? But considering that the ink on their contract was of the nonerasable variety, he could just deal with it until she made an actual termination-worthy error. At which point, Nina would be screwed and possibly homeless.

Right, moving on to a plan that involved making nice with her new boss and not ending up fired and homeless. She would be as personable and professional as possible, and Deacon would have no choice but to love her work. She would stop seeing imaginary shadow people. And she would stop reacting to the island and the people on it like one big exposed nerve.

"It would be a cliché for me to complain that this is what I use as bait to catch real food, right?" Cindy had whispered to Nina. "I mean, I like fish, but I'm more a beer-batter sort of gal."

"Yes, yes, it would," she'd whispered back. "But I brought the makings for blueberry waffles *and* my own waffle iron. And yes, I do consider waffle ingredients to be basic survival gear. So if you can hold out until the morning, I can arrange carb compensation."

"You're a good woman, and one day, people will

write songs about you," Cindy had said, poking half-heartedly at her green dragon roll.

Nina had made an airy gesture with her hands. "Yes, the Ballad of the Waffle-teer."

Cindy giggled, making Nina snicker. And when she'd looked up, Deacon was staring at her again. *Gah!*

Deacon had seemed to thaw a bit when the group started making checklists and plans—cooking rotations, the shower schedule, a "first-day to-do list" to determine exactly how over their heads they were with this project. So they'd finished dinner and settled down to brass tacks, each presenting his or her immediate plans for the house—stabilizing or rehabbing the interior structures, salvaging what few furnishings and antiques were left—and how they would work around one another to prevent delays and hissy fits involving power tools and garden implements.

Curled in her solitary iron bed that night, Nina had dreamed she was pulling the sheets tight over her mattress. The feather-tick mattress was hers. The sheets were hers. But the arms stretching out in front of her belonged to someone else. A large diamond flanked by sapphires winked on her ring finger. The sleeves of her dress were a beautifully embroidered blue muslin, with silver stitching at the cuffs. The soft white hands smoothed the counterpane. She was pleased that she was able to provide clean, comfortable rooms for her staff. She knew how hard the servants worked to keep a home running. And while she certainly didn't need to make up the beds, she found a certain satisfaction in seeing to them herself. She could walk down the rows of rooms, seeing a freshly made bed in each, and know that she'd done *something* productive with her day. Besides, the servants wouldn't arrive for a few days anyway. And it seemed inhospitable to welcome them to their new home with bare beds.

She bent over the far corner of the mattress, tucking the sheet tightly. And when she rose, she felt a large hand slide down the small of her back and give her backside a pinch. She squealed, and another hand clapped around her mouth, pressing her back against a broad male chest.

"Well, look at what I found here," a seductive voice whispered against her ear. "A pretty piece of skirt already bent over the bed."

A thrill of fear rippled up her spine as those hands slipped around her hips and pressed her bum against his solid frame. Teeth closed gently over her earlobe, tugging insistently. She relaxed into the masculine embrace, sighing as the mouth moved from her ear to her neck. The hand cupped her chin, tilting her head back toward him. The scene changed, and instead of a bright, sunlit room, she was outside in the dark, with the wind whipping at her skirts. The grip around her throat tightened, squeezing the breath from her lungs. She scratched and coughed and fought, but he was just too strong.

Suddenly, the pressure at her throat disappeared. She was falling, tumbling through space until she was underwater, watching waves roll over her head. She tried to swim to the surface, but she was held in place by growing pressure around her legs, tugging her down like an anchor, crawling up her body like greedy, grasping hands until it settled around her throat. She reached upward, trying to claw her way toward air, toward light, but was unable to make any progress. Now she saw herself, her arm extended over her head in a mockery of a ballerina's pose. Her delicate blue muslin sleeve fluttered against the water, and she stared at its motion as it slowly turned brown and disintegrated with age. The sleeve rotted away, leaving a grotesque, decaying limb behind, sloughing and dissolving until all that was left were bleached ivory bones reaching up toward the light.

In her head, she could hear screaming.

Nina had bolted upright, clawing at her throat and gasping for breath. She'd fought against the urge to turn on the little bedside lamp. The light would disturb Cindy, an admittedly light sleeper, slumbering just across the hallway, door wide open. Nina didn't want to explain why, at thirty-one, she needed a night-light. It was just anxiety, she'd assured herself. Just a new job and frayed nerves. She had nightmares all the time, and they had nothing to do with her surroundings. She'd sworn off the Xanax before arriving on Whitney Island, but sitting in the dark room with tension gnawing at her chest, she had wondered whether she should restart the pills.

HOURS LATER, IN the light of day, surrounded by freshly turned earth and mulch, it felt silly to have been so frightened by a bad dream. Nina pushed up from her knees, pressed her hands to the small of her back, and stretched, ignoring the house that loomed behind her. It was easy enough to do, since she didn't actually have to work *inside* the house—for which she was eternally grateful. She kept her eyes trained on the fountain, which, as it turned out, featured a beautifully rendered stone water sprite underneath a cocoon of brambles. She refused to look anywhere near the roof. She would not have a repeat of her shadow-person sighting. She would get through this first day, and then the next, for the rest of the summer, without having a ghost-based nervous breakdown in front of the rest of the staff, ruining what little reputation she had left.

Behind her, a smooth voice sounded. "That looks really nice."

Nina yelped, whirling around, clippers in hand. Deacon's eyes showed alarm, and he stepped out of range. "Sorry, sorry!" he exclaimed, holding up his hands in a defensive, *please don't clip me* gesture. "I thought you heard me."

Awesome. She had threatened her boss with sharp implements.

Despite the implement swinging, Nina was starting to like Deacon. He was kind and careful with the people around him. She'd read that when EyeDee first monetized and the worth of the company skyrocketed, Deacon gave out stock options to every employee, from the cleaning lady up. Increased shares were given to employees who had been with him since the company had started in Deacon's dorm room. Jake was given stock just for being the one who made sure Deacon occasionally ate and showered when he was doing the initial programming. And despite his financial difficulties early on, Deacon had never opened up the Crane's Nest to tours. He never let in one of those "paranormal hunters" reality shows, even though it would have been pretty lucrative for him to do so. That showed a certain amount of character.

"No, I'm sorry. I was in the thinking zone." Nina sighed, dropping the clippers into her tool basket and wiping her hands on her faded jeans.

"I get that way at work," he said, rubbing his hand against the back of his neck. "Back when I first started out, I'd stay up for three days straight, hopped up on Mountain Dew and espresso jelly beans, writing code. Jake said he could have thrown a brick at my head and I wouldn't have noticed. I guess I'm lucky he never tried." When she didn't respond, he cleared his throat a little and added, "Because, you know, damaged gray matter doesn't produce good HTML. It produces . . . something else . . ."

Nina's brow furrowed. Awkward small talk seemed to be something of an issue for Deacon. "Was there something you needed, Mr. Whitney?"

"Oh, I was just finished with my conference call and wanted some fresh air. The work you're doing, it looks nice," he told her.

"I'm just clearing away the weeds," Nina told him.

"Still, you're making a lot of progress for the first day," he said, nodding to the water sprite. "I remember her from the few times my parents forced me out to the house when I was a kid. She's Metis, one of the primordial figures in Greek mythology—"

"The first wife of Zeus," Nina said, yanking loose brambles away from the fountain and tossing them into a pile. "After he had his wicked godly way with her, Zeus feared a prophecy that Metis would give birth to children powerful enough to overthrow him. Of course, it didn't occur to him to worry about that *before* he had his wicked godly way with her, but that's beside the point. To work his way around the prophecy, he drank Metis in as water. A little while later, he had a splitting headache, literally, and Metis's daughter, Athena, sprang out of his skull and took her place as the goddess of wisdom and battle strategy."

Stop talking! Stop talking! Stop talking! Her brain screamed at her. *He's a product of several very fancy private schools, and he probably doesn't appreciate a lecture on stuff he learned in kindergarten!*

But there she was, giving him a speculative look, practically daring him to scoff at her retelling of one of the less offensive birth stories in the Greek canon.

Looking mildly impressed, Deacon pursed his lips. "I suppose with a company name like Demeter Designs, I should have known you would be familiar with Greek mythology."

"Ever since I was a kid," she said with a nod.

"That's sort of a weird subject for a kid to be interested in."

She gave a shrug that personified the word *noncommittal.* "Not really."

Deacon waited for a long moment, staring at her expectantly. "This would be the part where you tell me how you became interested in mythology."

Nina's full lips quirked, but she resisted the urge to smile. "It would be."

"Pardon me for saying so, Ms. Linden, but you seem a little . . . 'Twitchy' would be an offensive term to use, wouldn't it?"

Nina's first instinct was to snort-giggle, but she tamped it down. "Yes."

"OK, you seem edgy, then, and not just in the 'spending extended amounts of time with one of the *Forbes* top ten entrepreneurs' way. Like in an honest, 'I am so uncomfortable right now, I wish your face would melt like something out of *Flash Gordon*' sort of way."

She sighed. "I never pictured your face melting like General Kala's."

An impish grin brightened his whole face, and she felt the tension in her shoulders relax by degrees. "You know *Flash Gordon*?"

"My mom had an abiding, irrational love of Queen's music," she told him, narrowing her eyes. "Did you really just drop that *Forbes* reference on me?"

"I think in some cases, I should be allowed to use that *Forbes* reference," he said, shrugging. "It makes some people nervous."

"So why would you bring it up?" she said.

"A little conversational quirk of mine," he muttered. "No matter what I'm talking about, if I start thinking about the things I *don't* want to say, that's what I blurt out. I think, 'Don't try to impress her with lame media references,' and that's the first thing that pops out of my mouth. It's made meetings with investors a living hell."

She laughed.

"So, I've shared one of my psychologically formative secrets with you, not to mention made myself sound like a bit of a tool with the *Forbes* thing. The least you can do is tell me how young Nina Linden became so interested in Greek mythology that she named her business after the goddess of the harvest."

She offered him a shy smile. "When I was seven, I got the chicken pox. It was just awful, one of the worst cases my pediatrician had ever seen. I had them in my ears, on the soles of my feet, just *everywhere*. I was miserable and itchy, and I was making my parents equally miserable. And one day, my dad brought home a big stack of videos from the Rental Hut. *Annie*, *The Apple Dumpling Gang*, *Teenage Mutant Ninja Turtles*, anything to keep me quiet and still for a few minutes at a time. But the one I watched over and over, to the point where my mom was afraid that I was going to wear the tape out, was this weird animated collection of Greek myths. Hercules and the twelve labors. Icarus and his melting wax wings. King Midas and the golden touch. And my personal favorite, Hades tricking Persephone into staying in the depths of the Underworld three months a year, making her mother, Demeter, so miserable that she kills off all the plants and creates winter."

"Sort of dark for a seven-year-old."

"It was," Nina agreed. "But I was hooked, couldn't stop watching it, which was probably not healthy for me. Dad ended up having to buy the video from the store or pay more in late fees than the tape was worth. I started reading everything I could find in the library on Greek myths. I learned all about the gods and goddesses and their symbols and alliances and powers. And I loved the idea that Demeter had a fairly wimpy power—plants not being as lethal as lightning or the sun or the ocean—but she managed to bring the whole world to a stop because she was ticked off about her daughter being taken away. I started growing beans and avocados in cups on my windowsill, which led to my next crazy phase, gardening."

"And you turned out to be a nice, normal girl, so clearly the overindulgence in animated mythology didn't warp you too much," he said, grinning at her, making her insides turn all warm and fluttery. That wasn't good.

"What makes you think I'm nice and normal?" she asked, her tone far more challenging than what was advisable.

"Extensive background checks." Deacon's cheeks flushed, although Nina couldn't tell whether it was embarrassment or sunburn. "You know, I tried to send you an EyeContact request to help us keep in touch during the project, but I couldn't find you. Even with my supersecret admin privileges."

Nina was willing to let the background-check comment slide for now. She had expected as much, dealing with someone as rich and security-conscious as Deacon. What surprised her was that she'd passed the check. She pasted on a cheeky smile, even if she wasn't feeling quite sassy yet. "Well, this is probably going to hurt my chances of continued employment, but I don't have a profile on EyeDee."

Deacon's jaw dropped, and it was his turn to laugh.

He had a very nice laugh, Nina noted. It made his whole face relax into something just a little younger, a little less burdened. And she resolved that she would try to make that happen at least once a day, if for no other reason than that it might keep her in a job that much longer. Gardener-slash-court-jester was a perfectly respectable position, right?

"I don't know whether to feel insulted on a professional level or worried about hiring a hermit."

Nina scoffed. "I'm not a hermit! I just don't have that many people I want to keep up with from high school. I have friends, and when I want to talk to them, I have this new invention, it's called a phone. It's like magic. I hit these little buttons, and suddenly, my friend's voice comes out." She pulled her thick, early-model cell phone from her pocket.

Deacon's mouth remained open as he marveled at the relic in her hand. "Is that a Zack Morris phone? Seriously, Ms. Linden? Are you going to call for a carryout order from the Maxx?"

"It's just a phone." She sighed. "It works. That's all I ask of it."

He shook it like a faulty flashlight. "Can you even get text messages on this thing?"

She snatched the phone back and crossed her arms, peering up at him. She'd changed her mind. She wouldn't make him smile anymore, particularly if she was to be the source of his amusement. Because right now, that smile was doing funny things to her belly and making her knees all jellied. And surely, throwing herself at her boss while shouting *Flash Gordon* quotes was not the mark of a composed professional.

She needed to think of something else to talk about, something business-related, something that would catch his somewhat scattered attention and redirect it from her cave-phone.

"Why did you hire me?" she blurted out. "There

were much larger firms up for the job. Firms that have more of a track record with large estates. Why me?"

Really, brain? She huffed internally. *That's what you came up with? Making him question why he hired you in the first place?*

And there was the boyish grin again. "Plant samples. You were the only landscaper I met who thought to bring plant samples, so I could grasp what the gardens would smell like. I liked that. It showed an attention to detail I thought was lacking in the other presentations."

"Oh." She chuckled, surprised and pleased that he'd noticed. He rubbed the back of his neck, staring down at his feet. "And is there a reason you haven't hired a security staff? If nothing else, I'd assume that you'd be a prime kidnapping target. What with the *Forbes* top ten entrepreneurs list and everything. I mean, if I were a criminal, I would kidnap you."

Oh, dear God, brain, we are not friends anymore. Clearly, my id is going to take the wheel from here.

She cleared her throat. "Anyway, you've isolated yourself out here in the middle of nowhere without protection. Why not keep the security team on site?"

"It seemed unfriendly," he said. Nina snorted, which made him smile. "Not that many people know I'm out here. Besides, before we arrived, I had a security system installed. It's armed every time the day crews leave the island. Any motion within twenty yards of the shoreline sets off the sensors, and I get an alert on my phone, which includes a live feed from a nearby video camera. There's a panic room installed just behind my office. There are cameras focused on every square inch of the property. And this little button on my watch? There's a

private SWAT team standing by at an undisclosed location on the mainland who can make it here in six
minutes by helicopter."

"I don't know whether to be impressed or terrified."

"Maybe a mix of both?" he suggested. "You could be
imperrified."

Nina laughed. "That's awful. I hereby forbid you to
create portmanteaus. It's for the greater good."

"Well, you know what the word 'portmanteau'
means, which is one up on, oh, ninety percent of the
population."

"So if we have the SWAT team on the six-minute
call window, why can't Anthony stay on the island?
Surely, scary military personnel could handle a medical
evacuation."

Deacon nodded. "They could. And I added a medical
rescue service when I found out about Anthony's heart
condition. He's the best, and he came highly recom-
mended by Jake, so I wanted him. But his wife, Marie,
would worry herself sick if she couldn't see him every
day, and that seemed cruel."

"That was very kind of you."

"Not really," Deacon protested. "Marie brought
three dozen of her indescribably awesome Italian
lemon-drop cookies by my office and promised me
another two dozen every week for the next year if I let
her Tony stay at home while he worked on my 'little
house project.'"

"Really?" Nina cackled. "She bought you with
cookies?"

"Every man has his weakness," he said. "Mine happens to be delicious homemade baked goods."

"Well, if I ever foul up the flower beds, I'll just whip up a batch of snickerdoodles."

An expression of pure want flashed across his eyes, and Nina felt vaguely insulted that said expression centered on cookies. He pressed his hand over his heart. "Don't toy with me, Ms. Linden."

"I never joke about my snickerdoodles," she said, her voice dropping to a seductive, teasing octave that even she didn't recognize.

Tugging at his collar, Deacon cleared his throat. "Jake said you've been uneasy about the house?"

Nina's flirty tone disappeared. She cleared her throat. "I thought I saw something yesterday, but it was probably just a trick of light or a hallucination brought on by seasickness meds. Really."

"I know the house has a reputation," he said, carefully placing his hand on her shoulder. And then, remembering his own scrupulously written corporate policies on sexual harassment in the workplace—even if that workplace was his own backyard—he quickly pulled his hand away and held it behind his back. "And that can put people on edge, make them misinterpret things or see things that aren't there. But really, it's just an old, beat-up house on an old, beat-up island. There's nothing supernatural going on here."

There was a desperate tone in his assurance, Nina thought, as if he was trying to convince himself as much as her. She asked, "If it's just an old, beat-up house on an old, beat-up island, why do you want to live here?"

"A convoluted idea of family loyalty?" he said, perching on the edge of the fountain and squinting up at her.

She fished around in her tool kit until she found a faded green baseball cap embroidered with the lotus-like Demeter Designs logo. She pressed it into his hands and sent a significant look at his high, surprisingly elegant forehead.

AFTER A MOMENT of debating whether Jake would make fun of him for wearing it, Deacon slapped the cap onto his head. There were a lot of reasons for wanting to reclaim Whitney Island, but he doubted that sweet-faced, skittish Nina had the patience to hear that particular dissertation.

He'd anticipated complications with this project. One didn't simply walk into Mordor, and one didn't restore a one-hundred-plus-year-old house without some problems. He knew it was optimistic to expect to carry a full workload while he was staying on the island, which was why he had promoted Vi from his assistant to vice president of "distance operations," covering the holes in Deacon's schedule and chain of command while he was off getting closure. Vi now had her own assistant and a corner office with a mini-fridge stocked with her favorite obscure Jones sodas. He shuddered. Gravy should not be a soda flavor.

Deacon had grown up with a name that had traditionally meant wealth and privilege to many in Newport. Unfortunately, tradition and present-day reality weren't necessarily the same thing. The reality was like being the crown prince of a defunct country. Deacon was raised on tales of what could have been, what should have been. His dad had made a decent living practicing law, but his income wasn't what his Main

Line Philadelphia–born *Mayflower* mother was used to, and she couldn't seem to adjust her spending habits. The fights about money were constant, loud, and sometimes public. His parents were more than well-educated. They could order dinner in several languages. They could traverse the social landscape of their moneyed neighbors, but they just couldn't seem to get a grasp on ordinary adult obligations—such as the mortgage, car payments, or insurance. Somehow, his mother's outstanding accounts at Saks and Elizabeth Arden took precedence. And his father couldn't allow the family membership at the Newport Country Club to lapse. That would be shameful.

His father couldn't let go of the "Whitney tradition," even when it would have been more practical for the family to live in a smaller house or for Deacon to go to public school instead of the fancy private school the family's "peers" attended. So Deacon was treated to condescending stares and outright hostility from his classmates, as if they thought "poor" was contagious.

When he earned a computer-science scholarship to Harvard, the only school his father would consider letting him attend, kids from the same old-money families looked down their noses at him, the kid whose parents' car was repossessed from the school parking lot at parent-teacher night, the kid who bought school uniforms secondhand. Other scholarship kids resented him for stealing a spot from an underprivileged student. Mothers at the country club prayed he wouldn't notice their daughters.

The only thing the family had to its name was this

particular pile of rocks under his feet, which was held in a trust that wouldn't let it be sold. So when they had money troubles that couldn't be solved by opening a credit card in Deacon's name, his parents honored the family tradition of rummaging through the house for any overlooked knickknacks that could be hocked or sold outright.

Nina's background check had been an interesting, but troubling, read. He knew about the bankruptcy, the fraud charges, the trouble she'd had obtaining her own business loans and license. He felt a certain kinship with her. That combined with the fact that she was so lushly beautiful had made him fidgety and somewhat awkward during their initial interview at his office. He'd tried to converse with her professionally, as if she was any other contractor involved in the Crane's Nest project, but he'd ended up dropping the cup of piping-hot espresso his assistant had just delivered directly onto his left hand. Nina had rounded the desk in no time, quietly and competently using her purse-sized first-aid kit to apply ointment and a bandage to his burned skin. The fact that she was so ill at ease but still managed to function and care for another person told him all he needed to know about Nina Linden.

But still, possible shared trauma and his family's sordid financial history seemed like a lot of information to pile into a near-stranger's lap. So instead, he finally answered, "For years, this house was a symbol of my family's bad luck, of failure, shame, tragedy. I want to be able to show people that things have changed, to restore the family name to where it was, maybe even a little bit better."

"I suppose adding 'because now you have more money than they do' is a vulgar way to put it?"

Deacon chuckled. "Probably, but no less vulgar than me wanting to prove that I've made something of myself. Genes, even if they link you to some of the unluckiest bastards on the planet, do not determine destiny. So we're going to fix this place up and prove it to the world."

Nina's expression slid from concerned to slightly disappointed. His answer made sense. It was a crappy, shallow answer, but it made sense.

Deacon noticed Nina's frown. "Hoping for something a little more altruistic?"

Before she could respond to his oh-so-cheerful observations, Nina turned toward the sound of loud arguing as Cindy and Jake, yelling at the top of their lungs, were practically jogging across the lawn toward the fountain, arms waving. Anthony followed at a leisurely pace, as if his colleagues weren't going insane before his very eyes. Deacon sighed and walked toward them.

"What now?" he huffed.

Anthony continued past them, taking a seat next to Nina on the fountain. "Did Jake go too far with his version of quote-unquote flirting?" she asked quietly.

Anthony shook his balding gray head, folding his hands over his beer belly. "I'm not sure. I was in the grand ballroom with my crew and ran to do damage control when I heard the yelling. Blood is hell to get out of parquet flooring."

"Surely it won't go that far," Nina murmured.

"You missed the part where she threatened him with grout cleaner."

"Well, there's a complex history there," she started, but Anthony cut her off.

"They'll either stab each other or sleep together before the first month is out. Given the grout cleaner, I'd be willing to put a twenty on stabbing."

"That would be completely wrong and unethical and . . ." Nina said just as Cindy called Jake an "overgelled, classless troll" in a tone so sweet it sounded like a compliment. Nina lowered her voice to say, "I'll put thirty on sleeping together."

Anthony gave an exaggerated mock gasp. "And you seem like such a nice girl!"

"Whit, would you tell this woman that she has no right to move entire rooms around on my blueprints?" Jake demanded.

Cindy was all acidic smiles and saccharine sweetness. "Mr. Whitney, would you please explain to your architect that these storage areas are part of an organization plan that you approved?" she practically cooed. "You asked Anthony to knock out one of the walls between guest rooms to create storage and display space for your collectibles."

"Collectibles?" Nina whispered.

"I've seen the sketches," Anthony whispered back. "The guy's a *big* fan of those weird sci-fi/fantasy movies. *Flash Gordon. Krull. Tron. Ladyhawke.* Did you know they made *Krull* action figures? Because I sure didn't. I've never even heard of that movie."

Nina shook her head. "I did not know that. But now that I know that there's a tiny posable Liam Neeson out there, I sort of want one." The look Anthony gave her was equal parts confusion and speculation. She just shrugged. "Don't judge me."

Deacon asked. "Jake, didn't we have this conversation about the storage rooms last week?"

"Yeah, but I didn't think you were serious!" Jake exclaimed.

"Why not?" Deacon asked.

"Because when you told me about those plans, I said, 'That's fine, as long as you're OK with two of the guest rooms collapsing on themselves, because you're removing a load-bearing wall.' Remember?"

Deacon frowned. "No, I'm pretty sure I tuned you out after you said, 'That's fine.' "

"*Gah!*" Jake threw his arms skyward. At Nina's snicker, he turned on her. "Quiet, you."

Nina mimed zipping her lips and tossing the key to Anthony, who "caught" it.

"I was up to my ears in code!" Deacon exclaimed. "You know we have that new EyeChat feature launching—"

"I knew you weren't listening!" Jake cried, scraping his fingers through his thick sandy hair, making it stand up.

"Can't you make up some sort of hand signal or something so I know when a conversation is important and I need to pay attention?"

"Most people don't need hand signals to listen when their best friend is speaking, they just pay attention, whether it's critical or not," Jake grumped.

Deacon sighed and turned. "Cindy, I'm sorry. It seems that our plans for expanding the guest room into a collectibles room are not possible due to a structural issue. Would you mind looking into an alternative space in the family wing? Maybe the bedroom on the southwest corner of the third floor?"

Cindy nodded and gave Deacon a sunny smile. "Absolutely. That's no problem."

Jake sputtered indignantly, "Wha— Why does he get 'That's no problem' and a smile? I asked you to do the same thing, and you threated to grout my face."

"Because he explained it to me in a rational, polite fashion," she said. "And he signs my checks. Also, I like him better than you."

Dotty by Nature

JAKE AND CINDY eventually calmed down because Deacon offered to share some of his ill-gotten cookies from Marie. Delicious baked goods were the great workplace hostility equalizer, no matter how unorthodox the workplace.

The days that followed were strained, with Cindy and Jake pointedly avoiding each other in the house and ignoring each other completely at dinner unless asked a direct work-related question. Deacon and Nina had to find something to talk about, or meals would have been completely silent, convent-like affairs. So they talked about their mutual love of *Flash Gordon*, which led to an in-depth discussion of 1980s cartoons and Nina's inappropriate attachment to Popples. Nothing, including baiting Jake about the size of his Garbage Pail Kids card collection, could draw the other two into the conversation. Nina was grateful that Deacon was willing to return to the servants' quarters at a decent hour each night; otherwise, she would have been better off having dinner with the garden statuary.

When Jake wasn't around, Cindy became her usual talkative and cheerful self. Without a TV to keep them entertained, the ladies usually retreated into the female staff quarters each night to watch DVDs on Cindy's laptop while snacking on popcorn and sodas liberated from Deacon's stash. Cindy had a weakness for old black-and-white movies, anything involving Bette Davis, Billy Wilder, or Alfred Hitchcock—although considering their surroundings, they did skip *Psycho*. They wanted to be able to shower without a buddy system.

They fell into a daily routine—wake up at six, group breakfast and discussion of plans for the day's progress, wait for the construction crews to arrive on the ferry at eight sharp, work until five, break for dinner and progress reports. Lather, rinse, repeat. Anthony's arrival each morning seemed to bring normalcy, or at least good cookies. Marie's much appreciated contributions were kept in an R2-D2-shaped cookie jar on the shared kitchen counter.

They weren't exactly gelling as a team.

Deacon threatened to send the lot of them to some sort of hellish team-building retreat involving trust falls and high-ropes courses, but that seemed counterproductive to the whole *completing construction on deadline* objective. And they were getting the work done. The rooms were being systematically and meticulously cleaned, their contents catalogued. The grounds crew had cleared the debris and were digging new beds and reseeding the lawn. Anthony's people were through with making sure the roof wouldn't fall on their heads and were finally getting around to structural changes.

According to Jake, Vi had led a rebellion against Deacon at the EyeDee office when he'd tried to organize a retreat with his staff involving a rock-climbing wall. He'd almost lost his graphic-design department. And the use of his left foot. Vi did not suffer fools or trust falls gladly.

As for Nina, she suffered through the same dream on the nights she'd worked herself into exhaustion and slept deeply. It was always the same. She made the bed, arms trapped her from behind, and she felt hands close around her throat. And just when she couldn't bear the pressure around her neck another moment, she was underwater, watching her hands floating above her head. She didn't know what she was supposed to be learning from this dream. Or even if she was supposed to be learning something or her subconscious was just sort of a jerk.

So she avoided going into the house, keeping her back turned to it whenever possible so she wouldn't see imaginary people-shapes roaming the roofline. The dread she felt about potential dark-figure sightings outweighed any curiosity about the wonders inside, even when Cindy described the broken-down solarium with its old copper pots full of long-dormant soil. She had plenty of excuses for not going inside, since her work involved the yard. But the house loomed at the edge of her awareness, a constant foreboding presence that gnawed at the edges of her concentration while she worked the soil. She could swear she felt it watching her, nudging at her, trying to get her attention, like a child tugging at his mother's skirts.

Of course, Nina suspected that telling the others these thoughts would result in the loss of her job *and* a one-way trip to the loony bin. So she took to working with her earbuds in and music blasting to keep herself distracted.

Nina's growing friendship with Cindy was a comfort to her. She didn't ask why Nina was always up long before early-riser Cindy was out of bed. She simply accepted the cup of coffee Nina had brewed and asked Nina random questions, about the day she had planned, about her parents, anything to draw Nina out of her contemplative funk and into the real world. Nina came to admire Cindy's practical nature, her snarky sense of humor, her refusal to back down from a project, even when it was intimidating as all hell. Cindy Ellis had steely spine to spare. If she could just get Cindy and Jake to stop fighting like rabid squirrel monkeys every time they made eye contact, life on the island would be relatively peaceful. Almost.

FRIDAY MORNING WAS witness to yet another Cindy-Jake blowup. Anthony and Nina were standing outside the broken remains of the greenhouses, discussing how they might restore one to working order immediately so that she would have some indoor potting and workspace. Deacon had taken a break to give his input. Nina found the timing a little suspicious, since Deacon mentioned that he was supposed to be on an international conference call involving Guam that morning. Yet there he was, making suggestions on using the UV-treated glass in the panes to create the most growth-friendly environment for Nina's seedlings.

"Really, a regular old greenhouse will be fine," she assured Deacon. "These methods have worked for centuries. If it isn't broken, there's no reason to fix it."

"Well, with that sort of thinking, we would still be playing Atari and telling people how we feel face-to-face instead of posting it to our EyeDee status," Deacon teased her. "In which case, I wouldn't have any money, and you wouldn't be here with me right now, so . . . there."

Nina snorted. "All right, all right, order your fancy-schmancy glass."

"You're a very open-minded Luddite," he told her, in a tone he clearly meant as a compliment.

"I am not a Luddite!"

"The brick-sized phone you're carrying around says otherwise."

Nina lightly smacked his arm, which made Deacon throw his head back and laugh. And suddenly, Anthony found a reason to walk around the greenhouse, giving them a moment alone.

Deacon cleared his throat. "Cindy says you two have been watching movies on her laptop every night. If you want, you could use my office in the house. I have a flat-screen installed, and there's a generator in there to power it. It would probably be more comfortable than crouching around a computer."

Nina gave him a brilliant smile. "That's so sweet of you! But we couldn't use your office. That wouldn't be—"

"Deacon!" Jake yelled, rounding the greenhouse with

Cindy nipping at his heels. "Will you tell this woman that the crews will finish the wall treatments in the ballroom when they finish them and not before?"

Deacon and Nina groaned in unison. Nina adored Cindy, she really did, but she wished that her favorite organizer would pull some sort of naked revenge on Jake and get it over with. The rising sexual tension was starting to become disruptive. Also, her standing wager with Anthony had them sleeping together by the end of the month or she lost thirty bucks.

"I have buffing and polishing the ballroom floor on my timeline for this week, Rumson. It's one of *my* crew's first major interior jobs. I can't help it if you didn't co-ordinate with my schedule when you pulled Anthony's guys out of the ballroom and reassigned them to the kitchen. I have a schedule to keep!"

"A part of the rear kitchen wall was on the verge of collapse from water damage!" Jake exclaimed. "We just found the problem on Wednesday. What was I supposed to do, ask Anthony to ignore it so the crew could keep painting the ballroom?"

"Well, I didn't know that, because you didn't bring it up at the morning meeting," Cindy shot back.

"Because you don't ever talk to me at the morning meetings!"

Cindy frowned. "Well, that is a valid point . . . But a better alternative might have been to hire *more* people to work on the kitchen and the ballroom simultaneously, so we don't fall behind." Cindy looked to Deacon. "If you're OK with more people being hired, that is."

Deacon shrugged. "As long as they pass the security checks."

"Well, that is a valid point, too," Jake agreed, his tone stiff and reluctant. "And something I probably should have done anyway."

Cindy's eyes rolled just a tiny bit as she huffed, "And I will start talking to you at morning meetings, so we can avoid situations like this in the future."

Jake pursed his lips, as if he was considering the offer. "That would be nice."

Cindy nodded. "So we're good?"

Jake stuck his hand out for a shake. "Yes."

Cindy's blond eyebrows rose. "Don't push it."

"Well, at least they're solving their own problems now," Deacon said. "They're a little loud about it, but it's still progress."

Nina had her hand over her mouth to suppress the laughing fit the whole scene had caused. Deacon tugged at her wrist gently, pulling her fingers away from her lips, but before Nina could comment, Jake's head snapped up, a curious expression on his face. "Did you hear something?"

"The sound of the waves?" Nina suggested, glancing toward the house.

"The wind?" Deacon added.

Jake shook his head. "No, for a second there, I thought I heard someone calling my name."

Cindy turned toward the house. "Maybe someone on the construction crew?"

"No, it was a woman's voice."

"Isn't this how *Clue* starts out?" Nina asked. "And *House on Haunted Hill*? And *The Haunting*?"

Deacon said, "I think *The Haunting* was more about sleep-deprivation psychosis."

"Well, that's comforting," Cindy muttered.

Nina stared at Deacon, eyebrows raised. "*The Haunting*? Really?"

"I like movies!" he said, his tone more than a little defensive. "And I heard that crack about a tiny posable Liam Neeson the other day. You stay away from my action figures."

Nina gave a grin that could be construed as sassy—saucy, even. "I make no promises."

Jake stared at a small figure circling the corner of the house, his eyes wide. "Uh, Whit?"

Deacon's normally composed visage slipped into a more natural irritated expression as he followed Jake's line of sight.

The group turned in unison as a penny-bright voice called over the expanse of lawn. "Yoo-hoo! Jake! Deacon! Didn't you hear me calling?"

A tall, willowy woman in enormous tortoiseshell sunglasses and a hair-camouflaging, rainbow-streaked scarf was standing at the edge of the gardens. She made a surprising sprint over the grass, apparently unfazed by skintight jeans and worn red cowboy boots. Nina had never before thought of the word *scampering* to describe the movements of a human being, but there was no other word for the lithe, hyper steps that propelled her across the grass. She was hopping up and down despite her multitude of bags, waving her arms and grinning like a mad jackrabbit as she ran.

"Deacon!" she shouted. "I'm here!"

Deacon ground his teeth and glared at Jake, who threw up his hands in a *not me* posture. "Hey, I told her not to come."

Nina and Cindy perched on the lip of the fountain to watch this new development play out. Who on God's green earth was this person, and why did Deacon have that pinched look, as if he'd just swallowed licorice jelly beans?

"Maybe she's an illegitimate fortune-seeking half sister?" Nina suggested.

"Crazy-ex-girlfriend-slash-disgraced-Victoria's-Secret-underwear-model?" Cindy countered quietly.

Nina tried again. "Or maybe a perfectly nice but very eager Mary Kay sales rep."

"Hi!" The mystery woman dropped her bags—everything from an old army duffel to a classic Louis Vuitton suitcase—to the ground with a *thump*. "Aren't you happy to see me?"

Deacon scowled. Nina and Cindy exchanged uncomfortable glances. Should they all suddenly find something else to do so their employer could tactfully eject the newcomer from the island? Nina moved closer to Deacon, feeling the urge to soothe his clearly jangled nerves.

"Trust me, Flower Power, don't get in the middle of it," Jake muttered, pulling her closer to Cindy. Engrossed by the unfolding scene, Cindy didn't think to step away from him.

"How did you get here, Dotty? I thought I bribed every boat captain between here and New York not to give you a rental or a ride out to the island."

"Deacon Francis Whitney!" the woman, who seemed to be both Dotty by name and dotty by nature, shot back. "You always say that! And what sort of greeting is this for your favorite cousin!"

Cindy snickered, murmuring Deacon's middle name under her breath. "Francis."

Deacon turned to glare at her. "People who live in glass houses shouldn't throw middle-name-shaped stones, Cynthia Agnes Ellis."

"Stupid background checks," Cindy muttered, kicking at the dirt with the toe of her bright white sneaker.

"Who's up for a drink?" Jake asked brightly. "We've been working for a whopping two hours. We deserve a break. Come on!"

Nodding, Deacon forged a path to the main house, not stopping to see if anyone was following. Nina frowned, dropping her hammer into her tool kit and trailing reluctantly after him. She stood on the doorstep, staring into the house, her pale lips pressed into tight lines.

"It's just a house, Nina," Cindy assured her. "I've been working here for days, and I haven't seen anything out of the ordinary. I'm not saying that you're being unreasonable, because I had all those same feelings when I got here. But really, it's just a house with terrible ambience."

Nina scrubbed a hand over her face. "I hate feeling this way. I hate being scared all the time, freezing up every time someone walks up behind me."

Cindy's golden eyebrow lifted. "Are we still talking about the house?"

Nina shook her head. "Not really."

Cindy put her hand on Nina's shoulder and squeezed gently. "Well, later, after we've figured out what the hell is going on with Deacon's scarf-crazed cousin, we will break out the bottle of tequila I have stashed in my room, and you will tell Auntie Cindy all about it, OK?"

"It will take two bottles."

Cindy hip-checked her. "That's the spirit."

"Please don't say 'spirit.'" Nina groaned as Cindy led her through the towering oak doors.

The Fall of the House of Whitney

NINA WAS SO caught up in goggling at the expansive entry hall that she stumbled over the threshold. Cindy's day crew was going to have their hands full with this place. The beautifully inlaid parquet floors were blanketed in a carpet of gray dust. The walls were heavy dark wood and dirty beige plaster, relieved occasionally by a panel of gold leaf. The pressed-relief ceilings were impossibly high, with arched entryways to every room and warren. Every step echoed as Nina moved farther into the house.

The empty fireplace at the far end of the entryway was dark and dirty. She could make out lighter places on the faded cream silk wallpaper where paintings had once hung. There were a few spots on the tables where rings of dust clung to the surface, indicating that some little objet d'art had once stood there but had been snatched years ago.

Even with Deacon's money, how would they ever make this place feel cozy? It was more than a matter of a few throw pillows and a photo collage. How were they ever supposed to make this tomb into a home? And then, she remembered, Deacon didn't really want a home. He wanted a showplace, and this house was definitely suited to *that* task.

"I know it doesn't look like we've made much progress," Cindy said. "Mr. Whitney wanted me to zero in on key areas of the house before we really got down to business."

Nina could see it in her head, the way it used to be, shining gold leaf and gleaming dark wood. She imagined what sorts of flowers would look best in an explosive arrangement over the round marble-top table. She would use freesia, for their sweet, light perfume, and the citrusy delight of commuter daylilies.

"So the decorating style was called Le Goût Rothschild, which, as far I can tell, means 'cram as much overpriced crap into your living space as possible,' " Cindy said, with the bored yet reverent air of a historical-society maven chosen to give summer tours of the Gilded Age monuments on the mainland. "Unfortunately, generations of Whitneys have been sneaking into the house over the years and picking off the most obvious valuables, whatever was left after the bank took its share from Gerald. But Mr. Whitney insists that he wants to keep the style a bit more contemporary anyway. Everything else is going to be restored and scattered around the house or shipped off to said thieving relatives."

As Cindy led Nina toward large double doors on the

left, from behind which could be heard the murmur of male voices, Nina's attention was captured by the dark grand staircase that swept majestically from the center of the room to the next landing, splitting in two before ascending to the second floor. It was the sort of staircase that an old black-and-white movie queen might descend wearing a Charles Worth–style gown, to be swept off her feet or devastated by some heartless cad. Had Catherine Whitney ever come down those stairs to make her entrance into a room full of admirers? Her tenure as mistress of the house had been so short. And it sounded as if she'd been so unhappy while she was here. It was doubtful that Catherine had much opportunity to make good memories.

Nina could hear the music in her head, a sedate waltz to give the ladies a chance to show off their carefully practiced skills. She could hear the tinkling of crystal punch cups and murmured conversation. She could feel the warmth of wax tapers and dozens of bodies pressed into the entryway as they waited for the famed Mrs. Whitney to open the first dance. From the corner of her eye, she could see a dark shape hovering at the banister, a feminine shape, from the hips down, a series of tiered, swishing skirts. But the figure had no—

"Hey, we're going this way," Cindy said, making Nina jump.

"Sorry." Nina drew a shaky breath and nodded, trying to keep her face impassive. "Just got distracted."

"Yeah, dust bunnies the size of tumbleweeds send my OCD tendencies jangling, too. Don't worry, my crew will get it straightened out," Cindy said, pulling on Nina's arm until they entered what was once the music room. The windows stretched from floor to ceiling, letting grime-filtered light tumble over the remains of moldering couches and battered musical instruments. A grand piano stood collapsed in a corner, one leg bent out from under it. Above their heads, the ceiling was pressed tin, with molded plaster cherub faces in the center of every square.

Nina stared up at the multitude of white babies, frozen with perpetual smiles. "So . . . there's that."

"I spent about a day trying to find an explanation for it," Cindy said, shaking her head. "And then I realized that would only upset me more. Anthony assured me they're coming down soon. And then they will be destroyed with fire on holy ground."

Nina and Cindy shuddered in tandem. In the meantime, Deacon was pouring himself what looked like an enormous amount of vodka from an improvised wet bar on a defunct harpsichord.

"Dude!" Jake cried. "It's eleven o'clock! When I said 'have a drink,' I meant soda or an iced tea or something."

Nina crossed her arms over the chest of her green Demeter Designs T-shirt. "He had liquor, and he put it in here? Why not in the staff quarters?"

"Oh, there's a bar in the staff quarters, too," Cindy told her. "On the men's side."

"The boys have been holding out on us!" Nina grumbled.

"Well, I stole their tequila yesterday morning, so I think that makes us even. We're making margaritas this weekend, lady."

Jake took the bottle out of Deacon's hand when their

fearless leader began pouring himself a second shot. "Seriously, man, it's not that bad! You love Dotty. I love Dotty. I don't see why you're upset. It will be just like old times, having her around."

"Just like old times?" Deacon scoffed, snagging the vodka bottle out of his friend's hand. "Oh, you mean like the time Dotty convinced us that the polo ponies at the club were being mistreated, so we should set them all free? I got grounded for two months!"

"We were eight!" Jake exclaimed.

"I missed space camp!" Deacon shot back. "Or how about our junior year, when Dotty got it into her head that you and Genevieve Malloy were some sort of star-crossed supercouple, so she set up some John Hughes machination to make sure you ended up together on prom night?"

"That one wasn't that bad, actually." Jake shook his head.

"Yeah, until Genevieve's Cro-Magnon gorilla of a boyfriend saw you and tried to kick your ass. I jumped in, like an idiot, to defend you and ended up with fourteen stitches in my scalp. Or how about when we were in college, and Dotty decided I needed a tattoo, got me drunk, and took me to 'her' tattoo guy?"

"OK, OK, I get the point," Jake said, snagging the bottle out of Deacon's hands.

"Misspelled!" Deacon exclaimed, gesturing at his shoulder blade. "In two places!"

"In her defense, it's binary code, so no one knows that it's misspelled. And technically, it's not misspelled; some of the numbers are just out of order. So it's misnumbered."

"*I* know it's misnumbered!" Deacon groused. "It's not that I don't love my cousin. You know that I do. It's just that she sows destruction and chaos wherever she goes. She's like a chipper, chirpy goddess Kali."

"Try saying that three times fast," Jake muttered.

"Deacon, what is your problem with me being here?" Dotty demanded from the doorway, hands on hips. She'd removed the colorful scarves, revealing a wild shoulder-length mane of dark chestnut hair streaked with purple and red. The eyes that had been hidden by oversized sunglasses were so blue they were practically Liz Taylor violet. She looked like a delicate, whimsical—and at the moment, very pissed-off—creature from the Irish fairy tales that Nina's nana used to tell her. All puckish good humor until you crossed her, and then she salted your farmland and turned your milk cows sour.

Jake stood behind Dotty, arms crossed and leaning against the doorframe, surveying the scene with a shell-shocked expression as Dotty stood toe-to-toe with her cousin and poked him in the chest.

"You know how seriously I'm taking this book project. You know how important it is to me to finish it before you toss our family history into the Dumpster."

"First, that family-history crack was uncalled for," Deacon told her, poking his finger at her forehead. He did it without much force, but it seemed to annoy Dotty thoroughly. "And second, pardon me if I don't take your commitment to this project very seriously. Oh, I know, it's very important to you. Just like it was very important to you to spend eight months documenting the deterioration of cave paintings in Australia, which became less important when you decided to do a coffee-table book on the annual migration of red crabs across Christmas Island, which became less important when you decided to do a book on modern-day prospectors in Alaska. And then you decided to take off to Mexico to do sunrise studies of ancient Mayan ruins, which somehow ended up becoming a two-month-long trip down to Brazil because you met a guy who owned an emerald mine. Look, I love you, but writing this book you've planned is going to be another thing that turns out to be less important than whatever comes up next. And in the meantime, you're distracting my staff, interfering with my progress, and generally being a pain in my ass. And frankly, I'm getting a little tired of being the guy who cleans up your messes, bails you out of jail, or ends up with a misspelled tattoo!"

"He bailed you out of jail?" Nina asked, frowning.

"It was just a little protest on my college campus," Dotty assured her. "No big deal. The campus security guards had no sense of humor."

"She was naked," Deacon told Nina.

"I was a little naked," Dotty admitted. "But it was for a good cause."

"You were protesting the use of hormone-injected chicken in the campus cafeteria. How did that cause require you to be naked?" Jake asked, giving in to the need for a large drink.

"I think we're going to like her," Cindy told Nina.

Nina raised her hand. "I have a question. You're going to write a book about the house?"

Dotty beamed at Nina and practically skipped across the music room to throw her arms around her. She gave her a tight hug and then moved on to give Cindy similar treatment. Jake immediately poured Nina and Cindy their own drinks. "Yes! Well, it's not so much a book about the house as it is about our family. I'm a writer and photographer—"

This declaration was met by weary groans from Jake and Deacon.

Dotty glared at both of them. "Shut it, you two."

Shooing Jake away from the bar, Cindy poured Dotty a large drink of her own.

Dotty continued, "I'm a writer and a photographer, an art form I *happen* to take very seriously. I plan on documenting the entire renovation process, showing the house in its present decayed state and then whatever Deacon decides to do with it. I want to publish the pictures in a book explaining the house's history and how its construction affected our family."

"Air out our family laundry, you mean?" Deacon flopped into a nearby wingback chair, which buckled even under his slight weight.

"Deacon, it's been a hundred years. Trust me, that laundry's flapped in the breeze for quite a while. If anything, a book like this might clear up some of the more salacious rumors. And once I get my hands on Great-great-grandmother Catherine's diary—"

"Which has never been found," Deacon interjected.

Dotty glared at him. "And sorted through the family photos and documents—"

"Which have been ransacked and scattered all over the house by our dear relatives."

"I'm sure I'll be able to put together a more accurate picture of Catherine and Gerald," Dotty finished huffily. "And I'm sure I'll be able to explain the Whitney curse and why you seem to have been able to break it."

"There's no Whitney curse!" Deacon scowled.

"Oh, and there are no ghosts roaming the halls of the Crane's Nest, right?" Dotty shot back. "Despite the fact that almost every person who has visited this house in the last hundred years has had some sort of unsettling experience here. And I'm sorry, but what do you call it when—with the exception of you—no Whitneys have been able to make anything of themselves since Gerald Whitney? Any time a Whitney descendant starts a business venture or marries into a prominent family, that venture or that family is bankrupt within a year. The Whitney curse. Pretty soon, not even the pedigree was enough to tempt rich suitors or investors. The only thing the family has left is the island, this house, and what's left of its contents. And the only reason the family was able to hold on to it was that it was a land trust from the governor. Deacon here somehow broke the chain. I'm hoping that researching the book will help me figure out why."

Deacon drained his glass. "You are aware that there have already been three books published about Catherine and Gerald."

Dotty huffed out an irritated breath. A series of nasty pulp tell-all paperbacks had "reimagined" their great-great-grandmother's bitter end every twenty years or so. The first, in the 1940s, was the least offensive, postulating that Gerald had killed Catherine in a fit of jealous rage over her star-crossed love affair with Jack Donovan, the architect of the Crane's Nest and a former childhood friend of Mrs. Whitney's, and then used the fire in the south wing to distract the staff long enough to dump her body offshore. In the early 1960s, another book insisted that mounting debts and the sheer, overwhelming expense of building the house had sent Gerald into a resentful, murderous tailspin. Hollywood attempted to adapt that version into a thinly veiled feature film, which was slated to star Marilyn Monroe until her death shut down production. And in the late 1970s, the last, most vicious author to rewrite Whitney history accused Gerald of murdering Catherine in an opium-fueled rage after he found her in flagrante with her lady's maid.

For the first time since her arrival, Dotty frowned, muttering into her tumbler of vodka. "Yeah, and personally, I find it depressing, not just that the slander was so thorough but that investigators refused to deviate from the idea that Gerald killed his wife. No other suspect would do. It's closed-minded, which isn't tolerable. But it's also unimaginative, which is downright unforgivable. And none of those books was written with a family perspective. Face it, Deacon, I have just as much right to be here as you do. I don't resent you getting the house. Your dad was the oldest, and it was right that it passed to him, then you. But you know that you don't have it in that logical, mathematical heart of yours to shut me out. You need me here. Jake and I keep you human."

"You and Jake keep my insurance adjusters busy." Deacon snorted.

Jake made an indignant sound. "That's not— Wait, OK, that's fair."

"Fourth of July party?" Dotty guessed, giggling as Jake nodded. Realizing that Deacon was glaring at her, she stifled it, pulling a more penitent face. She may or may not have pouted her lips the slightest bit. When Deacon failed to respond, she made the pout more pronounced. Deacon grimaced. She ratcheted up the pout even more. Deacon groaned. For the others, it was like watching a ping-pong match consisting solely of facial expressions.

"The first time you mess up the construction schedule, you're out of here," Deacon warned her.

"You won't even know I'm here." Dotty giggled, hopping into Deacon's lap and giving him a world-class noogie. Deacon's eyes rolled toward the creepy cherubs, who remained unhelpful and silent on the subject of his cousin.

NINA WASN'T SURE what to make of Dotty Whitney. This was a woman who clearly had old blue blood flowing through her veins. She carried herself with that innate grace and assurance that old-money girls seemed to learn in their first days at prep school. Even the bohemian mishmash of tights, clashing scarves, and a loose man's shirt looked magazine-shoot-ready for some feature titled "Yard Sale Chic." But instead of turning her nose up at the accommodations in the staff quarters, she'd immediately starting adjusting the feng shui of her dorm bedroom.

"I could do yours, too," she offered, shoving her iron bedframe diagonally from the door in what she called the "commanding position" for energy restoration and calm.

"I'm good," Cindy said. "Nina?"

Nina was staring through the window at the main house. While a part of her still dreaded the idea of going inside, some peculiar, compulsive part of her brain was urging her back toward the house, to find out whether the smoky figure she'd seen was real or the imaginings of a brain pushed a little too far. There were so many things she hadn't seen in the house, so many rooms to explore. She could just walk across the lawn anytime she wanted and walk in. Why had she waited so long? She could go right now, if she wanted to, so why didn't she—

"Nina?" Cindy touched her arm. "You OK?"

"Oh, no." Nina put her hands up in a warding-off gesture. "Uh, I was just feng shuied last week."

Cindy noticed a well-crafted leather journal open on Dotty's bed. On the page there was a photo of the Eiffel Tower, shot at some distance, and another of a slim pair of feet clad in ballet flats on a cobblestone street. She crept a little closer and flipped to the next page, and the next. The book contained an extensive collection of black-and-white and color shots. A field of wheat with cypress trees spiking up from the golden waves. Black-and-white stills of the streets of Paris, a child eating an apple with an open-air market in the background.

"That is my portfolio," Dotty said. "I have some basic skill with a camera. So I've taken an obnoxious number of pictures while I have traveled. But I'm no Galen Rowell."

"You said something about a book?" Cindy asked.

"I want to document the whole renovation process,

and everybody involved, so release forms are coming your way, thank you very much. And I'll be going through the trunks and documents in the attic, looking for information about my great-great-grandparents and their marriage. I want to write about how the events of the past have affected our family over the years, how they're still affecting us, and how Deacon is trying to go about changing that. He'll hate every minute of being interviewed, but he'll get over it."

"Do you really want to dig up all that family dirt—" Nina cleared her throat. "I mean, history?"

Dotty threw a scarf decorated with multicolored skulls over the lamp on her nightstand. "Sometimes the dirt needs to be dug up."

Cindy's plump pink lips quirked. "Well, I can help you with the relics. I've already saved a few documents from an old desk of Gerald's that you might be interested in."

Dotty opened her shoulder bag and rummaged, muttering. "I have a whole list of items I'm looking for—diaries, housekeeping ledgers, visitor books, anything from the architect Jack Donovan's office on the property. If he kept a journal about the building process, that would be even better."

Cindy nodded. She'd seen plenty of old books around the house, some of them with handwritten pages. And as long as it was OK with Mr. Whitney, she didn't mind handing them over to another "on-site" Whitney for inspection before they were catalogued.

"I know that the house has been picked over pretty thoroughly over the years, so you can't promise much. Would you believe our parents had to actually chase some historical-society ladies off the island once because Deacon's dad caught them trying to 'claim' documents for their collections of artifacts? Of course, Deacon's dad wasn't supposed to be out here looking for valuables, either, but that's neither here nor there. Dang it!"

When she couldn't find what she wanted, she sighed, dug into her jeans pocket, and fished out what looked like a Starbucks napkin. She smiled triumphantly and handed her "list" over to Cindy. "And while you're at it, I need you to keep an eye out for these . . ." Dotty plopped onto her bed, kicking off her shoes and digging into her army duffel to pull out a sketchbook that she handed to Nina. Nina was beginning to wonder if it was like Mary Poppins's bottomless bag, with an endless supply of gypsy travel supplies.

She flipped through the sketchbook until she found several pages on which Dotty had fixed frayed, yellowed sketches of elaborate pieces of jewelry. A chunky bracelet made from diamond daisies. A choker consisting of two ropes of pearls holding in place a large citrine in a sunburst setting. A golden peacock brooch with emeralds and sapphires set in the tail. A multipaneled Bohemian-style garnet necklace.

"This is Catherine Whitney's fabled jewelry collection. Gerald may have been stingy with his affections, but he was a pioneer of the theory that diamonds make up for everything. Men of a certain class liked their peers to know they could afford to keep their wives and mistresses swimming in jewels. After search parties found her body and the maids were packing up her belongings, they realized the collection was

missing. Catherine's wedding-ring set was also missing from her hand when they found her, which just
reinforced the notion that she'd left her husband. Like
she'd ripped them off and thrown them at him in a
final 'eff you.' "

Nina peered down at the detailed sketch of a diamond ring set with sapphires. The sketch was marked
"Wedding set." Something about the ring was very familiar, but she couldn't quite place it. Maybe she had
seen something like it in a movie? She asked, "The
jewelry that she left behind, were they her costume
pieces?"

Dotty's eyebrows rose. "Why do you ask?"

Nina shrugged. "I just figured Gerald probably
didn't keep a lot of cash around the house. I've noticed
rich people tend not to. And if he did, Catherine probably didn't have access to it. So if she was about to bolt,
she probably took anything she could sell for traveling
money. If I'm running from a husband I resent and I
have a collection of expensive, easy-to-pawn jewels,
that's what I'm selling to get away with the man I
love. Said resented husband knows that not only have
I escaped him, but he funded my getaway with his
presents. It's the final 'up yours.' "

Dotty tilted her head as she looked Nina over.
"Once you relax a little, you don't pull any punches,
do you?"

"Neither do you," Nina retorted, her chin set in a
stubborn line. It was the sort of posture that would
have been natural—instinctual, even—just a few years
ago. Now it felt awkward, like stretching an unused
muscle. Dotty didn't seem offended. Her friendly smile

only stretched wider as she dug through her bottomless bag.

"The pieces she took were the real deal," Dotty assured her. "Back before the family fortune went belly-up, the Whitneys were what you might call conspicuous consumers, investing in some very flashy accessories for Catherine. And a good chunk of Catherine's jewelry collection was missing. But it wasn't found on her body. The police believed Gerald found her as she was making her escape, probably by the boat they found stashed on the far side of the island, and he killed her in a jealous rage, then dropped her into the water, thinking that she'd be carried out to sea. Family legend held that Gerald might have stashed the jewelry somewhere on the island after he killed her."

"Why would he have done that?"

"To conceal his involvement? To make it look like Catherine had been robbed once she reached the mainland? Because a man who strangles his own wife in a rage probably isn't great at long-term planning and impulse control? When you consider how desperately poor some of the descendants were, it was more of a fairy tale than anything else, some small hope that they could recover a piece of their legacy."

Cindy frowned. "The family had no problem believing that Gerald killed her?"

Dotty shook her head. "I think that's the part that bothers me the most. That it was so easy to accept that one of our own was capable of killing someone he'd promised to love, honor, and all that. It shows an incredible lack of trust, which after all the years, you'd think I would be used to, but still . . . it just hurts. And I think it hurts Gerald, too."

" 'Hurts' in the present tense?" Nina asked, lifting an eyebrow.

"You've heard the stories, of course," Dotty said. "The strange noises, the lights, the phantom voices. Unfortunately, Deacon and his parents have always refused to allow paranormal investigators onto the property to prove it, but there are several restless spirits wandering the house. Can't you feel them?"

The fact was, both Cindy and Nina could feel the heavy energy on the island, but neither was willing to admit it openly. Desperate to steer the conversation back to more neutral territory, Nina asked, "What were you saying about the jewelry?"

Dotty held up her hands. "I hope that if I find the jewelry, it will prove that there was some other motive to Catherine's death, some other sequence of events, or maybe even a new suspect."

"Not to mention the small fortune they're worth, right?" Cindy noted.

"Finding buried treasure would be nice. I mean, my relatives have been searching for those jewels ever since the 'Whitney curse' theory was born. My own granddad was convinced that if he found the jewelry, the curse would be broken and the family fortunes would reverse. Mostly, he just drove himself crazy and got a lot of splinters, digging up floorboards. But I think finding out that my great-great-grandfather wasn't a murderer would be pretty valuable, too. I think it would go a long way in clearing out some of the angry, frustrated spirit energy in this place and make it a lot safer for Deacon to live here."

"And what if you don't?" Cindy asked. "What if all you find is evidence that the stories about Gerald Whitney are true?"

Dotty shrugged and popped a soy crisp into her mouth from a container in her bag. "At least I'll know, and I can stop feeling indignant about the books and the ghost stories and the fact that a theme park offered to buy this place ten years ago to stage murder-mystery dinner reenactments during the summer."

"That would sting," Nina said, *tsk*ing sympathetically. "I can't imagine how I would feel if people trotted out my family's dysfunctional holiday dramas as entertainment. No one's been killed or anything, but we did have a wishbone-related stabbing once." Cindy and Dotty stared at her. "I mean, someone was stabbed *over* a wishbone, not *with* a wishbone. That would be weird."

Dotty—ignoring social convention and personal-space bubbles—wrapped her long, elegant fingers around Nina's wrist, pulling her hand away from her lips. "Sweetie, I bet you've got a great laugh. Stop covering it up."

"Even if you *are* a snorter," Cindy told her. "It's still a good laugh. Besides, in the next couple of months, I bet we're going to find out all sorts of embarrassing things about one another. Snort-laughs will be the least of our worries."

Since her ordeal with Rick, Nina had shrunk in on herself, trying not to laugh too loudly, smile too brightly, or do anything that would draw too much attention to herself. One of the things Rick had criticized most about her was her "Pollyanna" tendencies. She was too chirpy, too cheerful, too much to deal with first thing in the morning. She had become more subdued, more "mature," so she would be more presentable.

Nina let herself giggle a bit. Cindy rolled her eyes and dug her fingers into Nina's ribs, making her howl. She didn't hold back the half-joyful, half-anguished noise. She ducked away, holding her hands up in a defensive posture. "OK, OK. I'm ticklish. Cut it out."

Cindy shook her head and continued her assault on Nina's sides. "Not until—"

Nina sidestepped and pranced out of range but not before she let loose a loud, distinct snort. Dotty doubled over laughing, propping herself against her knees while Cindy dissolved into guffaws.

"You two . . . suck," Nina groused, although a genuine smile stretched her mouth so wide it nearly hurt.

"Watch the language there, Red, there are *ladies* present." Cindy gasped, her hand clapped to her mouth.

"Well, when I spot them, I'll be sure to censor myself," Nina retorted.

Dotty wiped at her eyes, while Cindy chuckled. The room fell silent in that special, awkward way that follows shared humor between near-strangers. Dotty had already decided she was going to like these women, come hell, high water, or snort-laughing. She had a feeling they would be key players in helping her nudge the ghosts from the Crane's Nest.

THE MAN CROUCHING just a hundred yards from the Crane's Nest was tall, dark, and handsome. But he was also hunched in the dry, tangled undergrowth between the untamed woods and the lawn proper, watching the staff quarters through binoculars, which didn't say much for his character.

Through the windows, he could see the women sitting around the ladies' kitchen area, drinking iced tea and eating cookies. The hippie girl with the wild hair was sitting cross-legged on the long kitchen table, telling some story that involved puffing out her cheeks and waving her hands like an idiot. The blonde burst out laughing, writhing and jiggling as she damn near fell over. Nina, as always, was slow to respond. She sat there like a bump on a log, practically asking for permission before working up the nerve to smile at the hippie girl's antics.

The hippie rolled her eyes, jostling Nina's arm and topping off her tea. Nina ducked her head, but he could make out the curve of her lips through the binoculars.

The man sniffed, his handsome face twisted into a mocking sneer as he watched the girls raise their glasses together. Well, wasn't that just precious? He was sitting out here in the heat, sweating his sack off, and Miss Priss was joining her Girl Scout troop for tea and cookies in the nice, cool house. She was rubbing elbows with the rich and famous, and he was hiding in the bushes like some nobody.

It wasn't fair. This wasn't the way it was supposed to turn out. Nina thought she could just walk away? She thought she could steal jobs from him and show him up? Not in this lifetime.

Make her pay, a voice whispered in his ear.

He started, looking around for whoever had whispered in his ear. He waved his hand, as if an errant mosquito were buzzing nearby in the fading light of afternoon. He focused his binoculars on the window, watching Nina sip her tea and delicately dab at her lips with a napkin.

Always so polite. He sneered. Always so prim and proper. She wouldn't say "shit" if she stepped in it. She was too good for that. It was what made her so easy to push around, her refusal to make a fuss even when she got trampled. Then again, the Virgin Mary act was also what had made her such a convincing little victim when she finally went to the cops to file her bullshit complaints against him. Conniving bitch.

Make her pay.

It wasn't a bad idea, he mused.

Nina should pay. She'd used her big doe eyes and her poor-orphan-victim routine to fool Deacon Whitney into hiring her, when she knew *he* was bidding for this job. The lack of loyalty shocked him, pissed him off. The minute she saw his name on the list of bidders, she should have stepped aside. He thought he'd made that clear with all the trouble he'd caused her, but she obviously hadn't understood the message, because here she was, on Whitney Island, where she had no business being.

Make her pay.

Yes, he would do that. He could show her, once and for all, who was in charge. He'd let her have her little moment now. He'd let her relax and think that maybe her stupid little business might make a go of it. But then he would crush her, just like he had at all the other job sites. He would fix it so that Nina was too much trouble to keep around. He would make Deacon Whitney feel unsafe having her on his staff. And who would be ready to step in and take over the mediocre work she'd done? He would.

Make her pay. The dark, seductive voice seemed to slither through his mind, worming its way into the cells and making them its own. *Show her who's in charge.*

He nodded slowly. It had been easy enough to sneak onto the island, even with the motion detectors and security cameras Whitney's people had arranged around the perimeter of the property. He'd simply followed the charter boat rented by the hippie girl and then veered south before they reached the shore. As he crept along the shoreline, he'd managed to spot every hidden piece of surveillance equipment. It was if he were being led along a safe path, allowing him to spy on the Whitney Island team undisturbed. The island, the house, wanted him here, he could feel it. A sly, rasping voice from the recesses of his brain told him so.

You're doing the right thing. You're putting her in her place. It wouldn't be so easy if you weren't doing the right thing. Whitney will probably thank you later.

He smiled, raising the binoculars to his eyes. Nina would be sorry that she ever crossed him. She would pay.

Sending Ghostly Tantrum
Throwers to Time-Out

CINDY HADN'T BEEN entirely honest when she told Nina that she hadn't felt anything out of the ordinary at the Crane's Nest. Since her initial walk-through, she'd felt eyes sliding over her skin like eels. She was used to people looking at her. You didn't spend your middle-school years in a D-cup without developing a sort of sixth sense for skeeviness. But in the Crane's Nest, she felt as if she was being studied, examined like prey from every alcove and cubby in the house. She sensed shadowy blurs at the corners of her eyes, but when she turned her head, they were gone. She tried blaming the unnatural chill of the rooms for the goose bumps and the feeling that someone was standing behind her, but her stubborn fight-or-flight response wasn't buying it.

Despite her fairy-tale face, Cindy Ellis wasn't one for

flights of fancy. Growing up, she hadn't had the time to waste. And now she didn't have the patience for anything that stood in the way of her goals. She'd purposefully ignored the Crow's Nest's unsavory reputation while composing her bid, because it didn't fit her overall agenda to shy away from such a potential career boost. Like every skeptical Newport local, she'd scoffed at the ghost stories connected to the house. Rich people and their nonsense, her father had called it, a waste of a perfectly good house, sitting out in the middle of nowhere, rotting away because of greed and ego. John Ellis had never had time for either. His girl was too smart to let something like "bad vibes" get in the way of doing a job right. An Ellis didn't back down from a challenge, even when the challenge was accompanied by goose bumps and foreboding. She could get over both with a stiff drink and a mushy Sandra Bullock movie.

But now that she was actually on the island, Cindy couldn't shake the feeling that there was something very wrong with this house.

And she wasn't alone. Cindy had lost two day-crew employees within the first three days on the job. She wasn't about to tell Mr. Whitney. She simply replaced them with other members of her team and continued the preliminary cleanup. She couldn't blame her employees for their sudden departure. They'd reported inexplicable cold spots, the sensation of being watched, footsteps in rooms where they were the only occupants. On the third morning, Greta and Maria, two of Cindy's most reliable cleaners, had abandoned the entry hall and run for the dock, purses in hand, to wait for the next ferry—which wasn't due for six hours.

Greta would only say that she wouldn't continue working in the house, and if that meant she was fired, she would accept that. Maria was considerably more descriptive, chattering nervously as Cindy tried to coax them back into the house.

"This is a bad place, Miss Ellis," Maria had told her, clutching the little gold crucifix around her throat. "Watching, everything is watching, waiting, for the right time to reach out. You don't want to be reached."

And now, as she was sorting through furniture in one of the second-floor guest rooms, she was moving around the bright, airy room, in the process of whipping a dusty storage sheet off a piece of mystery furniture, and she could clearly hear the faint echo of footsteps moving around on the third floor. And no one was supposed to be working on the third floor.

Cindy stood slowly, staring up at the plastered-medallion ceiling. Maybe it was a worker doing some sort of preliminary inspection? Or maybe it was just the house settling. She'd worked in enough old houses to know what noises they made when they shifted. She'd almost talked herself into ignoring it and continuing on with her work, when the ceiling right above her head groaned under the moving burden of some heavy wooden object. It sounded as if someone was moving furniture up there, something she had specifically instructed Anthony's crew not to do, as she had to sort through and label everything from its original position, per the requirements of the Whitney family's lawyer. And they were doing it in Mrs. Whitney's bedroom, which was one of the most contentious areas of the house. Aside from the dresses, costume jewelry, and antiques, the room contained personal mementos such as a hope chest filled with Mrs. Whitney's trousseau. Several Whitney relatives were petitioning for the right to run through that room like a Macy's white sale. So properly cataloging the Whitney boudoir before it could be ransacked was priority one.

Cindy nervously swiped her hands along the burnished gold tendrils that had escaped from her tight French braid. She really didn't want to go upstairs, particularly by herself, but the possibility of the furniture being moved without her approval was enough to get her feet moving toward the second-story landing. "Hey!" she called. "This is Cindy. I don't know who's up there, but you're not supposed to be moving anything."

No response.

A cold trickle of sweat ran down her spine, soaking into her blue Cinderella Cleaning T-shirt. Over the faint reports of nail guns and the muffled conversations of the workers, she could hear a strange cyclical humming of air. It was as if the house was breathing. Cindy waited for a long moment, praying that the noise would stop so she could forget about the whole incident. But there it was again, the scraping of furniture against the floor, farther down the hall now.

"Hello?" Cindy called.

The silence seemed to stretch out forever, mocking her. She stepped onto the stairs for the third floor, the air growing heavier, pressing against her from all sides, as if she were climbing through thick syrup. Instinctively, she stepped back and was ashamed that a staircase and a few bumps and thumps had her wanting to bolt for the main floor and the safety of other people.

"Hey!" she called again, her voice pitching higher. "Answer me, damn it!"

And through her shame came a bolstering tickle of anger. She was an Ellis. An Ellis didn't back down. Whoever was up there didn't know who they were dealing with. Cindy placed a foot on the first stair, gripping the banister, her knuckles white.

She felt the first impact in her stomach, as if she'd been sucker punched by some unseen fist. She wheezed, barely able to brace herself against the banister and avoid tumbling down the stairs. Her head swam, and her throat closed up, sinking her in a swampy mire of pain and confusion. What was this? What was happening to her?

The world seemed to spin. Her head rolled, and her eyesight blurred. She clung to consciousness, all that prevented her from taking a header down the steps.

"Help—" She started to scream, but a sudden, unexpected pressure at her throat stole her breath. It felt as if she were drowning, strangling, unable to draw air. She stumbled back a step, which made the pressure ease a bit. She rubbed at her throat and gasped, but the moment the air passed her lips, she fell to her knees, fighting the invisible blockage in her airway.

Clawing at the ancient carpeting, she felt her insides go cold. Tears slid down her cheeks as she writhed against the stairs. *Somebody help me.* She begged no one in particular. *Please let someone find me. Anybody, please.*

Cindy heard the rapid fire of footsteps on the stairs and a familiar, panicked voice. "Cindy! What happened?"

Anybody but Jake.

Jake pulled her toward him and into the cradle of his lap. The grip at her throat eased, and a small but steady stream of oxygen flowed into her lungs. The spasming in her chest finally relaxed, and she breathed deeply for the first time in what felt like an eternity.

Her eyelids fluttered open, and she saw Jake hovering over her, his face awash in concern as he pushed a tangle of hair out of her eyes.

The baby blues hadn't hurt, of course, but Cindy had agreed to that first date with him because she'd thought he was different from the yacht-club guys. And then, of course, he'd proven her wrong.

Jake was still staring at her. And the house had tried to kill her. *Right. Focus on the murderous house.*

"I'm fine," she said, her voice coming across as an indignant croak. "I just tripped."

"In a way that left a bright red mark on your throat?"

Her hand flew to cover the sore strip of skin where she'd clawed her own neck. "Yep."

"OK, we'll just pretend I buy that for now." He moved to help her up, but she shrugged him off, using the stair rail as leverage. She rubbed at her neck.

It was her imagination. She had to believe it. She had to write off that crushing, breath-free vacuum as something innocuous; otherwise, she would have to run screaming from this island and the payday she needed to keep her business prospering for years to come. She just had an overactive imagination combined with dust allergies that made her feel as if she was choking. Of course, she'd never had dust allergies before, but that didn't mean anything.

And in general, dust allergies didn't make one so dizzy that one missed a step and tumbled face-forward down a flight of stairs.

"Hey!" Jake exclaimed, barely catching her by the elbows and yanking her to his chest, sending both of them crashing backward onto the staircase. Cindy landed in his lap with an "*ungfh*," her head lolling back against Jake's shoulder.

Jake's arms tightened around her. And even in Cindy's woozy state, she noted that he was packing some pretty impressive biceps under the ridiculous pastel-green tennis shirt. It was galling to still be attracted to him, to see him being all concerned and knight-in-Polo-armor when she knew what he was really like. She was woefully familiar with how quickly he lost interest when he didn't get what he wanted. It made her want to smack that far-too-close-to-sincere anxious expression right off his handsome face.

His stupid, beguiling, handsome-as-all-hell face.

But before the smacking could commence, Jake swept her hair back from her eyes and seemed to check her over from head to toe for injuries. He shifted her in his lap so she was more comfortable and cradled her as if she was made of the same delicate porcelain as the furnishings downstairs. It made her feel safer than she had in years, more cherished since she had during her failure of an engagement, since before her father got so sick—

No.

Cindy peeled his hands away from her arms and would have stood if her legs hadn't folded under her like a cheap accordion. Jake frowned, and before she could wriggle out of his grip, he murmured, "You really don't like me, do you?"

The wounded, lost tone of his voice shook her resolve more than she cared to admit. She didn't like hurting him, no matter what Nina thought. She just didn't want to be bothered with his feelings. She wanted separation, distance, the objectivity she needed to do her job in a professional, memorable manner that would lead to referrals and further expansion of her business.

Getting out of his lap would probably be a good start.

She grasped the banister, gingerly lifting herself off Jake. He steadied her with a light touch at her spine. She covered the resulting shiver with a roll of her shoulders, as if she could push her vertebrae back into a reasonable configuration and rid herself of her puppyish response to Jake's touch all in one movement.

"I don't know you well enough not to like you," she said, without looking back. "I don't know you at all."

I never got the chance, a bitter voice added in her head.

"Well, you can get to know me," Jake said cheerfully, helping her navigate the stairs without further incident. "And in the meantime, maybe you can get some rest and fluids in your system, maybe a CAT scan just to be safe."

Cindy snorted but allowed Jake's hand at her elbow to steady her in her descent to the main floor of the house. Oddly, she wanted Nina. She'd only known the woman for a short time, but she wanted the redhead's quiet, calming influence to help figure out what had just happened to her.

Not that she would tell Nina about her near-asphyxiation on the stairs—or Dotty, for that matter. Nina was already skittish about the house. Dotty would latch onto the incident as some sort of proof that the house contained restless, hoping-to-be-aided-from-beyond-the-grave spirits. And while Deacon seemed to feel obliged to keep his crazy cousin on the island, Cindy didn't want to be kicked off this project herself for having a tragic case of the batshit crazies. But she knew that Nina would know how to make her feel better, whether it was a sympathetic hug or some of that soothing rose-hip tea that Cindy was convinced contained some form of natural narcotics.

For now, she could only permit herself to be supported down the stairs by the insistently cheerful Jake.

And when they reached the main floor, Jake damn near dropped her.

Cindy would swear later that she actually felt the fibers of the carpet brush her face before Jake caught her again and set her on her feet. Her already unsteady equilibrium barely registered Deacon standing in the entryway. Nina and Dotty were framed in the doorway, a rare irritated expression on Dotty's face as she watched Deacon talking to a sleek, reed-thin woman with a shiny bob of raven hair. The strange woman turned toward the staircase just as Cindy stumbled from the stairs.

"*Dar*-ling!" The newcomer didn't walk, she undulated, as if the reptiles sacrificed to make her sky-high heels had some sort of sympathetic magic locked in their skin. Her dress—a dizzying black, purple, and white zigzag pattern—was tight and draped precisely to show off a body honed by ruthless attention to calories and a trainer who showed no mercy.

A chain of intricately patterned silver, set with amethyst and onyx, stretched in a sinuous line across her collarbone, matching the stark onyx drops at her lobes. Her makeup was simple yet dramatic. Her boldly painted red mouth curved into a calculating smile. She might have been Snow White to Cindy's Cinderella. But that smile made her more of an Evil Queen.

"Oh, it's so good to see you!" the woman cooed, giving Jake an air-kiss that just missed his cheek. It was casual but somehow struck Cindy as staking a claim, an unladylike marking of territory. "It's been too long, darling, really. Mother was just saying the other day that we never see you! The Lilac Ball at the club. Our annual lawn party. You've turned down all of our invitations. If you're not careful, you're going to hurt our feelings. I'm going to start thinking you've lost interest in me."

The woman poked out her ruby-stained bottom lip in a perfectly practiced pout. For his part, Jake looked horror-struck, his shocked gaze drifting between this woman and Cindy without managing to land. He started to say something several times and then closed his mouth, only to open it again. Cindy supposed this was one of Jake's many quote-unquote girlfriends. No wonder he seemed nervous about being seen holding her. Or maybe he didn't want someone who was obviously a friend of his fancy-pants family seeing him cuddling the "help"?

Seeming reluctant to let go of Cindy's arm, Jake had little choice when the woman hooked her arm through his and led him back to where Deacon stood.

As the newcomer gushed over how *thrilled* she was to be involved and that she just couldn't wait to get started, which was why she'd shown up weeks ahead of schedule to present Deacon with her design ideas for the interior, Cindy rolled her eyes. Typical. Now that this barracuda with the telltale red-soled shoes was in the picture, he'd dropped Cindy and moved on.

Cindy pursed her lips, steadied herself against the banister for a moment. It sucked to be right all the time.

Resolving to forget the entire "tripping" episode, Cindy made her way to the opposite side of the room, where Dotty and Nina were whispering quietly.

"The insecure preadolescent girl inside of me is curled up in the fetal position," Nina grumbled, noting with inexplicable irritation the way the new arrival was practically standing on Deacon's feet, murmuring to him in low, familiar tones; until the moment Jake had walked in, anyway, which was the moment she launched herself at *him*. Poor Anthony had been standing off to the side, intently staring at the blueprints of the house so he could look anywhere besides at his boss getting kitten-whispered. And Deacon looked . . .

Well, maybe Nina didn't know Deacon well enough to gauge his facial expressions. He seemed impassive, even bored. He hadn't exactly been leaning into the lady's aural assault, but his face didn't give off a *Get thee away from me, you fashion-forward she-beast!* vibe, either.

In Nina's mind, Indignant Deacon spoke like a character from *Game of Thrones*.

"Oh, honey, she doesn't deserve your head space." Dotty sighed. "That's just Regina Van Hauten. We've known her since, oh, two or three noses ago." When Cindy lifted an eyebrow, Dotty clarified, "Since high school. Her family is close to Deacon's and Jake's parents."

"And why is she here?" Cindy asked.

Dotty's facial expression wasn't hard to decipher at all, with her mouth pinched into a derisive frown. "Regina's supposedly an interior designer, but judging by the hatchet job she did on Deacon's corporate offices, I'm betting she got her training from one of those videos you can order from an infomercial."

"Uncomfortable seating and abstract art?" Nina guessed.

"There's an 'installation' of discarded Starbucks cups in the lobby by some artist from Hoboken. It's called 'The Globalization of Mediocrity.' The janitor kept trying to throw it away, so Regina's idea was to put up a sign that says, 'Please don't recycle the art.' "

Cindy bit her lip before a snicker could escape. Dotty grinned at her, even as Regina sent the pair a scathing look. Nina noted that Regina hadn't bothered introducing herself to Nina or Cindy.

Dotty muttered, "I told Deacon not to hire her, but he said he 'has his reasons' for letting her ruin both his offices *and* his home. And when I press him, he refuses to answer, which is saying something, because I can *always* get Deacon to fess up. Just for your information, he is very ticklish."

"How will that information ever be of use to me?" Nina asked.

Dotty wriggled her eyebrows. "I can think of a few ways." Nina stared at her, adopting Deacon's "impassive" expression. "Oh, come on, I've seen the two of you together. It's like watching a nature documentary on scientists trying to get the two most socially awkward people in the world to mate."

"Not true!" Nina whispered back. "We talk about work-related subjects, that's all."

Just then, Deacon looked up from Regina's papers and gave Nina a lingering look, as if she were the only thing giving him the strength to continue his conversation with his decorator. Nina's face flushed bright red, and Dotty fanned her cheeks with Cindy's clipboard.

"Oh, hush, the both of you," Nina muttered.

"You made my cousin *smolder*," Dotty whispered in awe. "Until two years ago, he didn't wear matching socks half the time. He actually pays someone to match his clothes for him. So for him to throw any sort of swagger at you, that's sort of a miracle."

"He probably just had something in his eye," Nina protested softly. "Now, be quiet before someone hears you. This is a foyer, not a cone of silence."

"You're right, he did have something in his eye," Cindy singsonged. "You."

Nina groaned.

"Sweetheart, I'm going to insist that you ride that man like a pony," Cindy added. "For the good of mankind, technological advancement, and America's place in the worldwide economy. Think of the gadgetry he could come up with if he had a little stress relief."

Nina poked at Cindy's arm. "You are all class, my friend."

"Anyway, back to Regina," Dotty interjected, although she continued to fan Nina's pink face with her hands. "She makes a halfhearted effort at seducing Deacon, but the real prize is the house. I'm guessing she thinks revamping the place, emphasis on the 'vamp,' will put her on the cover of *Town and Country* or *Architectural Digest.*"

Nina shook her head, staring up at the seashell design on the ceiling. It was almost a relief to be back inside the house. Ever since her first visit, on the day of Dotty's arrival, she'd had a constant, nagging, almost compulsive urge to go back inside. Standing there in the main hall put a stop to the buzzing loop of need in the corners of her brain. She wasn't frightened. She wasn't nervous. In fact, other than the weird social pressure of having the living embodiment of all her female insecurities hanging all over Deacon's arm, she felt pretty darn relaxed. "I'm sure she won't want to change too much about the house. It's already beautiful; it just needs to be freshened up a bit."

But twenty minutes later, as Regina unveiled her presentation boards in the library, all hope for a refurbished masterpiece filled with lovingly restored antiques died a horrific death. Regina's proposal showed red walls with a vinyl-slick finish for the library. An oversized black lacquer table took up most of the space in front of the entryway fireplace. A bizarrely sculpted brushed-metal light fixture would replace the chandelier in the foyer. The other rooms weren't much better. Unrelenting supermodern patterns of black, white, and red. White and black plastic furniture that looked like the ugly love child of Danish Modern and Barbie's Dreamhouse. Spiky modern metal sculptures that would require anyone in a two-mile radius to get a tetanus shot.

Nina didn't know much about interior decorating, but she knew ugly, expensive, and uncomfortable when she saw it. And Regina's sketches hit the trifecta.

"Why, Deacon, you're so quiet. What do you think?" Regina demanded in a teasing tone.

DEACON WAS STARING at the presentation boards, his mouth hanging open like the anguished figure in Edvard Munch's *The Scream*. In fact, hanging *The Scream* in his living room would probably create a much more restful space in his home than the majority of Regina's designs. He squirmed in his seat, clearing his throat and crossing his arms over his chest. This had been a huge mistake. He'd given Regina this job to settle their debt once and for all, but what she'd produced was completely off the mark. It was as if she had photocopied the designs from his office and simply thrown them up on the imagined walls of the Crane's Nest. Even if he were only planning to use the house as a showplace, this design was cold, sterile, and completely incongruent with the exterior. What was worse, the designs were lazy and unimaginative, and that was something Deacon would not tolerate. However, he wouldn't humiliate Regina in front of the rest of the team. Not living on the island full-time, she had already pointedly mentioned, she was at a disadvantage compared with the rest of the team. Giving her designs the much-deserved red X of rejection in front of the others would make her that much more difficult to work with. He just needed to survive this renovation so he could cut the last string between them and move on with his life. He didn't like loose ends.

"It's interesting," he said. "But to be honest, I was

thinking of something a little less geometric . . . and less plastic. I'd like to keep some impression of the house's original design."

"Of course, of course," Regina said breezily. "It will take some back-and-forth to refine the plans, but it's so good to know you like my overall concept. I'll move forward with this theme in mind."

"That's actually the exact opposite of what I just said," Deacon noted. "If I'm not making myself clear, we can sit down right now and review the parameters of the project."

"We'll discuss it," Regina assured him. "Just let the concept simmer in your imagination for a bit, and we'll revisit the boards in a week. Now, let's talk about the plans for the ballroom, because Jake is being very stubborn about the window issue."

Regina looped her arm through his and sauntered down the hallway toward the ballroom. Deacon glanced over his shoulder at Nina and noticed with some apprehension that she, Cindy, and Dotty had their heads together, whispering animatedly among themselves. He couldn't make out what the girls were saying, but he was sure that they weren't planning a session of pedicures and margaritas.

This was going to get complicated.

THE TRIO OF ladies stood before the design boards, and despite the fact that they didn't share a single gene, they somehow managed matching expressions of horrified disbelief.

"She's going to turn it into the house from *Beetlejuice*," Nina hissed.

"We have to stop her," Cindy insisted. "Or kill her. Or both."

"Well, if you want to get away with a gruesome murder, this is clearly the place," Nina muttered, glancing around the library. "Sorry, Dotty."

Dotty shrugged. "I'm just trying to figure out how we can make it look like an accident or maybe a shark attack. *Jaws* was set in New England, so it's plausible. All we need to do is call in a few fake great white sightings and bend the tips of Nina's garden tools into triangle shapes so we can make the little bite marks. Then—" She paused when she realized that the other two were staring at her, mouths agape. "I went too far, didn't I?"

Nina patted her hand. "You had me until the mangled gardening tools."

Ninja Death Squad Buttons: The Latest in Modern Romantic Gestures

NINA STOOD IN the filtered light of the solarium, rubbing the skin along her arms.

It should have been warm. The room had floor-to-ceiling windows on all sides, letting sunlight flood through the fly-specked glass. In fact, the ceiling was made up of windows, arching out from the stone structure like a closed eyelid.

But there was little warmth to be found here. This place was almost as spooky as the baby-face-ceiling room. The roots of long-dead vines snaking up the walls and the remains of overturned planters were bad enough. The scent of dry rot and decay filled her nostrils, making her bite back a gag. Nina knew that plant death and composting were all part of the growth cycle, but this was waste. Whatever had been planted here had been abandoned, left behind without care, and that tugged at Nina's heart. But the truly creepy feature of the room, the heart of well-lit darkness, was the two carved stone figures that stood in the middle of the tiled floor, frozen mid-step.

The statue was of two small children, playing, their little hands reaching to the sky for something they were chasing. A kite? A butterfly? Their little faces were carved in expressions of joy. It was the only nonmythological statue in the house. Had Catherine based it on her own children? Had she hoped for them to play near their stone avatar, or had she meant for the statue to serve as a reminder of her children's innocent days? Somehow, that made it even sadder. Somehow, Nina's heart ached for those children, whose mother had loved them so much but was never able to see them grow up. The statue was a perfect representation of life at the Crane's Nest, forever stuck and then abandoned from the moment Catherine Whitney disappeared.

Tiny floor tiles of sandy beige met a rippling line of weathered blue glaze that had once been glistening cobalt.

"It looks like a beach," she said, turning to Deacon, who was watching her wander around the room while gnawing at her bottom lip.

THE LIP WORRYING should not have been as cute as it was. Deacon felt a pang of guilt for asking Nina into the house when she was so uncomfortable. He knew he was making excuses—*flimsy* excuses—to spend time with her. But he wanted to assure himself that she was all right. He'd been having a strange recurring dream for weeks, ever since Dotty's arrival. He was standing on the roof of the Crane's Nest, a delicately curved feminine figure in front of him, silhouetted against the orange-gold sunset. Her light blue skirts whipped in the wind. He could see the sparkle of silver embroidery at her sleeves. He was happy to see this woman, content to walk up behind her and wrap his arms around her lithe form. She sighed and relaxed back into him.

Catherine Whitney was a great beauty, there was no doubt of it. Her dark golden hair framed a face that was classically beautiful, with a full Cupid's-bow mouth, high cheekbones, and wide, deep-set eyes that were closed against the fading light. He saw his hands sliding up to cup Catherine's face, cradling her cheeks in his palm. She smiled up at him, leaning into the caress like a cat. He loved this woman, as much as he could love anyone. But she wanted to leave him. She thought she had the right. He would not let her go. No matter what she said, no matter whom she claimed her heart belonged to, she would always be his. And he never gave up what was his.

In the dream, Deacon watched his neatly manicured hands skimming down Catherine's neck, his thumbs tracing the depression at the hollow of her throat. He pressed in, watching her eyes snap open in alarm as he increased the pressure. She cried out, clawing at his hands as he squeezed her throat.

Catherine fought, as she always fought him, but in the end, he was too strong. He choked the life from her body and dropped her to the tiled widow's walk. Deacon watched in horror as Catherine's hair bled into a burnt auburn. Her still, blue-tinged face shifted into Nina's delicate features.

Deacon would wake up, drenched in sweat, with the image of Nina's still, broken body burned into his brain. He'd asked her to accompany him into the house that morning after a particularly vivid bout with the dream. He could still feel the way the muscles of her throat rippled as she struggled to draw breath. He needed to see her, to have a concrete touchstone to assure himself that she was safe, that she was well.

But seeing her now, penny-bright against the background of disorder and decline, he felt as if he'd betrayed her somehow. He should have guessed that she would find it painful to see a room meant to grow and nurture life now so empty and decrepit. Nina Linden was almost entirely made up of reminders of her vitality—rosy lips, marigold hair, dreamy eyes the color of new moss. And yes, he realized it was prosaic to refer to Nina in plant terms, but he couldn't help but think pretty floral thoughts whenever she was near. Moss wasn't strictly floral, but . . . and now she was staring at him.

He cleared his throat. "My parents said Catherine wanted her children to have a place to play in the sun, even if the weather turned cool. She had to fight for it, because back then, children were to be seen and not heard. To devote any room besides the nursery to them, much less a first-floor room that could be seen by guests, was almost unheard of."

Nina smiled at him. "Don't take this the wrong way, but if you tell me you want to turn this into a media room or something, I won't be responsible for my own actions. There will be a trowel involved."

"No," he said, raising his hands as if to defend his face from her, making her smile. The smile did funny things to his heart and its ability to keep an even rhythm. "I would like to keep the room pretty close to its original purpose, a place to soak up some sun and relax a little, read, work, whatever. Nothing crazy. I was thinking you might come up with some sort of indoor garden. Set it up however you'd like."

"I don't know if this is going to fit with the concept that Regina has planned. She doesn't seem to like . . . living things."

Deacon winced. "The presentation boards?"

"They were very specific, concept-wise."

"Yes, they were," he said, his lips twitching as Nina laughed. "I let Regina and Jake install my office when we first started working on the house, because I wanted it up and running before I moved out here for the renovations. The electricians got as far as updating the wiring and finishing the drywall before the house's reputation scared them off. Jake and I had to install all the hardware ourselves. But Regina seemed to get the idea that I want everything to look like this, which explains that rather horrific presentation she just gave. And so I spent a good three hours in videoconference with her this morning, going over the changes I want to her designs."

"But you didn't reject the ideas outright when she was standing right in front of you." Nina seemed to think about that for a long moment. "Because she would take correction over the Internet more graciously than in front of the rest of us."

"Exactly. I've persuaded her to go in a completely different direction, something called Mediterranean

Coastal Modern. All I know is that nothing will be made of vinyl, and I will be able to sit on the furniture."

"Impressive."

"It was a nightmare," he said. "I never want to see another fabric sample in HD."

Nina's brow furrowed. "So wait, we're living in relative unrehabilitated squalor in the staff quarters, and you've got high-speed Wi-Fi in your office? Have you ever heard of priorities?"

"I consider high-speed Wi-Fi to be a priority!" he exclaimed.

When Nina burst out laughing, he grinned. "It helps me to have a space here that reminds me of my office. I feel at home, and I work a lot faster."

"Oh, fine, bring logic and business sense into it. You know I can't argue with that," Nina huffed good-naturedly. She crossed her arms and turned around, scanning the space. "Well, the tropical thing has been done to death. You could always go Asian Modern, have Anthony's crews dig a koi pond in the floor, plant some weeping cherry trees. You don't have to do the full Zen rock garden and put up little concrete pagodas, but you can keep it restful, meditative. Or skip the Asian thing entirely, and you could go with the theme of your office and make it a full-on Bond-villain lair. We could put a button over there that summons your ninja death squad."

"Ugh," he groaned, making her blush. "I don't know what's weirder. The fact that it makes perfect sense to install the ninja death squad button in my indoor garden or the fact that I'm considering doing it just because it would make you laugh."

A genuinely pleased smile had Nina ducking her head. "Well, flowers and candy have been overdone, I think."

Deacon made a mental note to have ninja death squad buttons installed in every room of the Crane's Nest.

CATHERINE WHITNEY'S BEDROOM was elegant in its decay. Long ago, it had been an airy, sparsely decorated room done in feminine shades of blue, green, and cream. Unlike the more ornate, slightly Gothic pieces downstairs, the furniture was slender and sleekly lined. The bedposts were carved to resemble dryads—another creature prone to abuse from rutting gods, Dotty noted.

While Deacon had been frightened and upset by his childhood experiences at the Crane's Nest, Dotty cherished the memories of running amok in the old house. It had never felt haunted or even unfriendly. She only remembered exploring the rooms, admiring what few knickknacks and treasures were left, and finding little nooks and crannies where she and Deacon could hide from the bickering adults. It felt like a very formal playground. And now Dotty was just as comfortable as ever in the neglected rooms.

On one level, she was grateful not to experience the fear that Deacon and the others felt in the house. Dotty was an emotionally open person, and negative emotions were always more difficult to process than positive ones. And given the negative emotions that were no doubt lurking within the walls of the Crane's Nest, the impact on her could be overwhelming. But it was also frustrating that the spirits were ignoring the one person on the island who believed in them. She was starting to wonder if she should play hard to get like Deacon and loudly proclaim that she didn't believe in silly things like ghosts.

But Dotty did believe. Even in the face of Jake's teasing and Deacon's skepticism, she was a believer—in spirits, in love at first sight, and in destiny. She'd always known Deacon was destined for great things, crazy, world-altering developments in technology, just as she'd always known it was her destiny to help bring the Whitney family curse to an end. She didn't know how, and she knew she wouldn't do it alone, but she would help find what was needed to bring Catherine Whitney's soul to rest.

And it would start in this room. Catherine's suite was one of the places she and Deacon hadn't been allowed to enter when they were children. There were too many still potentially valuable items in the room, and their parents hadn't wanted to risk the kids damaging them during hide-and-seek. Dotty carefully sat on the ancient mattress and studied the figures, their graceful arms raised over their heads, becoming tree limbs that supported the canopy. Dotty had to stare at the carefully crafted limbs for a long time before she could decide where the carvings made the transition from flesh to wood. Soft folds of translucent mauve material hung loose from the bed like a shroud. A creamy silk-covered settee was placed in front of the large picture window. Several small volumes of poetry were stacked on a little table nearby.

Mr. Whitney's room was adjacent to Catherine's, separated only by a shared dressing room. A most civilized way for old-fashioned couples to maintain privacy while keeping channels of "communication" open. Sitting now on Catherine Whitney's bed, Dotty tried to imagine what it must have been like to live this way.

What would it be like, she wondered, to wake up every morning to this sort of luxury? Dotty hadn't grown up poor, exactly, but her parents certainly hadn't been able to afford anything like the Whitney manse. What did women like Catherine Whitney do all day? She'd seen enough *Downton Abbey* to visualize a lot of costume changes, dressing appropriately for various meals and activities of the day.

Speaking of which, where were all of Catherine's clothes? According to Jake's blueprints, there was a dressing room between Mr. and Mrs. Whitney's rooms. If she was a woman of means, she would have wanted to keep her clothes and accessories as close together as possible. Could the jewelry be hidden in some secret compartment in her closet?

Dotty crossed the room and opened the door opposite the bed. She coughed, waving the flurry of dust away from her face. A stained-glass window depicting a golden-haired woman in a flowing blue Greek gown provided the only light, giving the room a faint azure glow. Other than a vanity and an enormous floor-to-ceiling gilt mirror, every inch of the walls was occupied by paneled cabinets. No doubt, the clothes were stored in those, keeping the dressing room uncluttered. A dress dummy lurked in the corner, its disembodied presence giving Dotty her first pangs of unease. Catherine's maid would have hung whatever ensemble Catherine had planned for the evening meal or other affair over the model. But still, it was creepy as all hell.

What had it been like for Catherine Whitney to get dressed in this room every day? Didn't she ever want to throw on some comfy clothes and eat cookies? Did she have comfy clothes? In spite of considerable wealth, her life didn't seem particularly comfortable. What would it be like to spend every moment of your life being watched?

She shivered, turning her attention back to the cabinets. Where to start? She'd read up on what passed for security systems in the Gilded Age. While heavy-duty vaults were still entrusted with major financial holdings, Dotty also knew that the rich kept smaller caches in hiding places in their close quarters. Cabinets, dressers, desks. Furniture makers who could specialize in artful pieces with hidden compartments were in high demand.

Dotty studied the cabinets. The panels were carved with designs, but dust obscured them. Dotty tugged her scarf from her neck and began swiping at the panel closest to the vanity. In the dim light, she could see elaborately curlicued waves and seashells emerging. As she moved closer to the mirror, she uncovered the beginning of a much larger seashell and a pair of feet rising from the shell. Judging by the other mythological themes found around the rest of the house, she would guess that the carving was of Aphrodite, goddess of love and beauty, a rather unimaginative motif for a dressing room. She was a little disappointed in Catherine for being so prosaic in her decor.

Dotty rubbed a little harder at the curls circling the

goddess's knees and flowing down to her feet. At the very bottom of the panel, about three feet from the floor, she felt a tug on her scarf. Dotty stepped back. Had she snagged something? Pursing her lips, she continued to scrub at the carved feet. The cloth snagged again, and she yanked hard to pull it free. Somewhere under the panel, she heard a distinct click and the whir of rollers. She glanced down just in time to see what looked like some sort of support beam for the cabinets pop out. She danced out of the way before it whacked her in the shins.

Realizing what she'd uncovered, she shouted, "Destiny, you sneaky little bitch!"

LUGGING THE HEAVY cube-shaped box under one arm, Dotty was perfectly comfortable walking through the series of doors and false walls that led into Deacon's new private office. Tucked behind the library, the ten-by-twenty room had once served as a secret storage place for spirits, as Gerald Whitney didn't like the idea of leaving his personal stash of Scotch housed in the wine cellar. It was one of many secret rooms and passageways the original architect had tucked around the house. Dotty and Deacon had discovered most of them as children.

Dotty punched the entry code into the security panel mounted outside his door. Without being told, she knew it would be 51939—the release date of the first *Batman* comic. He'd used some variation of the code for his high school locker combination, ATM PIN, and garage-door key. The oak-paneled door slid left with a hiss.

Dotty rolled her eyes heavenward. Only her cousin would put a comic-book spin on an antique door. Even after spending time in Deacon's just-short-of-the-holodeck-on-the-starship-*Enterprise* offices in Boston, she still was stunned by the contrast between his office and the rest of the house. Unlike the elegant decay of the mansion's other rooms, the walls here were painted a smooth, blinding white, with huge high-definition panel screens covering nearly every inch from waist height to her line of sight. Instead of sports on every screen, Dotty spotted the EyeDee home page, Deacon's personal e-mail account, his business e-mail, and his Twitter feed.

On the screens closest to the sleek white-and-chrome desk were complicated chains of numbers and letters that were complete gobbledygook to Dotty. Deacon was hunched in his white leather captain's chair, frowning over a wireless keyboard, biting his lip in concentration. Dotty was struck by an image of Deacon in a mad scientist's lab coat, tinkering with his creature before shouting, "It's alive! It's *alive!*"

Smiling to herself, she set the box on a table and cleared her throat. Deacon didn't look up. She cleared her throat a little louder. Still nothing. She picked up a plush green doll and tossed it at his head. She tried not to let the flash of annoyance flickering across his features hurt her feelings. After all, she had just tossed a Yoda at him.

"Is *this* really what the rest of the house will look like? Because I was hoping that our great-great-grandparents' house would end up looking like a doctors' waiting room. On a spaceship. In a future without comfortable furniture."

Deacon gave her a flat, unreadable expression. She gave it right back to him. He sighed and stood up from his desk. "No, I've explained to Regina that if she doesn't significantly change her designs, her work on this project is over. Is this really why you broke into my office? To insult me and my furniture?"

"No. I *walked* into your office to talk to you about the book."

He sighed. "Dotty, I don't want to hurt you, but we both know this new book isn't ever going to get off the ground. You'll make a mess of whatever progress Cindy is trying to make organizing the house, lose interest in a few months, and be off to do something else."

Dotty would allow that, considering that she had cut and run on several projects in the past. "Not this time, Deacon. It's too personal. I think it's important to me and to you that we sort through this family stuff once and for all. I mean, how many times did we try to talk to our parents about it, only to have them shut us down and tell us it was too hurtful to talk about?"

Deacon frowned at her. "Uh, that would be never, because my parents didn't actually talk to me about anything."

There were times when Dotty hated her aunt and uncle, she really did. Her own parents were decent enough, she supposed. But they were absent, hard to pin down, moving from place to place, because "starting over" in each new exclusive community gave them a new audience for whom they pretend they were the affluent, high-flying Whitneys. Uncle Robert was cold, selfish, and willing to sacrifice his own son's financial well-being to keep up appearances. When Deacon had made his money a few years ago, Robert was the first one to come to Deacon with his hand out, claiming that he was owed a share of his son's success for all of his parental sacrifices.

"It's important, Deacon. We need to know why this happened to our family, why the effects have rippled through the generations. Is it a curse? Bad karma? Or do we just have unlucky genes? Don't you want to know?"

"Why is it so important to you to prove that there's a curse?" Deacon demanded. "Your parents still speak to you. You had a relatively stable childhood, even if they move around a lot now. I don't get why you need some curse to blame for how your life turned out."

"Oh, my God, you enormous idiot!"

Deacon frowned. "Well, that was . . . unexpectedly harsh."

"I'm not looking to blame something for *my* messed-up life. I'm looking for some cause for *your* messed-up life."

"Uh, Dotty. My life isn't miserable. I have four houses, the largest collection of *Flash Gordon* memorabilia in the continental United States, and one of the original Batmobiles. William Shatner sang 'Rocket Man' at my last birthday party."

"First of all, that's a sad commentary on what you think makes a person happy. And second, he didn't sing it. He *spoke* it."

"Did I mention I own my own chocolate factory?"

"Deacon!"

He sighed, flopping back into his chair. "Fine."

"Despite that rather upsetting list of assets you just mentioned, Deacon, you still act like you expect everything to just—*poof*—up and disappear. Because of the curse, you think you're going to lose everything."

"That's ridiculous."

"Really? You don't think that investing a crapload of money to restore our great-great-grandparents' cursed house is some sort of subconscious curse-breaking gesture?"

"I think that was a crapload of pop psychology."

She picked up a stress ball shaped like a Storm Trooper and threw it at his head. "Ugh, you are so frustrating. You haven't dated anyone for more than a few months since college, because you're afraid to get married and start a family. You bought those houses as an investment, and you haven't been to any of them except this one. You stay holed up in your apartment because you knew the super before you started making money, and you know he won't evict you if the worst happened. And the only people you spend any time with are your coworkers, me, and Jake. Everybody else you keep at an arm's length, because you don't want to find out whether they'll stick around if you lose your money. You don't want to know if they're true friends."

He would have whacked his forehead against the desk, but it would have given her too much satisfaction. "I hate it when you're insightful."

"Look, the good news is that if there is a curse—which there is—then by the rules of the universe, we can break it. And then maybe you'll stop waiting for the other shoe to drop and start to really live your life. Maybe with a certain shy redheaded landscape architect who for reasons I don't understand finds your particular brand of social ineptitude adorkable. "

Instead of protesting, as Dotty expected, Deacon sat straight up in his chair with a suddenly serious expression. "Did she say something?"

Dotty nodded. "I know it's been a while, doll, but when a woman spends that much time staring at your mouth, it's not because she's wondering what sort of ChapStick you're wearing. She's been throwing serious come-hither vibes your way, in a socially awkward, almost indecipherable way that most people wouldn't be able to pick up on."

"No, really, did she say something?" he asked absently.

"Several things, none of which I am willing to tell you."

"Because that would be too simple and straightforward?"

"Because that would ruin my fun." Dotty picked up the cube Deacon was just now noticing on his side table. "Also because I just found this giant box hidden in Catherine Whitney's room, and I'm pretty sure it's going to help me figure out what happened to her right before she disappeared." And with that, she left.

"WHAT? DOTTY!" DEACON flopped back into his captain's chair and started talking to himself. "She wants me to follow her. She wants to draw me into this *Scooby-Doo* mystery mess. She wants to Dottify me, once again. So I'm just going to sit here and do my work and stay sane." He nodded sharply and sat up, pulling his wireless keyboard into place. "Right, good plan."

Then again, Nina would probably be there when Dotty opened up the box. She seemed just as interested in this family-history bit as Dotty and Cindy. Her big green eyes would probably be bright with curiosity and excitement. And her cheeks would be all flushed . . . and her mouth . . .

"Damn it." He sprang up from his chair and followed after Dotty.

NINA AND CINDY were taking their lunch break in the ladies' quarters, relaxing at the long table and eating pasta left over from the previous night's dinner. Jake, the Wednesday-night cook, knew his way around a carb, so it was worth revisiting.

"Hey, look what I found—aw, are you eating the last of the primavera?"

"And I'm not even sorry," Cindy told Dotty, slurping a noodle into her mouth.

"I saved you a plate," Nina said, hopping up and cuffing Cindy lightly on the back of her head.

Dotty dropped the heavy box onto the table.

"What's that?" Cindy asked through a mouthful of pasta, nodding toward the cobweb-covered cube.

"I don't know. I found it in Catherine's dressing room. I was going to open it, but now that I know where I fall in your friends-versus-delicious-Alfredo-covered-pasta lineup, I don't think I'm going to share this with you. Clearly, Nina is a better friend than you."

"We knew that anyway," Cindy said dismissively. "Come on, it could be the jewels!"

Cindy disappeared into her room and returned with a pink toolbox.

"Really?" Dotty laughed. "A pink toolbox?"

"It comes in handy," Cindy told her. "You never know when you're going to have to hammer in frame hangers or dismantle some ugly entertainment center."

"They didn't have one covered in glitter?" Nina asked, smirking at her.

"With *My Little Pony* decals?" Dotty added.

"If you don't want these bolt cutters to chop that padlock off, keep talking," Cindy said, holding up the pink-handled tool and nodding toward the rusted brass clasp on the box.

"I don't need your bolt cutters, thank you very much," Dotty said primly as she fished a small screwdriver and a long, skinny awl out of her bag. "They don't make locks like this anymore. We can't cut it. I can get it unlocked some other way."

Dotty inserted the tools into the lock and manipulated them back and forth, listening for the telltale *click*. She was so concentrated on the task at hand she didn't even flinch when Deacon and Jake pushed their way through the servants' entrance. Deacon sat next to Nina on the long dining table, and she gave him a smile that made his run across the island worth it.

"What are we doing?" Jake whispered, standing over Cindy's shoulder.

"Watching Dotty perpetrate an act of extreme optimism," Cindy said, waving her bolt cutters at Dotty with an expectant expression. "Sweetie, the lock is probably rusted shut."

"Why do you have pink bolt cutters?" Deacon asked, just as the lock clicked, opened, and fell to the floor. Nina's jaw dropped, her eyes oscillating between a triumphant Dotty and the defeated lock.

Dotty winked cheekily and lifted the lid of the box. Jake jumped to his feet. Cindy squealed and clapped her hands, only to let loose a disappointed "*hmph*" when the contents turned out to be stacks of small booklets with matching brown leather covers. At least twenty of them. Each one was stamped "CGW" at the bottom right corner.

Catherine Grayson Whitney.

"Diaries," Dotty said, flipping through the inside covers, checking the dates that had been painstakingly inscribed on the first page of each. Even in the thrill of discovery, Dotty couldn't help but marvel at Catherine's neatly looped, even script. Her own handwriting was a chaotic mix of cursive, block print, and shorthand. Product of a different generation and school system, she supposed. "Catherine's diaries, starting years before her death. This could be her complete journal collection for her adult life."

"Not as cool as jewelry but still exciting," Cindy conceded, trying not to let her disappointment show.

"Yes, Dotty has given us the gift of reading," Jake said with a shudder. "Reading really old, cramped, faded cursive."

"This is exactly what I was hoping for!" Dotty exclaimed, launching herself across the room and throwing her arms around Cindy. The blonde's knees buckled under the force of Dotty's enthusiasm, and the women went sprawling to the floor.

"I'm sorry." Dotty giggled as Jake helped the girls extract themselves from their person pretzel. "I just can't believe it! I found my great-great-grandmother's diaries, which no one in my grasping, devious family has managed to locate in almost one hundred years. That's huge!"

"How did you find it?" Deacon asked, laughing

when Cindy's and Dotty's legs tangled together and they fell back to the floor in a heap.

"I'm just that good," Dotty told him as solemnly as she could from the bottom of the person tangle. And when Deacon gave her the now-familiar deadpan face, Dotty added, "My scarf caught the corner of a false wall panel, popped it loose."

"Jack Donovan designed a lot of little hiding places around the house, the passages between the floors, but I doubt half of them are actually shown on the blueprints," Jake said, thumbing through one of the journals. "There's a wall in Gerald Whitney's library that revolves so he could access a direct stairway to the master suite. And there's a hallway from Mrs. Whitney's room to the children's wing. I guess it was so she could bypass a couple of staircases to get directly to their rooms at night or when they were sick."

"Secret passages and revolving walls? Suddenly, my *Scooby-Doo* jokes don't seem so lame," Cindy mused.

"It was *en vogue* at the time to add an air of mystery to one's home," Dotty said, searching through the diaries for the latest date. "And when one's home is this large, it makes sense to try to skip a few hallways to save time. Plus, rich people tended to have a lot of secrets."

Dotty frowned, absently tucking her candy-colored hair behind her ears as she sorted through the diaries.

"What's with the pout?" Cindy asked. "You were so excited a few minutes ago."

"Oh, I still am," Dotty assured her. "But I can't find the last diary. You'd think it would be near the top of the box. But the latest one I can find is about six months before she died."

"Well, she probably wrote in it every day, right?" Cindy said. "She wouldn't go to the trouble of breaking into her secret lockbox every evening. She probably kept it somewhere she could get to it easily, like her nightstand or her vanity."

"Probably," Dotty said, frowning again as she searched the bottom of the box for the first volume. "But trust me, those would have been the first places my relatives would look for valuables. And no one has ever mentioned finding a diary. It would have provided some valuable insight into what was going on in her head." Dotty fished the earliest volume from the box and placed it on top. "In the meantime, I can start at the beginning and get some idea of what Catherine's marriage to Gerald was like . . . and maybe I'll skip a little, because I'm one of those people who read the last chapter of a murder mystery first."

"That's just wrong," Cindy said, shaking her head.

"Of all the things she just said, skipping to the end of a book is what bothers you most?" Jake asked.

Cindy crossed her arms and set her chin. "I hate spoilers."

Marriage Counseling for the Ancient Greeks

CINDY ENJOYED CLEANING windows. She didn't see why so many people made cracks about not doing them. She found it soothing, wiping layers of grime away to reveal a clear, shining surface. Few people were blessed enough to see tangible evidence of the difference they made with their work every day. She swore by an equal mixture of white vinegar and dish soap, which took longer to clean but left a brilliant shine behind.

It was like a meditation exercise. When she was finished, she felt relaxed and at peace. So even though she didn't necessarily have to clean the windows in the family wing, she found herself with her trusty newspaper clutched in one hand, moving it in slow, sure circles as she stared out through the glass. Her mind wandered over the day's to-do list, Jake's many vaguely inappropriate requests for dates, what it might take for her to say yes to one of those requests. Slowly, the light outside shifted from the clear, sharp air of late morning to the golden blaze of full afternoon. Cindy was so zoned out she barely noticed the difference.

And then she heard an angry shout from outside. Her eyes scanned the lawn to find a woman in an ornate, high-waisted blue gown arguing with a dark-haired man with a mustache. Cindy looked down and saw a dingy rag in her hand. Her sleeve was black cotton, connected to a plain dress and a starched white apron.

A maid's uniform.

Cindy peered through the glass. The man seemed to be pleading with the woman, gesturing toward the house and then between the two of them. The woman was shaking her head, trying to pull her hands from his grasp. He pressed her hands to his chest and gently kissed her fingertips, but she jerked away from him and turned toward the house.

Cindy finally got a look at the woman's face, a face she recognized from photographs and paintings all over the house. The tear-stained face of Catherine Whitney.

The sound of glass shattering on the floor brought Cindy out of the vision.

Jake stood behind her, a pitcher of iced tea in one hand and a drinking glass in the other. His other glass lay shattered at his feet. Jake's usually tanned face turned pale, and his pupils were the size of olives. "You saw it, too, didn't you?" he whispered.

"Saw what?" she asked carefully. There was no reason to admit her vision until he tipped his hand in this game of Who's a Thundering Loony?

"Out on the lawn," he said, stepping closer to her. "I was bringing you something to drink, and I saw a woman who looked like the old pictures of Deacon's great-great-grandmother."

"Arguing with a dark-haired man in a vest and tie?" Cindy asked.

Jake nodded, and his hands started to shake.

Cindy took the pitcher and the glass from him and set them aside. "Were you wearing a maid's uniform?"

Jake frowned. "No. I just looked through the window, over your shoulder. I didn't see what I was wearing." He shivered. "Why would we both see something like that? Why? I mean, if it was dark outside, I could just say that we were scared and misjudged what we saw or that someone was playing a trick on us. But it was in broad daylight, Cindy. How did we see that?"

Cindy shook her head. "It felt like a memory, like we were seeing someone else's memories."

"It probably was. Anything's possible here. I hate this house," Jake confessed. "I have since I was a kid. I'm only here because Whit's my best friend, and he asked me for help. I've always felt like someone was watching, waiting for me to drop my guard. I would see things, shadows shifting, things moving from where we'd left them. I'd hear angry footsteps on the landing by the third floor, though no one was there to make any noises. But I could never tell Deacon, because it would stress him out, or he would just write it off as me being paranoid. I know he's seen things here, too, but he just can't bring himself to admit it. Because his rational, math-fueled brain will not accept it. Also, it's not very manly to admit that you're afraid of ghosts."

Cindy smiled at him, remembering the sweet boy she'd accepted a date from, the boy who wasn't afraid to admit that he couldn't dance and brought her a box of Junior Mints because he remembered that she liked them. "Do you know who the dark-haired man was?"

"He looked like the old tintypes of Jack Donovan, the original architect for the house."

"It didn't look like they were talking about construction scheduling," Cindy muttered. Why had Catherine been so upset by a conversation with her architect? It seemed that the rumors about Catherine getting "close" with a man other than her husband were true. The poor soul had looked devastated, and Catherine had seemed . . . irritated. She hadn't looked heartbroken by love that could never be. She looked annoyed. Was it because she was afraid her husband would see them from the house?

"It did look pretty personal," he admitted. "If you think about that, it makes sense. If she was going to have an extracurricular activity, it probably would have been with him. Donovan would have been in frequent contact with Mrs. Whitney as he built the house. He probably stayed here on the island with the family in the last few months of completion work, right before Catherine died."

"We have to tell somebody about this," Cindy insisted. "We made a mistake before, not telling them about my little episode on the stairs, which I can now admit was *not* dust allergies. We have to let the others know what's going on so they can be prepared."

"With what? Holy water and crosses?"

"That only works on vampires," she retorted. "And no. But I do think that it would be safer for everybody if they knew they could feel or experience something freaky. They may not overreact and hurt themselves if they know what's coming."

"I'm not going to Deacon to tell him that I witnessed an argument that happened more than a hundred years ago. He'll think we're nuts."

"We just had a full-on shared hallucination. Do you have any idea how rare and weird that is?"

"Yes, which is why I'm not eager to go around claiming that it happened!" he exclaimed.

"If you help me talk to the others about this, I will go out on that date with you."

His blue eyes narrowed with suspicion. "OK, first of all, that's massively unfair. And second, it's sort of insulting that you think the promise of a date is enough to make me sacrifice my own dignity. And third . . . well, I can't think of a third, because I'm probably going to fold and accept anyway."

"Take it or leave it."

"I'll take it," he grumbled. "But I'm not going into great detail about Catherine's possibly straying with the architect. There's only so much news Deacon can take."

"Deal. And we have to stay on the island for our date."

"What?" Jake cried.

"I don't want you to try to razzle-dazzle me with fancy restaurants and maître d's who know you by name. If you're going to woo me, you're doing it here. No resources. No false fanciness. It's like *Survivorman*, only with dating."

"Cindy!"

"Those are my terms."

Jake slapped some dust off his khakis. "Deacon should hire you for his legal department."

Cindy preened a bit and tried to tamp down the frisson of excitement in her belly. And then a thought occurred to her. "Oh, come on, I was possessed by a spirit, had a ghostly flashback, and I'm still a *maid*?"

ELSEWHERE ON THE island, the day was shaping up to be a bright one for Nina. The indoor garden room was almost cleared and ready for the renovations she'd discussed with Anthony. The water features were refilled and ready for the water lilies. And the crews were clearing the tiered gardens leading to the east side of the house, which would entail planting a variety of spring- and summer-blooming plants, which would blossom on a rotating basis. Nina always enjoyed the challenge of choosing and placing such plants so the transition was seamless. And today she would remove the plants from their peat pots and begin organizing them into the appropriate groupings.

But first, she was meeting with Deacon and Cindy to discuss the careful cleaning process for the stained, bird-soiled marble statuary around the grounds . . . except that Cindy was late, and Deacon had decided to use this time as his lunch break, so he was chewing his way through a large veggie sub. He'd offered to split it with Nina, but she found the amount of wasabi he used to be a violation of the term *condiment*. And Nina kept getting distracted by a weird itching sensation in the corner of her brain, as if she was looking at some pattern she should recognize, but it wasn't coming to her.

It was becoming a familiar state, this strange *could I be having déjà vu but not really?* feeling. Ever since she started having the recurring dream about making beds in the staff quarters, only to be accosted from behind, she felt as if there was something about the house that she should understand but didn't. And it was getting a little frustrating. Every time she had the dream, she saw and felt a little more, and *was felt* a little more by the man who snuck up behind her. The woman in the dream didn't seem frightened of the man, until, of course, he started choking her. But she never saw who it was. Nothing about him was distinctive, other than his large, warm, very talented hands.

Still, it was less fun to have those hands wrapped around her throat.

Mid-bite, Deacon waved his free hand in front of Nina's face, breaking her line of sight to a statue of Medea pouring water into the lily pond. "Earth to Nina, come in, Nina."

"Have you noticed a theme with the statues in the gardens?" Nina asked.

"No, but I'm sure you have." Deacon chuckled, prompting Nina to whack him with her clipboard. "Nina, your observations are usually pretty interesting. Please proceed without smacking me with office supplies," he amended, wrapping the remains of his sandwich in cling-wrap and giving her his full attention.

"OK, the fountain out in front of the house, that's Metis, the first wife of Zeus, and clearly, everything didn't turn out happily ever after for them. We've talked about this. This is Aphrodite, a pretty traditional statue as far as the time period goes but also the wife of Hephaestus, a powerful, technologically advanced god who spent most of his time devising traps to humiliate his wife with her various lovers. Not a happy bride. Over there? That's Medea, wife of Jason, who was so devastated when her husband betrayed her that she killed her own children. And there? That's Helen of Troy. For all the romance of running off with Paris and launching a thousand ships, she started off as the wife of Menelaus, who thought that being a good host meant trotting his naked, humiliated spouse out for his guests to ogle. So what do we see when we look at the big picture?"

"The Greek gods were in desperate need of marriage counseling?" When Nina whacked him with the clipboard again, he exclaimed, "Ow! That's it, I'm taking the clipboard."

"Over my dead body," she told him, trying in vain to hold it out of reach. He humored her and didn't try too hard to retrieve it. Honestly, the man had the wingspan of a condor. "Whoever designed the original gardens surrounded the house with images of women trapped in unhappy marriages to powerful men."

"Well, it would have been Catherine, right?" Deacon supposed. "She was the one who supervised the construction of the house. Do you think she was trying to tell Gerald something?"

"Could be," Nina said. "But if that was the case, wouldn't she pick more triumphant figures? Hera, who managed to get revenge on Zeus for his affairs by turning his lovers into animals or tying their legs in knots to prevent them from having Zeus's babies. Clytemnestra, Helen's sister-in-law, who wrapped her cheating, child-murdering husband, Agamemnon, in a special royal robe she designed so he couldn't fight back when she stabbed him."

"Were there *any* happy stories in Greek mythology?" Deacon asked. "I can't seem to remember any."

Nina shook her head. "Not so much. I just can't shake the feeling that the message in the garden isn't *from* Catherine, it's *to* Catherine."

While she was distracted by that cheerful thought, Deacon snatched the clipboard out of her hands. She glared at him, but there was no real heat in it. Deacon grinned cheekily and handed the board back. "Well, as much as I have enjoyed sharing a nonlunch and upsetting Greek marriage history with you, I have to get back inside."

"Fine, then, go develop world-altering social technology! Just leave me alone with my thoughts on the creepy statues!" Nina called after him. He waved back at her, laughing.

With her silly grin still in place, Nina strolled to the back of the house. One of Anthony's crews had replaced all of the broken panes in the largest greenhouse, and Nina had a lovely makeshift potting shed there. She was practically skipping when she opened the doors, humming a happy Irish folk tune. But the moment she stepped into the warm, humid space, her foot skidded across the floor, making her stumble into one of the potting tables.

"Mother fudger!" she yelped, rubbing at her hip where she'd whacked it against the corner.

How the heck had she managed to slip on a textured concrete floor? She looked down at her feet. Beneath her shoe was a large, curving shard of terra-cotta. One of many shards of broken planting pots scattered across the floor. It took Nina a full minute to process what she was seeing. It looked as if a bomb had gone off in her greenhouse. Broken pots and potting soil lay scattered and broken on the floor. Every seedling she'd nurtured was flattened into the black potting soil. Her plans for the gardens had been ripped off the walls and tossed to the ground.

Nina stooped to pick up the curved piece of planter. The all-too-familiar sense of panic burst through the wall of calm she'd built up and burned through her chest like acid. It was happening again. How had he gotten onto the island without setting off the security equipment? This was how it had started before. Ruined work sites, damaged equipment, carefully planted flowers dug up overnight. She should consider herself lucky that she didn't have a truck on site to smash. She would lose this job. She would become too much trouble, and Deacon would drop her like a hot rock when he realized the security threat she posed. She would lose her business. She would lose her apartment. She would lose the friendships she'd built with everyone here. Deacon. The tender green shoots of whatever this *thing* was that was growing between them would be trampled.

Hot, angry tears welling in her eyes, Nina slung the shard against the wall and reveled in its satisfying crunch.

"Nina?" Deacon called. "Hey, I forgot to ask— What the hell? Are you all right?"

Nina's face was beet-red and twisted into a furious, un-Nina-like expression. She hunched against her workbench, staring at the mess in the greenhouse as if it was responsible for the national debt *and* movies based on video games.

"Nina."

When she didn't respond, Deacon turned her to face him. But he wasn't entirely sure she was seeing him.

"Nina, don't take what I'm about to do personally."

He took the remains of his sandwich out of its bag and waved it under her nose. The bright sting of the wasabi struck her full in the nostrils, and Nina inhaled sharply, her face wrinkling in distaste. "Good sweet Lord!"

Deacon grinned at her. "There she is."

"You're going to burn off your taste buds if you keep eating that stuff."

"Yeah, yeah. Now, what's going on in here?"

Nina hadn't even realized the tears were coursing down her cheeks. "Damn it," she growled, wiping at her face.

"Did you have an accident? Did you fall and knock something over?" Deacon asked, gesturing to the mess. "Several times?"

Nina shook her head, her teeth grinding together as she snatched another piece of pottery from the floor. "Stupid asshole."

Deacon's mouth fell open. "I'm sorry?"

"Not you," she insisted, the color draining from her face. "The asshole who did this. He's the asshole."

Deacon shook her gently and hooked his hands under her arms. "Nina, snap out of it. Oh, hell, look at your hand."

Nina glanced down at her palm, where a deep puncture was welling blood. She hadn't even realized she was holding the jagged piece of pottery in her palm. At the sight of her torn flesh, she burst into wracking sobs. "Damn it! Just—damn it!"

"Hey." Deacon hugged her to his chest. She was trembling, as if her anger couldn't be contained by her body and was threatening to shake its way loose from her very muscle fibers. "Hey, come on, now. I don't know what's bothering you, but there's no reason to Hulk out on poor, innocent plants. This isn't like you."

He tucked her head under his chin. He rubbed his hands along her back, stroking her hair. Her chilled, trembling hands stilled as she blew out long, deep breaths. The orange-and-spice scent of her hair wafted up to meet his nose. He pressed his mouth to her temple. She leaned into the caress of his lips, angling her head until he was kissing her cheek. She turned her face toward him, as if she was searching his face for a quirk of the lip, a flicker of cruelty in his eyes, anything to show that he was manipulating her. He didn't have a mirror handy, but he was sure that all she saw was wide-eyed awe and lust. She inhaled sharply as he threaded his hands through her hair and pulled her closer.

The wreckage of the potting shed faded away, and Deacon's world shrank down to the nerve endings in his lips. Nina settled her weight against his thigh, pushing him back against the floor. Deacon rocked onto his back, pulling Nina down with him as he slid his tongue between her lips. Nina's fingers trailed down his abdomen until she brushed bare skin. He hissed at the icy contact against his skin, bucking his hips against her.

Nina plucked at the buttons of his shirt, pushing it aside and baring his pale, smooth skin. She laughed shamelessly as he writhed under her cold touch. His sharp white teeth nipped at her bottom lip, a bit of revenge for her torture, and he licked along the line of her throat, nibbling at her collarbone. She dragged her hand to the button of his jeans, toying with it. His hands splayed around her hips, molding her body to his, before pulling her shirt up her long, pale back and pulling it over her head. Nina gasped, rolling her hips as the hard curve of his desire drove against her center. His mouth rose to meet the cotton-covered swell of her breast, tugging the straps down her arms. But he fumbled with the clasp, unable to find the magical combination of undone hooks to make it open. He tried to regain his footing, smacking into a broken pot.

The clinking sound caught Nina's attention, and she retreated from the kiss. Her face flushed red and she scooted back, closer to the potting table. Deacon sat up, following her movement, but he knew that . . . whatever it was that they'd just done had come to an abrupt close. The spell had been broken. Clothes were being buttoned. And a bewildered Deacon would have gladly traded everything he owned to go back one minute in time.

"So, that happened," Nina said, biting her bottom lip as she searched for her shirt.

"Are you OK?"

She nodded. "This is my problem to deal with, Deacon. Don't worry about it."

"I meant, are you OK with the whole abrupt greenhouse semi-nudity?" he scoffed, making her laugh. "Also, there is no such thing as one person's problem when we're living out here on our own, especially when it makes you cry like this. You can tell me. You've known me for a while now, Nina. Do I strike you as someone who's going to spread gossip?"

She patted his large hand, which was cupped around her shoulder, and shook her head. "No."

"We'll go to the staff quarters and get your hand cleaned up, and you can tell me all about it. Unless you've been talking to Dotty and you believe that ghosts destroyed your greenhouse. If that's the case, she's dealing with blood-dirt-and-tears Nina."

Nina rolled her eyes, but she was smiling. "Don't patronize me."

"I like to think of it as emotional coddling."

"How is that better?"

"Six of one, half a dozen of the other," Deacon said, with a pat on her shoulder, leading her out of the wrecked greenhouse.

WITH A *SPONGEBOB* *SquarePants* bandage on her hand and a cold bottle of ginger ale resting against her thigh, Nina felt safer. Removed from the violent destruction of her plants, it felt less as if Rick was going to burst in at any moment and finish the job. She took a deep breath and tried to figure out how to explain all of this to Deacon.

"The beginning is usually the easiest place to start," he said, gently slipping his hand around her uninjured palm.

Nina nodded. "My former partner, Rick, was better

with people. We met a few months before I graduated from college. He was dating my roommate, and he cheated on her, if memory serves. Which should have been a major warning sign. I ignored it, of course. Rick's family owned a landscaping business in Providence, which basically boiled down to a lawn-mowing service. He saw some of my senior projects and asked me to help him out with a few sketches for some clients. A few sketches turned into full-time design work. And usually, while I was digging and planting, Rick was on the porch having lemonade with the client, giving the client all the highlights of the flower beds we were installing. He wasn't great with plants, but he was a hell of a salesman. He made everything sound magical, as if the client was just a few days away from backyard paradise. And he was usually able to upsell them into a water feature or a more expensive variety of plants.

"It worked. Business boomed. We started getting higher-income, higher-profile clients. Rick changed the name to something acceptable to our wealthy clients: Elegant Environments. He printed up new brochures and business cards, went to trade shows, and bought new equipment. And for a while, it worked. We were in demand. Rick presented himself as the local boy made good, creating magic out of dirt. We worked on larger and larger projects, some of which got publicity in some home-and-garden magazines. Rick did the interviews, of course, because he was the brains of the operation. I was more comfortable behind the scenes anyway, so I didn't mind. I did all of the designs, and eventually, I did more and more of the field work. Rick couldn't make it out to the sites, because he was too busy lunching with clients or going to chamber of commerce meetings and 'making contacts.'

"Rick was always telling me that we were barely breaking even, that he wasn't taking a paycheck, because he wanted to make sure I got paid along with our work crews. Everything we had was being invested back into the business, he said. Our overhead was overwhelming because of salaries, insurance, and the wear and tear on the equipment, he said. One morning, I showed up at his house to pick up some plans, and he had this brand-new Jet Ski hooked up to his truck. As a matter of fact, he had a new truck. He was driving the old one to work and keeping the nicer one at home for personal travel. And there was a brand-new bass boat parked next to his garage. He was funneling money from the business into his toys. Jet Skis, the boat, a new plasma-screen with surround sound, all the while telling me that he couldn't afford to give me a raise or the share in the business that he had promised me. He couldn't give away part of his family business, after all.

"When I saw what was happening, I asked him again, when would I get my raise? He didn't have an answer for me. When would I get a share of the business or even some controlling say in how the business was run? He didn't have an answer. So a few nights later, I snuck into our offices and looked at the books. I realized how much money he had sucked away. I may have lost my temper."

"Care to elaborate on that?" Deacon asked.

"I may have shattered the windshield of that brand-new truck," she admitted, biting her lip.

A delighted grin broke across Deacon's handsome face. "With what?"

"A concrete planter shaped like a dolphin."

Deacon snickered, and Nina gave a weak chuckle. She couldn't find the situation funny just yet. It was still too raw. For now, she was grateful to Deacon for hauling her up off the floor and distracting her with "abrupt greenhouse semi-nudity." It was some of the most enjoyable nudity of any degree she had ever experienced. She would focus on the electric tingles still zipping along her nerve endings, because she was getting to the more difficult part of the story. It was the part that had her spiraling into a near-fugue in the greenhouse, and part of her wished Deacon could kiss that and make it better, too.

Nina peeled the label loose from the ginger-ale bottle in long strips, fidgeting with the paper while she tried to find the right words. "I felt so stupid, so helpless. I had nothing to show for years of work. I didn't have a contract to show that I owned any part of the business or that I was guaranteed a share of the profits. It wasn't like Rick was going to give me a reference. I didn't have any reputation to speak of. But I figured, what else could I do? I had to work. My parents are lovely people, but I wasn't about to move in with them. So I scraped together every cent I could, cashed in savings bonds from my grandmother, borrowed money from my brother. There were some shameful incidents with cash advances on credit cards. And I started Demeter Designs.

"I tried to keep it low-key. I was afraid of advertising, for goodness sake, because I didn't want Rick to see it and get mad at me. But Rick just laughed. He said I would be closed within a year, so what did he care? It was like he forgot who had done all of the work at Elegant Environments. He started to believe his own hype. He presented mediocre designs to important clients and began losing jobs to firms he used to call 'rinky-dink.' I started getting more jobs, and eventually, I started swiping jobs out from under him. He was furious! He came into my office and pitched a royal hissy fit. 'Disloyal,' he called me. 'Petty, ungrateful, deceitful,' and a bunch of other words I shouldn't repeat. He threatened to sue me. When I laughed and reminded him that would be hard, considering we'd never signed a contract, he got this weird look on his face and just walked out.

"About a month later, I started getting weird bills in the mail. My credit report red-flagged a dozen or so new cards, store accounts, memberships to porn sites. My credit rating went into the toilet. I could never prove it, but Rick had destroyed me. He ran up huge debts in my name, ruined my credit. I think I had a mortgage for a hunting cabin in Utah. It took me more than a year to clear it up. Hell, I'm still clearing it up.

"My jobs got sabotaged. I would leave a pristine, beautiful garden, and the next morning, I would come back with the client to find the plants bleached and the flower beds torn up.

"I can't tell you how many equipment trailers I accumulated. They kept getting stolen out of my shed. And the worst part was that he'd steal my equipment, and then, after I'd reported it stolen, he'd sneak it back into my driveway before the cops arrived, and I would look like a nutcase.

"I felt so powerless all the time, so damn stupid. I almost didn't bid for the Crane's Nest job, because I didn't know if I would still be in business long enough to complete the work, and I knew Rick was bidding for the job, too. I knew if he saw me bidding for the same account, he would be furious."

"So why did you?"

"I wanted to make something great. I saw the pictures of the house. I saw the footprint of the original garden designs, and I knew I could do something extraordinary. I walked into your office and saw Rick sitting there, waiting for his appointment, and I almost turned around and ran out. Rick's design was awful." Nina snickered. "I got a peek at the presentation boards. It was tacky and out of place and ugly. He wanted to put in a succulent garden, can you believe it?"

"The nerve," Deacon said, shaking his head.

"You have no idea what I'm talking about, do you?" she asked, sniffing.

Deacon shook his head, brushing the mussed hair back from her face.

Nina clarified, "One New England winter, on an exposed location like this? It would put the 'suck' in 'succulent.'"

"Oh."

"And as he was walking out of the meeting, the jerk actually smirked at me while he did his usual 'frat guys all together' thing with you. I almost walked out of your office, because I was sure there was no way I was getting the job. But then you looked at me, right in the eye, and I figured running away like a little girl would be poor form."

"Definitely. You would have left me with a tacky, dead succulent garden. It would be a fate worse than death." Deacon wrapped his arm around Nina's shoulder and squeezed her gently. "Look, you're here because you belong here. Because I didn't trust anyone else with the job as much as I trust you. And my trust isn't something that I give easily. Now, the question is, what would you like to do about the Rick situation?"

"I'm assuming that you're not firing me? I would understand if you fired me. No hard feelings."

Deacon's eyes went saucer-sized. "No! Why would I fire you?"

"Because my presence on the island is inviting the violent attentions of a crazy man?"

"You still represent less of a threat than most of Jake's ex-girlfriends. And Dotty."

"OK," she said, nodding. "What are my options?"

"Well, I could try to find a way to file destruction-of-property charges against him. But that would require proof that he actually came onto the island. Or I could make a few phone calls and erase his digital presence from planet earth entirely."

"Is there some unhappy medium between the two?" she asked.

"Well, sure, if you want to take away all of my fun."

"Let me think about it," she said.

He pulled her close again, breathing in the citrus-spice scent of her hair. "It's going to be OK, Nina. You're not dealing with this alone anymore."

She glanced up at him, and he leaned back into an appropriate non-lawsuit-like space bubble. "You know, Cindy, Jake, and Dotty. They're going to want to help you, too."

"Of course," she said. "Thank you, Deacon. It feels good just to have talked to someone about it. What is it about you that makes people want to tell you everything? You should have been a priest or something."

"A priest?" he asked, lifting his eyebrows. "With a face this pretty and a mind this brilliant?"

"And modest, too." She sighed.

LEAVING NINA TO rest in the staff quarters, Deacon made it across the property to his office in record time. The moment he reached his desk, his fingers flew over the keyboard, calling up video feeds from cameras scanning the greenhouse area over the last twelve hours. He scrolled through the video at lightning speed, only pausing when someone crossed the screen. Nina, Jake, Anthony, a few of the landscaping day-crew members breaking for lunch. But no one entered the greenhouse. Frowning, he switched camera angles, scrolling through another feed until he saw a dark blur cross into the camera's view at around six A.M. He clicked on a tab to stop the scroll, then rewound, playing the section of footage at normal speed. A tall, dark figure darted across the lawn and opened the greenhouse door. Deacon stopped the footage. The man on the screen was wearing black from head to toe, his face hidden by a dark baseball cap. He also had his face turned away from the camera. In fact, the man managed to keep his face turned away from the camera throughout the clip, including his dash across the lawn. It was as if he knew where the cameras were.

Deacon sat back in his chair, turning the dilemma over in his head. He'd known about Nina's troubles with Rick Douglas, the bankruptcy, the vandalism, thanks to the background check he'd run before hiring her. Clearly, the cursory report he'd received didn't quite cover the extent of Douglas's tactics.

Deacon picked up the handset and dialed his corporate security chief's number. "Hey, Gabe, I need you to look into a guy named Rick Douglas. Also, review security footage in sectors A three to twelve from oh-four-hundred to seven-hundred hours. There's not much to see, but you can probably pick up on something I missed. When you find Rick Douglas, I want you to keep an eye on him, track his activities. I want pictures. And I want to know when he gets anywhere near the coastline."

Rick Douglas would never touch Nina. Deacon hung up the phone and tapped his fingers on his desktop. He tried to stay fluid and flexible. When you worked in an industry that could quite literally change overnight, you didn't make decisions that included the word *never* or *always*. But he simply couldn't have this.

He had to find a way to keep Nina safe. Nina was his, his to protect. She was his. Hissing, Deacon felt a sharp pain in his right hand. Glancing down, he saw that he was clutching a letter opener in his palm, the sharp edge biting into his skin. He dropped it onto the desk and scrubbed his uninjured hand over his face.

This wasn't like him, the drastic mood swings, the strange cyclical thinking that always seemed to come back to Nina. Hell, stripping down a woman who was technically his employee on the floor of an outdoor utility building was *definitely* a departure from his usual personality. Was it the isolation of the island? Being away from familiar surroundings and people who kept him grounded? Or was he too much like Gerald Whitney, possessive and too quick to act? Was it the house? Was the Crane's Nest destined to drive all of its Whitney residents insane?

It didn't matter. The curse, the emotional upheaval, none of it was as important as Nina's safety. Come house or high water, he would not allow Nina to be terrorized on his watch.

Brainstorming for Bogeymen

THAT NIGHT'S DINNER was the most awkward on record.

Nina made enchiladas, because it was her night on the schedule, and she couldn't screw up tortillas and beans even when her hands were trembling a bit. Cindy was ruthlessly polishing her silverware. Jake looked as if he was ready to jump out of his skin at any moment. Deacon was staring at Nina as if she possessed the secret cheat codes to video games that hadn't even been invented yet. Nina was avoiding eye contact, but he wasn't sure if that was because of the Rick problems or post-greenhouse semi-nudity awkwardness. Dotty seemed to be the only one not completely stressed out. Nina suspected some fairly strong herbal supplements were involved.

Halfway through the silent meal, Cindy gave Jake an emphatic nod toward Deacon. He frowned and shook his head no. Cindy made a circular, *come on with it* gesture. Jake shook his head again. By this time, they'd caught the others' attention and realized they weren't nearly as sneaky as they thought. Meanwhile, Deacon was watching Nina as if she would bolt at any moment And Nina kept her head bent over her plate as if she was praying for divine enchilada intervention.

Deacon cleared his throat and said, "Nina and I have something to tell you," just as Cindy said, "Jake and I have something we need to say."

"You're going to put us out of our misery and agree to go out with him?" Dotty asked, clapping and turning toward the others. "Who had three weeks in the betting pool?"

Deacon shook his head and said, "Me, but that's not really as important as Nina's issue."

"Our issue is pretty serious," Cindy countered.

"Well, so is Nina's." Deacon turned on the landscaper. "Nina, come on. We talked about this."

"Maybe we should let Nina go first," Jake suggested brightly.

"Jake, we talked about this," Cindy groused.

Nina suddenly blurted out, "I think my former boss snuck onto the island and destroyed my greenhouse."

Suddenly, Cindy's simultaneous declaration of "The house is definitely haunted" didn't seem so dramatic. Although it did make Deacon roll his eyes a little.

Cindy patted Nina's back. "She can go first."

Nina gave the brief, emotionless summary of events that she'd been practicing in her head since the afternoon.

Deacon added a comment about the state of the greenhouse and said that Anthony's crew had already cleaned out the mess.

It was strange to watch that livid flush creep into Nina's cheeks, to hear the flinty, pissed-off tone in her voice. Nina had reached her breaking point. And apparently, her chewy candy center was made up entirely of anger.

"I'm sorry that I brought this with me to the island," she practically spit. "And the offer to let you fire me stands. It wouldn't be the first job this jerk has ruined for me, not that I can prove it. I just have to work harder to make sure he can't ruin the next one."

"Nina, I'm not going to fire you," Deacon told her quietly. "It's not your fault. You can't control what some psycho does. I'm not angry with you. I'm a little angry with the people who installed my security system for not picking it up, but that's not something for you to worry about. I don't want you to worry, all right? Just focus on that water-garden thing, because I am very, very concerned about the possibility of living here without the right number of water lilies."

She offered him a tense imitation of a smile and nodded sharply.

"And I have a few Tasers in my bag. You and Cindy are more than welcome to keep them with you if you don't feel safe," Dotty offered.

"You have *a few* Tasers?" Jake exclaimed. "Who would give you more than one Taser?"

"Who would give you *one* Taser?" Deacon asked.

"Have you ever ridden on the Metro in Paris?" Dotty snarked. "Well, until you do, don't judge me."

"We're getting away from the point," Deacon retorted. "Maybe my security company can provide you with mace or personal alarms or a Taser that might not electrocute you when you try to use it because Dotty dropped it in a puddle once." He ignored the obscene gesture Dotty sent his way, tapping a few tabs on his phone to pull up a picture of Rick, which he promptly sent to all of the other team members' phones. "This is a picture of Rick Douglas. If you see him, come to me immediately, and we'll call my security team."

Nina shot Deacon an incredulous look. How did Deacon know who her former boss was and pull up a picture of him so quickly? She knew it was unwise to question the skills of a Web wizard, but it seemed suspiciously efficient.

"Until then, keep your eyes open, and if you see anything strange, report it immediately. I'm having five copies of my alarm watch made, so that each of you can call for help directly, if necessary. They should be here in a few days."

"That actually brings me to my point," Cindy said. "The reporting issue, that is."

Jake grimaced, as if he had hoped that Cindy would drop the subject in the face of Nina's problem.

"What's going on?" Deacon asked.

"Cindy and I had a, well, let's call it an episode this afternoon."

"An episode?"

"An incident," Jake amended.

Dotty held up one hand, as if waiting to be called on, before interjecting, "Is an incident better than an episode?"

"OK, are we just not going to talk about this out in the open?" Cindy demanded. "I know that nobody wants to use the g-word first, but I can't just ignore what I'm seeing and feeling. Jake and I saw two people on the lawn. We think it was Catherine Whitney and Jack Donovan, the original architect of the house. And it looked like they were having some sort of argument, maybe a lovers' quarrel. And since they've been dead for about a hundred years, I think we can assume that's not possible. A few weeks ago, I was on the steps to the third floor. I heard furniture moving upstairs, when no one was supposed to be up there. I tried to go upstairs to look around, and all of a sudden, I couldn't breathe. It felt like I was being choked. If Jake hadn't caught me, I would have fallen headfirst down the stairs. Now, I came onto this island as a complete skeptic. But those two experiences, plus the feeling that I'm being watched no matter where I go on this island, have made a believer out of me."

This pronouncement was met with a long, awkward silence.

Cindy looked up and down the table. "I can't be the only one who's seeing and feeling these things."

No one made eye contact with her.

"No one's willing to admit they've had an experience?" Her cheeks flushed red.

Maybe it was a mistake to be this candid with the others, particularly Deacon, who was looking at Cindy as if he smelled something funny. And that something was her termination notice. But damn it, she was fired up. She wasn't crazy. She knew what she saw. And all horror-movie jokes aside, she certainly hadn't walked onto this island expecting to see something. And she was seriously regretting accepting that date from Jake, who was turning out to be a bigger weasel than she originally thought, leaving her hanging out to dry like this.

"I haven't seen anything yet, but I wouldn't be afraid to admit it," Dotty said. "I understand if some of you are. Do we want to write down what's happened to us on slips of paper, and we can read them anonymously?"

"This isn't a sorority grievance circle," Deacon grumped. "Let's at least be men about this . . . or Cindy. We can be Cindy about it."

Cindy preened a bit before saying, "Wait, how do you know about sorority grievance circles?"

Deacon cleared his throat. "Moving on. I haven't seen anything." He cleared his throat, tugging at the collar of his T-shirt. "I've had some weird dreams, but I think they're just stress or . . . heavy psychological suggestions from my cousin over there."

"What kind of dreams?" Nina asked. "Are you making a bed in yours?"

"Uh, no," he said, shaking his head.

"Well, good, because it would probably be a little weird for you to dream about being felt up behind by a guy with sneaky hands."

"That would be weird," Deacon agreed.

"Wait, are you having multiple weird dreams or the same weird dream over and over?" Dotty asked.

"The same one over and over," Nina said. "I'm wearing an old-fashioned dress, making a bed here in the servants' quarters. A man comes up behind me and gets handsy. Everything changes, and I'm outside on the roof. I can't see his face, but the hands run up my neck and start to choke me. The next thing I know, I'm underwater, and I'm sinking."

"Anything else?" Jake asked.

"My flesh melts away, and I become a skeleton," she added, through pursed lips.

Cindy shuddered. "Gross."

"You asked!" Nina exclaimed.

"Jake asked," Cindy countered.

"Jake asked!" Nina amended, throwing up her hands.

"So you were choked and then thrown into water?" Dotty asked. "That sounds an awful lot like how Catherine died. But would Catherine be making beds in the servants' quarters?"

"Well, she was awfully happy to be making beds there, which seems unusual for a high-society wife," Nina said. "But at the same time, the sleeves on the dress I was wearing looked pretty fancy. Embroidered blue muslin, definitely too nice for a maid's dress."

"So unfair," Cindy muttered, still bitter about her own "flashback" experience.

"Did you say embroidered blue muslin?" Deacon asked. "With silver at the sleeves?"

Nina nodded.

Deacon flopped back into the chair. "Oh, hell."

"Why 'oh, hell'?" Cindy asked.

"Because I've been dreaming about a woman in a blue dress with silver embroidery at the sleeves. Catherine Whitney. She's standing up on the roof. I come up behind her, I'm about to kiss her, but instead, my hands close around her throat, and I choke her to death."

"How often would you say you're having this dream?" Dotty asked.

"A lot," Deacon said. "A few times a week."

"And you?" Dotty asked Nina.

"Once or twice a week. More when I get stressed out."

"So you're dreaming that you're Catherine," Dotty asked Nina, before turning to Deacon. "And you're dreaming that you're Gerald. Several times a week. And you didn't think you should mention it?"

"It could still be the power of suggestion, all of those stories and theories you fill our heads with day in and day out," Deacon protested. "Maybe Nina and I both saw a picture of Catherine wearing the same blue dress."

"Deacon, I've seen every picture of Catherine Whitney ever painted or photographed. There are no pictures of her in a blue muslin dress with silver embroidery at the sleeves," Dotty insisted. "And if you and Nina are having what sounds like the same recurring dream from different perspectives, several times a week, that has to mean something."

"I'm not sure that makes it better," Deacon said. "There's a considerable creep factor in choking your own great-great-grandmother several times a week. Especially now that I know that Nina is inside her body while I'm doing it. Sort of."

Jake raised his eyebrows. "So you're admitting that you may be part of all of this supernatural woo-woo crap?"

With a lingering look at Dotty, who was smirking enough for three triumphant Whitneys, Deacon growled, "No! Damn it. Maybe."

"Which means I win!" Dotty crowed, making Deacon thunk his head against the table.

While Dotty did a little victory dance, Cindy sent Jake a significant look. He shook his head. Cindy narrowed her eyes. Jake hesitated, dropped his fork onto his plate, and leaned back in his chair. "Fine. Cindy and I had an incident this afternoon."

"Aha!" Cindy crowed. "So you admit it!"

"Yes, yes, I admit it," Jake grumbled. Cindy's lips quirked into a smile. Perhaps he wasn't as rodent-like as she'd thought. Jake turned to Deacon. "I saw it, clear as day, Whit. They were as solid as you or me, and she looked just like the pictures of Catherine. Unless you've been experimenting with some sort of hologram technology or some extremely committed re-enactors snuck onto the island along with Nina's crazy ex-boss, I don't have an explanation that involves real, live humans."

"*Et tu*, Jake?" Deacon scrubbed his hands over his face.

"Me *tu*, bud. You know how much this house creeped me out when we were kids. This shouldn't come as a surprise to you."

Deacon groaned.

"Well, I hate to add to your ghostly stresses, but I don't think the shadow-woman I saw on the roof was the result of seasickness meds," Nina told him. "Especially when you consider that I saw her again on the main staircase the day Dotty showed up. I didn't see her full body that time, just the bottom of her skirt and her waist."

"Ghosts don't usually show up as full apparitions

with features and distinct clothes and all that," Jake told her. "You usually see a partial body or a shadow."

"How do you know that?" Deacon asked.

Jake's face flushed deep pink again. He sighed and pulled a copy of *Hauntings for Total Morons* from his laptop bag. "I bought it when I was hired. You know what kind of reputation this house has!"

"Keep that book away from Dotty," Deacon said, staring at the orange-and-white softcover manual as if it was an explosive device.

"I'm a little upset that I haven't had an experience yet," Dotty said. "I'm a wide-open channel and the most creeped-out I've felt so far was when I found that picture of our great-great-aunt Bernice."

Deacon and Jake shuddered simultaneously. "Not a handsome woman," Jake explained to Cindy.

"I do think it's interesting that Jake and Cindy are seeing the key figures—Catherine, Jack, Gerald—from the outside, as observers. But Deacon and Nina are experiencing things from the key figures' points of view. Maybe the house or Gerald and Catherine are trying to tell you two something," Dotty said.

Nina pondered that for a long moment. "Well, that is . . ."

"A singularly horrifying thought," Deacon finished for her.

Nina pointed a finger at him. "Yep."

"I think we need to keep track of who feels or sees what and when," Dotty said. "It would help, I think, as I'm writing."

"Oh, I know!" Cindy ran to Deacon's room and dragged his whiteboard back to the table. "We'll come up with a list of phenomena, type up the notes, and keep a record of what happens while we're here."

Jake chuckled. "You really can't help the organizational thing, can you?"

"Wait, we should have s'mores when we tell ghost stories," Nina insisted, perking up at the thought of caramelized marshmallows and melty chocolate. "Do we have the makings for s'mores?"

They all shook their heads.

Nina frowned in a way that made Cindy want to give her a pony or something. "Maybe next time."

Cindy cleaned the board and drew a rough timeline structure with a dry-erase marker. "OK, so who felt something first?"

"That would be Deacon," Dotty said. "He had nightmares for years about the—"

"Dotty!" Deacon exclaimed, shaking his head.

"Deacon, you haven't talked about it since we were kids. Pretending it away won't work. You have to talk about it."

"I was a kid!" Deacon protested. "I didn't know what was happening. I could have been having an asthma attack."

Dotty countered, "You don't *have* asthma."

"Whit, I think she's got a point," Jake said quietly. "I thought the whole point of coming back here was to prove that the house couldn't scare you anymore."

"I thought the point was to prove that your family's fortunes have been recovered," Nina said.

"There are several points!" Deacon exclaimed. But when faced with the knowing looks on both Dotty's and Jake's faces and the confused expression on Nina's, he sighed and finally said, "When I was a kid, I hated coming here. And not just because it was boring and there was no Internet connection. This place scared me. Mom and Dad would leave me in the entry hall while they skulked around the house, looking for silverware or art or—the holy grail of grasping Whitneys—Catherine's hidden stash of jewelry. I never felt safe here. I never wandered, because nothing about this place screamed, 'Hey, come explore!' But one afternoon, I walked up the grand staircase, looking for my mom, calling for her, trying to get her to come closer so I wouldn't have to walk farther into the house. I didn't notice how cold it was getting. I made it to the third landing, and all of a sudden, it was like I was walking through Jell-O. I couldn't move my arms or legs as fast as I should. And I was so busy panicking about that, that it took that much longer to register when *something* grabbed me by the shoulders and shook me. It was holding me from the front, but I couldn't see it. I couldn't breathe. I was only ten, but I could *feel* how much it hated me. It wanted me dead. It wanted to toss me down the stairs like a rag doll and break my neck. And I think that if my dad hadn't poked his head over the railing to check on me, it might have. But I was also a scared kid with an overactive imagination. I didn't see anything. I only felt it. And yes, part of the reason I started renovating the house was to prove that it can't scare me anymore."

"Which it totally does."

"Shut it, Dotty. I'm a rational person, a numbers guy," Deacon said. "I believe in the things I can see and hear and touch. It's hard for me to admit that I'm scared of a feeling."

"And you haven't had any 'feelings' since you came back here?" Nina asked gently.

He cleared his throat and shook his head. "No."

Meanwhile, Cindy had started her timeline, titling it "Perception" and marking the earliest known activity in the group, "Deacon (age ten)" with terms such as "Unexplained cold spots," "Sensation of being squeezed/shaken," and "Difficulty breathing." She drew a line to her spot on the timeline, which was also marked "Sensation of being strangled, difficulty breathing." She drew a separate timeline for "Visual" and noted Nina's shadow-woman sightings and the vision she and Jake shared. When she turned around, the group was staring at her, all wide-eyed.

"I like order," Cindy said, her tone defensive.

Dotty managed to wrestle the dry-erase marker from Cindy's hands. "Well, Cindy's compulsive tendencies aside, I think there are two components to the haunting."

"Do we have to call it a haunting?" Deacon whined.

"Yes!" the others chorused.

Dotty scribbled "Manifestation" and "Curse," in a crooked, loopy scrawl that made Cindy wince. "Hauntings work on a couple of different levels. All buildings absorb a certain amount of emotional energy expressed by the people within their walls. Some buildings—whether because of their location or because of traumatic events or because someone with strong psychic ability lived or lives there—absorb more energy than others."

Cindy nodded. "The Stone Tape theory, right? It's why hospitals and prisons are more likely to be haunted than other buildings."

The others turned to look at her.

"Yes, the pretty girl can read. Moving on." Dotty continued her lecture. "Sometimes a haunting can be residual or cyclical, where there's not really a spirit present. But some event, whether it's traumatic or happy, gets imprinted on the space and plays out over and over like a record. And other times, it's an actual spirit, which is a more interactive, intelligent haunting and tends to scare people a little more. And then the most malevolent haunting is demonic. It has nothing to do with the history of the house or the people in it; some negative force just takes up space in the house like an unwanted renter."

"The paranormal equivalent of a drummer sleeping on your couch." Cindy nodded sagely.

"So you're saying we have a demon squatter?" Deacon asked skeptically.

"No, I think we're dealing with residual and spiritual hauntings. It sounds like Cindy walked into a memory pocket when she saw the vision of Catherine and Jack on the lawn. Those are residual, but everything else? Spiritual."

"Do you think that if we resolve the issues, Catherine and her ghostly entourage will go away?"

"I don't think Catherine is the ringleader," Nina said quietly.

Jake's brows rose. "Why do you say that?"

"Cindy, when you had that vision of Catherine and Jack, where were you?"

"Gerald's room."

"OK, so if you saw Catherine and Jack arguing like a couple of not-terribly-discreet teenagers, then perhaps Gerald saw them, too. It would certainly explain the heavy, angry footsteps on the third floor, near Catherine's room. Who wouldn't be angry when he realized his wife was sleeping with someone he was paying large amounts of money? That's a double whammy. And with him being suspected of strangling his wife, the 'difficulty breathing' bit makes a lot of sense."

"She makes a good point," Jake said.

"If there are spirits in the house, I think Gerald is the one we have to worry about. Can we make him go away?"

"I don't know. We could have a priest come out to the house and bless it."

Deacon leaned back in his chair, arms crossed over his chest. "And then a news story runs on the wire under the headline 'EyeDee CEO hosts exorcism at haunted mansion.' No, thanks."

Cindy frowned. "OK, in movies and books, you find out what's bothering the ghost, and sometimes that ends it. But I don't know whether that's for literary license."

"I suppose that Gerald's problem is that he only got to strangle his wife once?" Jake asked. He cast a contrite look at Deacon. "Sorry, man."

"Actually, that brings us to the other issue." Dotty pointed at the word *curse*.

Cindy tried to commandeer the marker. "Let me just—"

Dotty smacked her hand away.

"Dotty, there's no such thing as the Whitney curse," Deacon told her, on autopilot.

"I'm asking a little bit much from you in terms of acceptance, huh?" Dotty nodded. "And by the way, there is a curse."

Attempting to steer the conversation back on track, Nina interjected, "So, say for argument's sake that at some point, during the last hundred years or so, someone uttered some sort of incantation, did some sort of blood-letting ritual, or just looked really hard at a picture of Ralph Fiennes, while thinking, 'I do not like the Whitneys very much. I don't wish them good things,' what do we do to break the curse?"

"Ralph Fiennes?" Deacon frowned.

Nina scowled. "He's shifty."

Dotty ignored them. "Usually, it involves bringing some hidden truth to light."

"Maybe Catherine's spirit wants us to prove without a doubt that Gerald killed her?" Cindy suggested.

"It doesn't seem to make much sense that Catherine cursed her own children and descendants," Jake said.

Dotty said, "They bore the name of the man who strangled her. It wouldn't be too far off to think she had a little anger bottled up when she died. That kind of energy carries."

"OK, well, how do we prove a one-hundred-year-old crime without a doubt?" Jake asked.

Deacon cried, "This is ridiculous. We're not detectives!"

"No, but we're intelligent people who have access to the only evidence left. This house. The grounds. Who knows what's hidden up in the attic?" Cindy said.

"We should be on the lookout for ledgers, day planners, household books, anything Catherine or Gerald might have doodled on. Dotty, you've been looking at Catherine's diaries. Have you read anything interesting so far?"

Dotty dashed back to her room, retrieving a few of the journals and the notebook she used for notations. Nina cleared the table, and Deacon attempted to help her, hoping to avoid this ghost discussion by hiding in the kitchen, but Dotty dragged both of them back for her presentation. She had several journals spread out on the long table. She explained that Catherine was from Albany originally. But her family moved to New York when she was a teenager to take advantage of the thriving economy. Gerald and Catherine met at a ball, one of the first of her debutante season, in an age where a very young girl marrying a much older, established businessman was considered a coup, rather than sly tabloid fodder.

"The first journal starts on the day of her wedding in 1894. She doesn't write like someone who's terrified of her future husband," Dotty said. "She sounds happy, hopeful, excited about her future, just how you'd hope your daughter would write on her wedding day."

Dotty pulled out a tintype portrait of Gerald and Catherine. Catherine had a sweet, open face, with wide, light eyes and elegantly twisted blond hair. Her delicate little hand rested on Gerald's arm as she smiled at the camera. Gerald looked so stern, Nina thought. Stern, no-nonsense, and cold. Handsome in a dignified, unmussed way but not exactly a guy you could see spooning someone on a couch under a comfy blanket.

Jake suggested, "Maybe because it was early days yet?"

"Could be." Dotty shrugged.

"How does she feel about Gerald?" Nina asked. She stared at the wedding portrait. Something about the photo was . . . well, not bothering her but bringing back that niggling, *I should remember this* sensation in her brain.

"Fond," Dotty said. "Not quite in love, but she talks about him being handsome and distinguished, funny and affectionate when they're in private. Not exactly an ogre. Our gal Catherine was a prolific writer. Some of her journals only cover a few months. It's why there are so many of them. I'm having a little bit of trouble putting them in order, because a few seem to be missing. But I did find an interesting entry dated about two years before the house was completed." She read aloud:

Gerald has announced that we will be building on an isolated island off the shore of Rhode Island proper. A new start, he called it. Anyone could build a mansion in Newport, he says, but a home on its own island is an estate, a country unto its own. I asked him if I was going to have to address him as Mr. President. Oddly, he didn't laugh.

I worry, diary, about living in this strange, isolated spit of land in the middle of nowhere's oceanic twin. What if I get angry with Gerald and cannot walk away from our argument because I am trapped on all sides by water? What if I just want a cup of tea with a friend? My entire sphere will be cut down to the children and the servants. And Gerald has made it quite clear how he feels about me making friends with them. How often will I be allowed to leave? To have visitors? Although I am sure that Gerald doesn't intend it this way, this change of household feels a bit like a punishment.

As an added irritant, Gerald is insisting on hiring a local builder for the house, while other first-circle families have hired the best in French and English architectural minds. I believe he wants to endear himself to our more "pastoral" neighbors, as we will be living in this location year-round and will need to maintain good relationships with them—even if we are separated from them by miles of ocean. However, he doesn't seem to understand that it makes him appear miserly to his peers, using an unknown, unproven name when our contemporaries have selected the masters of the field. He will be judged, whether he believes that is important or not, and he will be treated differently by the people with whom he would like to make connections. Oh, la—what a snob I am turning out to be! To think I used to be one of those more "pastoral" folks myself. Oh, bother, what's done is done. I hope that the builder's ideas will be so unique that his origins will be forgotten.

Nina glanced down at Catherine's hand, resting against Gerald's arm. And she realized what was bothering her. The ring. Catherine's wedding set. It was a large diamond ring set with sapphires. Just the like the ring she saw in her recurring bed-making dream. The woman in the dream was definitely Catherine Whitney.

"How soon after did they hire Jack Donovan?" Jake asked.

"A few weeks, but there was an added wrinkle for Catherine," Dotty said, flipping through the journal until she found the appropriate entry:

This morning marked our first meeting with the builder Gerald has hired for the Crane's Nest. Imagine my surprise when Gerald elected to hire Jack Donovan, the very same boy who used to sit on my front porch and steal kisses in between sips of lemonade. I hadn't realized that Jack had trained as a builder; we lost track of each other when he went off to university and my family moved away. I must confess, he is little altered since our brief "romance" when we were barely more than children. There is no great tale of loss here, diary. This morning, I told him that he was lucky that I hold no resentment for how easily he moved on and established himself after "breaking my heart." He merely laughed, while Gerald looked on in irritated confusion. He was—and is—a perfectly nice young man. He has the same dark good looks and easy smiles. Still, I cannot help but wonder how my life would be different had I waited for Jack—if my parents hadn't moved me to New York to put me in a more "suitable arrangement."

Would I have married Jack? Would I have been happy as his wife? Would I have been able to stand hearing about the fine houses he was building for other folks while we lived in a single room in some unremarkable section of town? Would I have continued loving him in that stubbornly romantic way only girls of seventeen master? Or would I eventually resent the loss of my "destiny" as the young heiress to Newport's upper circles?

So yes, Jack's presence has left me unsettled to the extreme.

Cindy blew out a low whistle. "So I guess the theory about Catherine's inappropriate relationship with the architect wasn't too far off the mark."

Nina thought of the way the dream man's hands fit over her body—*Catherine's* body—and blushed. She wanted to fan her hot cheeks but resisted the urge. She didn't want Dotty or Cindy to notice.

"Maybe, but that's one of the last entries of the diary, and I haven't found the next volume yet," Dotty said.

"Is it weird for us to be talking about this?" Cindy asked. "I don't want to offend you two."

"It's not as if I ever met them," Dotty said with a shrug. "And I'm just as interested in the story as you are. I've always been sort of morbidly interested in my ancestors. I mean, most people think of their great-great-grandparents as being these cute, cuddly, old folks, but mine were a tragic horror story. I have to wonder what drove Gerald to kill her. I mean, he looks so cold. Who would have thought he had it in him to strangle the mother of his children? Love, jealousy, anger, those are all very powerful, dangerous emotions. Imagine he had to be pretty desperate to do something like that. It doesn't justify it, but . . . Gerald never came across as a cruel man. Just cold. It's strange. I know she's not doing the right thing, or at least, it seems like she won't eventually, but I can't help but feel a little bit sorry for her. She's a young wife, and her occasionally emotionally unavailable husband's dragging her out to the middle of nowhere to build a house with her ex-boyfriend? That's got to be a bit of an ethical muddle. Deacon?"

Deacon nodded. "I thought I understood, but hearing it in her own words humanizes her. When you're finished with the diaries, would you mind if I read them?"

Dotty beamed at him. "Of course! In the meantime, we document everything. We journal all of the experiences, weird dreams, visions, eerie feelings, noises." She reached into her giant shoulder bag and pulled out blank steno pads, tossing one to each in the circle.

"First question: Who keeps five blank notebooks in their shoulder bag?" Jake asked as Dotty threw one at his head. "And second: We're just going to stumble through our days here waiting to get another glimpse of the possibly-not-real or, even better, get knocked down the stairs?"

"The physical interactions are an illusion," Dotty said, sounding incredibly self-assured for someone discussing ghostly assaults. "The apparitions can't really hurt us. Psychic energy can't interact with the physical plane. We may see it, we may feel it, but it's not real."

"Feels awfully real," Cindy murmured.

"Just remember to stay calm," Dotty told her. "Fear can cloud your judgment, amp what you're seeing and feeling. Focus on what you know is real. And if it goes too far, just tell the apparition, 'I don't welcome your energy. I banish you from my space.'"

DEACON RAISED HIS hand, as if he was about to launch into a list of reasons why this was an asinine suggestion, but Nina caught his wrist and pressed his hand to the table, shaking her head. He felt as if he'd been stunned by one of Dotty's possibly illegal Tasers, a warm, electric tingle that traveled up his arm and lodged in his chest. Nina's hand didn't move from his, holding it steadily as she laughed at his space-cadet cousin's ghost-busting advice and Jake's inevitable facial contortions. Deacon could feel his heart rate slow. He could actually sense the serotonin levels in his brain increase, giving him a sense of well-being and calm.

How did she do that? How did she make him feel better by simply touching his arm? He stared at her, watching the light from the refurbished ring fixture dance in her hair. Deacon's brain hadn't been calm since he'd discovered online gaming and Mountain Dew. He'd thrived on stress and caffeine for ten years. Hell, he needed his brain to fire on all cylinders.

Nina was dangerous, the ultimate unknown quantity. Anyone who could alternately make him murderous and blissed-out in a twelve-hour span was not someone with whom he should spend a lot of time.

And yet . . .

If he'd learned anything since "coming into money," it was that time was the most valuable commodity on earth. There was a limitless supply, but everybody had a finite amount assigned to him or her. And how you chose to spend that assigned amount defined your entire existence. If he could spend what time he had with Nina, feeling this strange, still serenity, he would consider that worthwhile. Of course, being able to kiss her again would be nice, too. Even if it did end in a very expensive lawsuit and/or eventual divorce.

"And yets" were a total pain in the ass.

"Hey, at least you're seeing something. I'm still sort of bummed that I haven't had an experience yet," Dotty said, nudging Cindy's ribs.

"Maybe you're too open to it," Jake suggested. "Maybe ghosts can smell desperation on you. Like single men and student-loan officers."

Dotty chucked an orange at him.

"Stop throwing things at my head!" Jake exclaimed.

You Only Snark the Ones You Love

JAKE KNEW THAT a gentleman would probably take Cindy's rejection at face value and give up. But Jake couldn't stand the idea that she didn't like him. Something about her compelled him to prove that he was a good guy. Although he would have to do it without tampering with Nina's flowers again, because she seemed pretty serious about that mini-rake thing.

So here he was, seeking out Cindy to surprise her with what he considered his most brilliant romantic gesture yet, something that would entice her into agreeing to a genuine date, one that would involve actually leaving the island and spending some time in the real world. He found her supervising her cleaning crew as they meticulously cleaned out a storage closet on the second floor in the master wing. He was surprised that she would go anywhere near this part of the house after her experience on the stairs. But then again, Cindy was too obstinate to give up, even when it could put her in danger. He tried to find that charming, but mostly, he was just annoyed that she would venture up there on her own just to spite the house.

"Jake," she said, with her usual amount of warmth toward him, which meant little to none.

"Hey, Cindy, I want to show you something," Jake told her.

"If this is about the satyr murals in the men's steam room, trust me, I'm aware," Cindy groused, dusting her hands off on her pants.

"No, come on."

Pulling her to her feet, he led her into the grand ballroom. It hardly resembled the grimy, decayed mess they'd walked into weeks before. The walls were spotless, scrubbed down to the plaster. The windows shone, even in the full glare of the midday sun. The floor had been ruthlessly swept and polished to a glossy shine. Her crews had worked with Anthony's to create the best possible strategy for restoring the floor. There was buffing, lots and lots of buffing. This was the first time Cindy had seen the whole picture.

"It's so beautiful," she breathed, turning in a circle so she could take in the full effect. "I'm sorry we got into such a fuss over it. I just get so focused on my goals and timelines that occasionally I get tunnel vision. Also, you drive me *nuts* sometimes."

Jake rolled his eyes heavenward. "It was almost a nice apology. You were so close."

Cindy blushed. "Well, I wouldn't have blamed you if you hadn't shared this with me."

"You really get a lot out of your work, don't you?"

Cindy was flushed with pride. "This is why I was hired. This is the sort of difference I love seeing in a home when I work. This house, for all its history and historical complexity, will be a better place after I leave it. And that means something to me."

"Hold on, you haven't seen anything yet." Jake yanked on a rope, and several heavy canvas drapes dropped from the ceiling, puddling on the floor with a soft *whump*. Cindy covered her mouth with her hands, gasping as golden, ethereal light flooded the room. The ballroom ceiling was made up of massive stained-glass panels. The repeating Venetian floral patterns in their jewel tones created a garden effect that was both dizzying and beautiful, leading to a dome that featured several alternating floral motifs.

"In case you're interested, that's Tiffany glass," he said. "Mrs. Whitney happened to be a friend of Louis Comfort Tiffany, so old Louis was happy to doodle her a little design for the dome and windows. We only had to replace a few panels, which is sort of remarkable given the time that's passed."

"It's a shame that you lose this effect at night." She sighed, rubbing her arms. It was lovely to have goose bumps for a positive reason for once. "It would have been such a beautiful setting for a fancy midnight ball."

"Actually, Mrs. Whitney thought of that," Jake said. "She had Jack Donovan install curved mobile metal panels around the exterior of the dome, and gaslights would shine through the stained glass at night, giving it this really cool, sunlit glow."

"Will you be able to do the same?" she asked.

"We install new gas lines in the morning. We're even

backlighting the ceiling panels to give them the same effect. This is the one room in the house where Regina showed some sense in her design. She's keeping the walls stark white, bringing in a little warmth with the color of the flooring, but the main color element in the room will be the windows. But before she could put her 'signature touch' on the space, Deacon and I were able to convince her that whiting out the stained glass would be a violation of the National Historic Mansion Registry's rules on antique windows."

"Is there such a thing as the National Historic Mansion Registry?"

He shook his head. "Nope. And they definitely don't have rules about antique windows."

She snickered. "Very clever."

"Now." He bowed over her hand, making her wish that she'd washed up before entering this cathedral-like space. "May I have this dance, milady?"

"What are you doing?" she asked, pulling her hand out of his grip, although she did it without her usual vehemence.

"You told me that I could have one date with you, but we had to stay on the island. So I'm taking you dancing—dancing. Ah! Knew I forgot something!" He jogged over to a heavy shrouded chair. If he had a violinist hidden under that tarp, Cindy would be deeply concerned. Instead, he pulled out an MP3 player and a docking station, cueing up a lilting, woodwind-heavy waltz.

"You couldn't have warned me about this quote-unquote date so I could clean up a little?" she asked sourly, glancing down at her dusty T-shirt and jeans.

"I was afraid you would find some reason to back out if I told you ahead of time," he said, holding his hand out to her.

A flash of guilt tugged at Cindy's chest. She hadn't been very nice to Jake. OK, sure, he'd been a jerk to her. But name one college-age boy who didn't go through a jerk phase. It wasn't like her to hold grudges. And it was beneath her to continually treat this man with contempt and an oversensitive, fault-finding eye.

She couldn't fault Jake for being unpleasant, really. In fact, other than their argument about the memorabilia room—which she was willing to admit she'd provoked on purpose because it amused her to see him wring his hands through his hair—he'd been pretty sweet. He was funny and kind and considerate, particularly of Nina, whom he seemed to have adopted like a kid sister or a stray kitten. If he was a blue-collar guy who worked down at the marina, she probably would have agreed to move in with him immediately and have a dozen of his beautiful blue-eyed babies. She supposed this was a shameful example of reverse classism, and she would take the time to feel bad about it at a later date.

"Look, it can't be a proper ballroom until Cinderella dances here. You're doing Deacon a favor. So may I have this dance, miss?"

Cindy nodded, curtsying the way she'd seen Keira Knightley do in that Jane Austen movie. Jake beamed and slid his arms around her waist, holding his hand at an angle so she could slip hers over his. His left hand remained at a completely respectful area near her waist. He stepped forward, leading her into a simple box step that eventually circulated into the waltz. He wasn't even counting under his breath.

"You took lessons for this, didn't you?" she asked, her snicker barely held in check.

Jake grimaced. "Might have, when I was a kid. My mom insisted that if I was going to play baseball or soccer, she wanted me to dance, too. She said it made me a well-rounded person. But then, when I was seventeen or so, I figured out that she just didn't want to be left without a partner at weddings or parties when my dad was off in the den drinking with the other masters of the universe."

Cindy frowned. She remembered Jake making a few comments about his parents on their first date. They'd talked about their families, and Jake had said his "hadn't spent enough time with him to be worth mentioning," then asked her another question about her beloved father.

They hadn't danced on that first date. And now Cindy regretted it. Jake moved smoothly, without being conscious about it. She tried to remember any time she'd seemed that comfortable in her skin and came up short. Nor could she remember the last time a man had bothered leading her in a dance that involved steps and not just grinding up on her or doing the standard "stand and sway."

She tried not to let it go to her head. The colors, the beautiful lush light, the smell and feel of the man in her arms. She had to keep herself grounded, remind herself why a real relationship between the two of them would never work out—like aversion therapy, only with skanky interior designers.

As they completed a circuit around the dance floor, Cindy peered up at Jake through her lashes and asked, "So, Regina, huh?"

"Let's not talk about that," he said. "That is definitely not good first-date conversation."

"If you want there to be a second date, I'd like to know where that stands."

"That was a long time ago," he assured her, his face flushed. "Regina's parents are friends with mine. We were thrown together a lot when we were kids."

"So she's not your type?" Cindy asked.

Jake smiled at her, somehow brightening the room even more. "Until recently, I was into women who were really driven, career-oriented. But now I've come to realize that I want something different. I want you."

Cindy's brow furrowed while she contemplated what the hell he meant by that. "So I'm not driven?"

He grinned at her. "No, you're happy with where you are. That's not a bad thing!"

She skidded to a halt, mindful of not leaving shoe marks on the gleaming floor. "Well, since I've settled into my place right here, why don't you go back to your friend Regina? She's made it pretty clear that she's ready to take you or Deacon on as fixer-uppers."

Jake frowned, not quite understanding why this conversation seemed to be rolling downhill so quickly. "I don't want Regina. She's just like every other girl I've ever dated. All polish and prospects. No fun. You're together. You know what you want, but you don't let it get in the way of having a good time. You don't let worrying about success or money drag you down. You don't have your whole life planned out."

Cindy was missing the part in this monologue of her virtues that was an actual compliment. Because so far, he was making her out to be some sort of free-wheeling, bubble-headed hippie type.

"Ambition. That's what it is," he said, grinning at her. "You don't let ambition run your life."

Cindy's eyebrows shot up so fast and so high she was surprised she didn't strain a muscle in her forehead. "So you're saying I don't having any ambition?"

"You're happy the way you are," he said, shrugging.

Cindy's eyes narrowed, flame-blue with fury. Gritting her teeth, she snatched up her cleaning tote and did her best to avoid flouncing as she stormed across the dance floor. She *lacked ambition*? Was that really what he thought of her? Did he even realize how insulting that was, to claim that she was somehow virtuous because he thought she wanted less from life? She didn't know what was worse, the smug elitist classism of it all or the fact that he'd misjudged her so badly. Of all the stupid, shallow, jackass things to say, that was what came out of his mouth?

She knew what her father would do in this situation. He would shove his foot up Jake's butt until the smarmy jerk tasted shoe leather. But this was—for all intents and purposes—her office, and she couldn't go around turning her coworkers into human penny loafers. And it singed her working-class, *nonambitious* sensibilities to the quick that he was going to get away with thinking that of her.

So really, it shouldn't have surprised her when her fingers wrapped around an empty can of floor polish and threw it across the room, beaning Jake's head with a solid *thunk*.

"Ow!" he yelped, clutching at his head. "What was that for?"

She almost let it go. She almost walked out of the room, letting the thrown household cleaners do the talking for her. But she'd held back for too long. She'd let him toddle along in blissful ignorance while she carried the burden of their past connection. And she was tired of doing all the heavy lifting. So she raced back across the dance floor on nimble feet, burying her finger in his chest and poking for all she was worth.

"For one thing, if you don't think I have any ambition, you've completely misunderstood every single conversation we've had, *ever*," she growled. "And that includes the ones you can't remember!"

Still rubbing at the side of his head, he spluttered, "OK, clearly, we got off on the wrong foot at some point along the way. Because I don't know about you, but most of my conversations don't end with someone getting a can of floor polish lobbed at his head. Why don't you like me?" Jake exclaimed. "I shouldn't have made that comment about your ambitions. That hurt your feelings, and I apologize. But this started way before that conversation. You've had your hate on for me ever since we stepped onto that boat. You like Anthony. You like Deacon. I expect you and Dotty and Nina to make one another friendship bracelets at any minute. I don't get it. Most people like me. But you treat me like I'm trying to sell you a time-share."

"You really don't remember, do you?" Cindy scoffed. "I mean, at first, I was willing to cut you some slack. But after a while, I thought maybe you remembered me but were too embarrassed to admit it after we'd been here for weeks. But you honestly do not remember me at all, do you?"

"If I say no, are you going to bean me with another can of floor polish?"

"Eight years ago. You took me to see a symphony concert at the park. There was a windstorm a few days before. I was wearing these really cute wedge sandals, and I was having trouble stepping around these big fallen limbs—"

Jake's mouth fell open, and he blurted out. "I picked you up and carried you over to the amphitheater. A little old lady told you to hold on to me because there weren't a lot of gentlemen left in the world."

Somehow, hearing the words come out of his mouth made a wave of pain rush through her chest. "Yeah."

"And then she pinched my butt," Jake said. "Really hard."

"I didn't know that part," she admitted, swiping at the tears gathering in her eyes. Why was she crying now? She hadn't cried over him in years. Maybe it was embarrassment, knowing that he was aware of their connection now and she would have to deal with his reaction. Or maybe living through the "abandonment" all over again was just playing with her already frayed nerves. Either way, it was a balm over whatever wounds were left on her heart when Jake offered her a handkerchief from his pocket. Manners, she thought; no matter what, the man had pretty manners.

The man was also shaking his head vehemently. "I thought your name was Cassie."

"Oh, you—What is wrong with you?" she exclaimed, turning on her heel and walking out of the room.

"Wait," he said, nimbly catching up to her in a few steps. He caught her arm and gently tugged at the elastic in her hair, pulling it out of its carefully woven French braid. He fluffed it out, arranging the golden waves around her shoulders. His eyes went wide. "Oh, my God, it *is* you."

She buried her face in her hands. "You didn't remember me because my hair was up? I'm going to murder you."

"Why didn't you *say* anything?"

"Because I didn't want to be the one who reminded you. I wanted you to remember me on your own."

"But I never went out with that girl again."

"Would you please stop calling me 'that girl'? I am a person. A person who is standing right here and can hear you!" she exclaimed.

"I never went out with *you* again. What happened?" he asked. "Why didn't you return my calls?"

"You tell me. You never called me again."

"There's no way I wouldn't call you again!" He gasped, his eyes bugging out. "Wait, wait, that was, what, June 2005, right? Oh, no. Oh, no no no no."

"That had better be Jake-speak for 'That's the month I was abducted by aliens and unspeakably probed.'"

He ran his hands through his hair, leaving it in Einstein-level disarray. "I'm an *idiot*. June of 2005. I was here for the summer with my parents. I'd just broken off with Madeline Taylor—again. It was the fourth or fifth time we'd broken things off, and that girl was just pure relationship evil. She kept pulling me back in, and no matter how many times I said no or told her I wasn't interested, she managed to convince me that even if I wasn't sure about *her* intentions, I should at least date her while I figured it out."

"None of this explains why you failed to call me."

"Right after our second date—I remember now, it was the second date, and I was just about to call you to set up the third—Madeline heard that I'd gone out on a few dates. She called me, trying to 'fix things' between us. And when that didn't work, she showed up at my parents' house, and the next thing I knew, we were dating again."

"So she destroyed your phone and your basic sense of courtesy?" Cindy asked.

"Actually, she did destroy my phone that year," Jake said. "But only a few months later, after we'd gone back to school."

"She sounds like a charmer."

"Well, what happened to you?" he demanded. "Why didn't you call me?"

"I had some personal problems," she said. "I got distracted."

She could practically see the panic spread across his face as he scanned his memory banks to determine whether her personal business could have included bearing his love child.

"My father got sick," she said indignantly. "I had to defer college and take care of him."

"Oh, I'm sorry to hear about that. Is he better?"

She shook her head. "He's been gone for about four years."

"I'm sorry I didn't call you again. I'm sorry I didn't get to take you out again. And I'm sorry I didn't remember you. I was young and stupid, not that it's any excuse. Forgive me?"

"I think there will be more groveling involved," she told him.

"You want more groveling?" he asked.

"I think a little extra groveling is called for."

He dropped to his knees, clasping her hands between his. "Please! Lady Cynthia! Forgive me for my grievous error!"

"Get up." She sighed, her cheeks turning red. "I did bean you in the head with floor polish. I'd say that probably makes us even."

"I really am sorry that I didn't call you again," he said. "And for forgetting you. That was a stupid, thoughtless thing to do. You'll be glad to know that I have matured into a wiser, less douchey person."

She tilted his head toward her, inspecting the respectable lump forming on his crown. "I'm sorry for hitting you in the head with a blunt object."

He grimaced. "I had it coming. And I'm sorry that I hurt your feelings with that 'ambition' comment. I really meant it to be a compliment. I like that you care about more than just your job. I just put it badly."

"You're forgiven. Mostly," she said. "And I overreacted. Can we start over?"

"Does starting over involve getting some ice for my head?"

"I'll wrap it in a towel and everything," she said, offering him her arm and leading him out of the ballroom. "So when was the last time you heard from Madeline?"

"Uh, she sent me an EyeContact request a few months ago," Jake said. "I declined it, but she sent it a few more times. And then she hired a private investigator to find my address and parked outside of my apartment building for a few nights running. I had to move in with Deacon for a while and change all the contact information on my accounts to a PO box. Other than that, nothing."

"Have you noticed that you tend to bring the crazy out in a girl?"

Love Letters from No One

The island is a beautiful, though lonely, place. Josephine is so happy here, running as fast as her chubby little legs will carry her across what will become our lawn.

My feelings about living in a place so remote are in a constant flux, much more so with every visit we make to the island for "progress reports." While it will be so alien to live without the clip-clop of horse hooves just outside the window or the murmur of conversation from the street, I must admit that Whitney Island is a peaceful place. None of the tedium of city life will find us here. No unexpected visits from neighbors. No calling cards. No worrying about being seen in the right shops, the right clubs.

And the house will further these advantages. The gardens will be second to none. There will be room for the children to play without worrying for their safety from *carriages, strangers. I feel that I will be able to breathe properly, for the first time in years. It will be a compromise, diary, one that I hope I am able to make.*

On that note, Gerald insists on the Crane's Nest having enough room to throw the elaborate parties that are becoming so fashionable. I don't know if I will ever have the desire to become a fixture on this circuit. I certainly don't want to compete with a Mrs. Astor or a Mrs. Vanderbilt. But if it will bring my husband some pleasure and help his business, I will do it gladly. I simply don't know if we need a ballroom that seats four hundred to accomplish it.

"Boooring!" Cindy called, yanking a box from under a tarp in the main attic. The finished, expansive space spread out over most of the main wing's square footage and was larger than the first floor of Nina's apartment building. "Get to something good!"

Nina thought about noting Cindy's good mood, a general upswing in her morale since she and Jake started going on "dates" around the island—long walks along the shore, dinner on the back porch at the main house, long talks on the dock. But Cindy refused to talk about it, because she didn't want to jinx it. And it didn't seem nice to provoke her. Especially since she hadn't told Dotty or Cindy about the kiss with Deacon in the greenhouse, and Nina knew that somehow, teasing Cindy would result in her own personal beans being spilled.

So instead, Nina flipped through the diary until she found a passage of Catherine's thoughts that seemed to hold more dramatic promise.

For the first time in my marriage, I have been dishonest with Gerald. He asked me how I knew Jack, and I lied. I told him he was simply a friend of the family. I don't know why I lied. Maybe I didn't want to admit that I had any romantic entanglements before him. Maybe I didn't want him to have any reason to doubt me. Or maybe I had some misguided need to protect Jack, to make sure he had this job and the opportunity to make a name for himself. Now I can't go back. If I admitted that I lied, Gerald would be furious, and worse, he would be hurt. He would wonder why I felt it necessary to lie, and I would not be able to answer.

It is strange seeing Jack so often. It seems that he visits our New York home at least once a day to discuss plans for the house, ideas for simplifying or expanding. As Gerald is often away on business—more and more lately, it seems—it has fallen to me to meet with Jack and approve the changes to the various stages of the house plans. I will be honest. At first, those plans seemed like a nonsensical web of blue-smudged paper. And at night, I have wept with the frustration of being expected to understand it all.

But as Jack very patiently explained the schematics to me and the construction process as a whole, it all started to make sense. I could see the house in my head, from the ground up. I could walk through its hallways and imagine its views from the windows and the widow's walk. It gave me an unexpected sense of power to be given control over the Crane's Nest. Gerald might be the owner of the house and Jack the architect, but I will be its creator.

Jack is just as he ever was, as charming as he could

possibly be. In the hours we have spent together, he has told me he's missed me, and he is glad that we will be spending so much time together. I will confess that it is pleasant to keep company with someone who knew me before my ascension to my "post" as Mrs. Whitney. He knew the awkward Catherine of coltish limbs and flyaway hair, and he still looks at me as if I am a sweet he is eagerly anticipating. He has been a comfort to me as I enter this new phase as mistress of a monolith.

Nina turned the diary over in her hands, the dim light of the afternoon sun shining through the rain-dappled attic window. "It's kind of sweet that Jack carried a torch for her all that time, since they were kids."

"It's kind of hot," Cindy said, conscientiously folding the sheet that had just covered a rather lovely cherry table with carved lions for legs. "Repressed sexual tension, corsets, and . . . blueprints."

Dotty's lips pursed into a knowing grin. "Really, blueprints are suddenly attractive to you? And that has nothing to do with you nursing a certain recently concussed architect back to health?"

Without even looking at Dotty, Cindy pointed at her. "Quiet, you."

Nina giggled, opening another of Catherine's diaries. Technically, Saturday was their day off. They could leave the island for the day to run errands or just get away from the house. But instead, the ladies had trekked up to the attic on this miserable, drizzly day to search through the treasures there. Reading through Catherine's diaries had left them with a gnawing curiosity about Mrs. Whitney. And Dotty was determined to find information that might be locked away in the attic's nooks and crannies. So far, they'd managed to find a lot of broken furniture, a hobby horse that had belonged to little Josephine Whitney, and several crates of chipped china with gold-plated rims surrounding a golden W. And Dotty had found an oversized hatbox containing an enormous, faded blue picture hat, which was now jauntily angled atop her head.

"Anyway," Cindy continued, "it definitely sounds like Jack and Catherine's decision to run off together wasn't a hasty one. They danced around each other from the beginning."

Dotty frowned, snagging a small digital recorder from the pocket of her hoodie and putting it on the floor next to her.

"What's that about?" Nina asked.

"I figured that it might be a good idea to record ourselves as we're talking about Catherine and Jack. I'm hoping the recorder will pick up messages that the naked ear couldn't pick up."

"Why would we want that?" Nina asked. "Doesn't it seem sort of reckless to try to communicate with whatever is going on in the house? I mean, why not just whip out a Ouija board and try to text with it?"

"Text with the ghost." Cindy snickered. When Nina and Dotty turned their attention to her, she shrugged. "It's funny, because it's sort of the same thing, but not really . . . Right, sorry, carry on."

For a moment, Nina was sorry that she'd mentioned the Ouija-board issue. She and Cindy had refused to participate in any sort of active provoking of the dead, including Ouija boards, attempted channeling, automatic writing, or just speaking rudely to empty rooms. Dotty was not happy, but she wasn't quite brave enough to try any sort of communication by herself. Besides, Nina and Cindy were more than willing to help her with her research, and that was a dirty, occasionally risky job (splinters, errant sharp objects, occasional possession by spirits). Dotty had created a timeline on their whiteboard, keying in important dates and events in Catherine and Gerald's relationship, then a separate timeline for Catherine and Jack's supposed relationship. So far, she'd found plenty of dates but no real clues about Catherine's death. And she certainly wasn't any closer to a supernatural explanation for her family's generational misfortune.

But at least she'd found a lovely hat.

"This is called EVP, electronic voice phenomena," Dotty said, waving the recorder. "Some people think that if you set out a recorder and ask a spirit questions, the recorder will pick up noises and answers from the spirits that the naked ear couldn't hear."

"What if you record something you don't want to hear?" Cindy asked.

"Still safer than a Ouija board," Dotty said. "Those things are like a giant, evil neon sign that says, 'Hey, undefined manifestations who mean us harm, here we are!'"

Nina laughed. "But don't people use EVP and electromagnetic meters and all that to confirm the presence of ghosts? I don't think we have to prove that they're here. We know they are. I think we need to know why and how to get rid of them."

"I don't want to communicate *with* the spirits,"

Dotty assured her. "But wouldn't it be nice if Catherine or Jack gave us some clue to where we should look for her jewelry or what we could do to undo the curse?"

"Or tell us that Paul is dead?" Nina suggested brightly.

"I think I liked you better when you were all meek and unassuming." Dotty grunted, lobbing a ball of tissue paper at her.

Nina easily ducked the ineffective projectile and turned her attention back to the diaries. "Here's another one," she said, reading aloud.

Jack kissed me today. Just writing those words is terrifying and makes me want to dash them with my pen. If Gerald were to ever find out . . . I shudder, diary, to think what his reaction would be.

It happened so quickly, and I was so shocked that I don't think I responded appropriately. We were standing at his draft table reviewing plans for my bedroom suite. He was asking me questions about the placement of the bed that I realize now could be construed as intimate. I felt his hand on the back of my neck, and before I knew it, he had turned me around, pressed me back against the table.

I pushed him away, but I am ashamed to say that I felt some stirring inside of me, the longing and giddy lightness of that young girl who once kissed Jack Donovan on her porch swing. All these years, I believed I would never be the sort of woman who welcomed attentions from men other than her husband. But Gerald is gone so often, and Jack is always here. Always.

I am so confused, as unsettled as the storm-tossed waves that eat away at the shores of our new home. Is

*my marriage so easily eroded? Could I break my bond
with Gerald so easily? What sort of woman am I becoming?*

Dotty's face became more unsettled with every
word. Nina immediately regretted reading that particular passage. Sometimes she forgot that they weren't just
speculating about characters from some long-forgotten
story but that these were Dotty and Deacon's relatives.
And of course, Dotty didn't want to hear in-depth detail about her great-great-grandmother's slide into an
adulterous affair.

Catherine Whitney had been a lonely woman, isolated with an old flame while undertaking an intimidating task. Of course, she turned to that old flame for
comfort. Nina didn't judge her for it, but she wouldn't
treat the romance as if it was the greatest love story ever
told—especially when Dotty or Deacon was around.

"So are we looking for anything in particular, or are
we just sifting through the rubble like prospectors?"
Nina asked, snapping the diary shut.

"Well, I was sifting, but while we're up here, I was
hoping to find Catherine's wedding trunk. When she
and Gerald got home from their extensive honeymoon,
she used it to save her wedding dress and sentimental
keepsakes. My grandmother told me about it when I
was a kid."

"How did your relatives not find and pawn this?"
Cindy asked.

Dotty began counting the wall panels, until she
found the fourth from the door. "Well, I'll be honest, as
much as she loved her husband, my grandmother saw

the direction the family was taking in my grandfather's generation. She didn't know what was in the wedding trunk, but she knew that it would be a shame to let it be pawned for cash that wouldn't sustain her spendthrift husband for more than a few months. So she took it." Dotty shoved a stack of cartons marked "Pots and Pans" away from the wall with a grunt. Hidden behind the stack, she found an old steamer trunk bearing customs stamps from Paris, Berlin, London, and Lisbon. "And she hid it behind a bunch of cartons no one would look at twice. Who wants to sort through old pots and pans when you're looking for treasures? And one rainy afternoon, right before she died, she told me where she'd hidden it. She made me promise I wouldn't tell my father or my uncle—whom she loved but didn't trust with anything valuable—but I had to swear that I'd share what I found with Deacon."

Nina helped her drag the trunk into an open space in the middle of the room. Dotty plucked a bobby pin from Cindy's hair with an apologetic shrug. She picked the trunk lock and popped the lid open, filling the attic with the scent of long-dried violets. Nina squealed in delight as they gently lifted a layer of yellowed tissue paper from the top tray, revealing a travel set of monogrammed silver brushes, combs, and a hand mirror. A tiny canister of violet-scented talc with powder puff, an ancient porcelain pot of lip rouge, and a set of pearl-studded hairpins completed the toiletry set. Dotty carefully lifted the tray from the trunk, revealing a carefully folded white satin bundle wrapped in more tissue paper. Nina helped her lift the heavy material from the trunk, unfolding it until it became a long, elegantly cut wedding gown with a high waist, lace sleeves pointed at the wrists, and a long, bell-shaped train.

"Wow," Cindy marveled. "They sure knew how to make a dress back then. You know, this was a Charles Worth design? He was the Tom Ford of his generation. You really had to rank in the four hundred to get an appointment with him."

"Gerald would have spared no expense for his bride." Dotty noticed that the liner of the trunk top didn't fit quite flush with the edges. She raised a hand to Cindy's head to search for another hairpin, but the blonde warned her, "If you rip more hair out of my head, you and I are going to have a problem."

Dotty *harrumph*ed and plucked a pin from the picture hat, then jammed it into the space between the lid and the liner. After a few wiggles, the lid popped loose, revealing a false top that provided a handy—if narrow—secret storage space. A bundle of papers fell into Dotty's hands.

"Jackpot, ladies!" she crowed, waving the packet over her head. The bundle of letters was tied with a bit of faded pinkish lace. She carefully untied the knotted lace and studied the dates scribbled on the back of the envelopes. "Letters to Catherine spanning, oh, three or four years!"

"Love letters?" Cindy asked.

Nina told her, "Well, I don't think you tie letters from your school friends up in pink lace and hide them in your wedding trunk. Nobody in this house trusted *anybody*."

"Good point. What do they say?"

Dotty very gingerly opened a random letter from the pile.

" 'Dearest Kitten,' " Dotty read. " 'The vision of me holding you in my arms—freely, without watchful eyes and interference—is the only thing that keeps me sane each day. When can we be together? I thought myself a good man, a patient man, a man of morals. But loving you has put every one of those misconceptions to the test. I need you, to touch you, to taste you. When can we give up all of this pretense? When will you be mine?' "

"Wow, that's pretty hot stuff for the time," Nina said. "Is it signed?"

Cindy let loose a silvery laugh. "No, the author signed it with a little sketch. It's a little bird. An ugly bird. The letter writer is a better wordsmith than an artist."

"It's a crane," Dotty said, her voice even more deflated than before. "Well, that's one way to keep from getting caught. It does seem fitting that Jack would use the crane as a symbol, considering the location. After all, the house brought them back together."

"Is it at all possible it's from her husband?" Nina asked, more for Dotty's benefit than for her own curiosity. Dotty seemed honestly disturbed by each new revelation about her ancestor.

"It doesn't sound like something Gerald would write," Dotty said, her tone skeptical. "I've read his business correspondence. Poetic lover he was not. The handwriting is similar, but everyone had lovely penmanship back then."

"You OK, Dot?" Cindy asked, nudging her arm.

Dotty's hat drooped as she nodded. "The more I learn about Catherine, the more it seems to make sense and then conflict. It just seems strange that a woman who would have a special passage built so she could go to her children instead of turning them over to nannies at night, who would give so much consideration to her servants' comfort, would cheat on her husband."

"Cheating on a spouse, particularly when that spouse is absent and—from what we've read—distant and cold, doesn't make you a bad person," Cindy told her. "It doesn't make you a *great* person, but I don't think you should think less of her because she was unhappy."

"I know," Dotty said. "Maybe I would feel better if we found something written from Gerald's perspective, something that showed him for a callous, unfeeling jerk who deserved to be cuckolded. Or maybe something from Jack that proved he was worthy of Catherine's love. Right now, everything feels off-balance."

"Have you thought about contacting Jack's family?" Nina asked.

Dotty shook her head, unleashing a small storm of dust from her picture hat. "There is no surviving family. He didn't have any children. Like I said, he pretty much disappeared from public life after Catherine's death. Some people claimed to have seen him in the days after her body was found. Even with the scandal, you'd think that he'd be able to parlay building one of the most luxurious homes in the country into more work, but he never did another high-profile project. Some doyenne in Virginia claimed to have hired him to build a summer home on the coast the following year and demanded repayment when he didn't complete the design. But that didn't work out, because she couldn't find him. It's like he just disappeared from the face of the earth."

"You can hardly blame him. The woman he loved died suddenly. And there was probably a bit of guilt, since her husband killed her over their affair. He may not have wanted to work again just because of the associations with Catherine."

"Do any of the letters say anything helpful?" Cindy asked, eager to break the somber mood. "Like, 'Gerald told me to meet him at the top of the stairs at nine P.M. so he can strangle me?'"

"Now, that would be too easy," Dotty huffed, carefully slipping the letter back into its aging yellow envelope. "Everything here—the letters, the diaries, the artifacts—they're pieces of the puzzle. I just have to find a way to make them fit."

"In the meantime, you do look rather fabulous in that satellite-sized hat," Cindy told her.

Dotty preened, putting on a brave, bright face. "Of course, I do, darling. I'm a Whitney."

Dotty of the Dead

NINA WAS LOOKING forward to her day, planting an array of annuals timed for different seasons, so that the beds would display different patterns and designs throughout the year. She loved the sturdy elegance of tulips and Johnny-jump-ups mixed with daffodils, which would give way to fiery splashes of snapdragons and poppies.

Ghostly issues aside, Nina was pretty content. She'd deposited Deacon's latest check, which allowed her to pay off the last of her remaining Rick debts. This made her bank account solvent for the first time in months. She immediately paid several outstanding personal bills online, paid off her credit cards, and rewarded the patience of the lovely folks at the garden center, who had floated her supplies for the last year.

She had no bills due from that very moment until the next payment from Deacon's office. She even had a little money to spare. She could buy herself something she *wanted* instead of the bare necessities. She could buy *shoes* . . . assuming that she managed to get off the island to a shoe store. She would never be able to thank Deacon enough for the difference he'd made in her life. If she had any success as a business owner, it would be as a result of his generosity. She felt a little weird, accepting money from someone she'd committed greenhouse frottage with, but she also knew that wasn't why Deacon had hired her. She knew she'd earned her place here. He wanted her on the job because she'd been clever and creative in her approach. She belonged here. Making out on the greenhouse floor was just a delightful side benefit.

On the slightly less normal side, she'd spent the previous evening updating her "ghost journal," something Dotty now insisted that they do at the end of every day. Even if the journal entry was "Nothing to report," Dotty wanted it documented. She knew Cindy occasionally made up entries, such as "Visited by the ghost of Elvis—may or may not be bearing his love child," but Nina tried to be as honest as possible. After all, poor Dotty was the only one in the group who hadn't had so much as an ominous goose bump. So Nina dutifully maintained her Diary of the Weird. Even if it was just a vague impression, like the time she thought she saw a pale, angry face pressed against the common-room window out of the corner of her eye, she wrote it down. She did, however, add a notation of "Probably my imagination" to these entries.

While Cindy maintained her surface sarcasm, she confided in Nina that she'd taken up her own "independent study" to try to find some evidence that Catherine and Gerald had shared some sort of affection during their marriage. Like Nina, Cindy had noticed Dotty's growing despair at the character sketch she was developing for Catherine—frustrated, lonely, increasingly bitter, and easily drawn into adultery. They both feared that this would lead to waning enthusiasm for the book project and that Dotty would eventually drop it, as she had dropped so many projects before.

Dotty needed to see a project through to completion. Nina was sure it would be good for her, that it would give her the confidence to get her floundering career on track. Dotty was a fabulous person and an even better friend, but she needed direction. And Nina believed it was good for Deacon to have his cousin around, as much as he protested. If Dotty didn't complete the book project, Nina wasn't sure that their relationship would survive Deacon's *I told you so*s. The family connection left both of them too raw to survive much teasing.

So while Dotty was sunning herself on a nearby towel, probably meditating on an image of finding Catherine's jewels or the final diary, Cindy sat on a stone bench, watching Nina plant her bulbs and reading through a few of the copied newspaper clippings and book excerpts her librarian friends had e-mailed the day before.

Nina suddenly stopped and looked up. "Wait, Gerald and Catherine only had two kids, right?"

Dotty nodded. "Gerald Junior and Josephine. They were sent to live with a distant aunt after their father died. By the time Gerald Junior was old enough to inherit the family business, it had already died a slow, painful death. He tried starting his own company, a munitions plant. He earned a government contract at the beginning of World War Two, and it looked like the family fortune might be rebuilt, but there were problems with the pig iron he was using, and the shells fell apart in the field. The government snatched the contract back faster than you could say 'barely escaped treason charges.' The plant was closed within a year. Josephine made her debut in Philadelphia. The aunt tried to introduce her into society, pretending nothing had changed. But Josephine didn't want any part of it. She was married quietly to the son of a family who owned a textile mill. But eventually, that family's fortunes failed as well. Josephine's husband died before they could have kids. And Gerald Junior and his wife had two children. His son was our grandfather."

"So how did you end up with so many long-lost cousins?"

"Distant second and third cousins from Gerald's line. They're not actually descended from Gerald and Catherine, but their fortunes were tied to his business ventures. So they suffered the same fate as the other Whitneys. Bankruptcy, desperation, pawning everything in sight. And they're not particularly pleased with Deacon's suddenly striking it rich. You wouldn't believe how they came out of the woodwork after his stock offering, reminding him of all the good times the family had at reunions and holidays, how they'd always believed he was something special. And then subtly informing him that their kid was starting college or that the mortgage on their house was past due. He felt so good about making his fortune that he wrote checks to the first few, and that started a sort of feeding frenzy. He had to start saying no, and when he did, it just got worse. Lawsuits, break-ins here at the house, the sense of entitlement and jealousy. It was overwhelming."

"But if all of these other cousins aren't direct descendants of Gerald Whitney, they couldn't have a claim on the house, right?"

"Of course, they don't, but that doesn't keep fringe relatives like our great-uncle Phillip from claiming that the idea of changing the house causes him deep personal distress. The court won't take him seriously, but filing the injunction—which he has done twice—will cause legal complications for Deacon and possibly delay construction. And he expects Deacon to cough up a few ducats to make 'the problem' go away."

"Will Deacon pay him?" Cindy asked.

"I don't know. He was awfully annoyed at having to pay him last time."

Nina shook her head sadly. "Poor Deacon."

Dotty smirked. "Don't let him hear you say that."

"It's just that everybody seems to want something from him. It's sad. It's like being the most popular kid in your class because you have a cupcake in your lunchbox. Pretty soon, the cupcake is gone, and you find out that nobody really liked you in the first place."

Cindy smiled brightly. "If you make that comparison to Deacon's face, I will give you a shiny nickel."

Nina tossed a clump of grass at Cindy, who ducked out of the way. "Not a chance, you career ruiner."

"Oh, here's something. Jennifer sent over pictures

from the Whitneys' first party here on the island, just after the house was completed," Cindy called to Dotty.

"It was their first and only party. Catherine was dead within a month," Dotty responded, not bothering to move from her comfortable position.

"So what happened at the party?" Nina asked as she raked a small section of dirt clear and prepped it for planting.

"It started off really well," Cindy answered, flipping through the carefully printed sheets. "It was a fairy-garden theme. Thanks to Mrs. Vanderbilt's costume parties, everybody was more than happy to dress up. Women showed up dressed as dryads and nymphs. The men sort of cheated and just wore masks with their tuxedos. Catherine had arranged for photographers to take the guests' portraits as they arrived, so they would be able to capture the costumes before they could be mussed." She showed the others some copied photos of stiff, bored-looking women in cellophane fairy wings. "This was a good time to you people?"

"Even when you're talking about the rich white sector of the population, I'm pretty sure 'you people' is considered offensive," Dotty told her.

Cindy frowned. "I will send you some lovely apology flowers."

"And yes, believe it or not, these women were probably having the time of their lives. Portraits were just a lot more formal then. They weren't encouraged to smile."

Dotty finally dragged her butt off her towel and crawled over to examine the photos.

"I've read about this. It was a very swanky do. Champagne from Paris and sweets from Switzerland. If guests arrived without costumes, they were immediately directed to a spare bedroom suite, where Catherine had hired seamstresses to fit them in a selection of very chic theme-appropriate frocks. Catherine had even arranged for acrobats to dangle from trapezes bolted into the ceiling of the ballroom."

"She let someone drill bolt holes into her brand-new ceilings?" Cindy asked.

"No, she arranged for the bolts to be built into the ceiling in the first place."

"She planned the theme that far ahead?"

Dotty shrugged. "She took this party very seriously. She knew that her future as a respected hostess among the very rich depended on a successful evening. Also, the plan was that she would hang chandeliers from the bolts later."

Cindy grumbled. "Rich people."

"Stop it." Nina poked her in the ribs.

Dotty slid her sunglasses on top of her head and sorted through Cindy's papers. "OK, so they're socializing in the foyer, in front of the grand staircase. Dinner is served, prepared by a fantastic French chef Catherine had lured from some upstart social-climbing family in New York. The dancing started, but Catherine had disappeared. This was unheard of. The hostess always led the first dance. It was quite the scandal.

"Gerald excused himself to go look for her. Several guests insisted they heard shouting from the garden, and a very pale Catherine rejoined the party to lead the dancing. Gerald wasn't seen for the rest of the night. The party never quite got back into swing, and the guests left early. It was reported in society pages to be 'one of the most uncomfortable evenings of the year.' Catherine was said to be devastated."

"So Catherine had the bad taste to leave her own party and meet her lover in the garden, and her husband caught her?" Nina asked.

"Sounds like it."

Cindy pursed her lips. "But Jack Donovan wasn't at the party. It says here in this gossip-column clipping, 'Notably absent from the disastrous soiree was Jack Donovan, the architect of this marvel of modern domestic engineering. Several guests were overheard stating that Mr. Donovan was not invited.' So she couldn't have been meeting Donovan in the garden."

"A second lover?" Nina suggested, eyeing Dotty carefully.

"No offense, Dotty, your great-great-grandmama was sort of a skank," Cindy marveled, wincing when Nina whacked her in the shoulder.

"Maybe," Dotty said, sliding her sunglasses back into place. "A few weeks later, Catherine disappeared. There was a frantic search, and then her body was found in the bay. Gerald insisted that when he arrived on the island, Catherine was nowhere to be found. The police insisted that he must have arrived earlier, killed Catherine, and then made a big show of arriving at the house and looking for her. Maybe Gerald was just pushed too far. First, Catherine takes up with the architect, and then, a few weeks later, it looks like she has someone else, too? Maybe that was more than Gerald could take." Dotty swiped at the hot tears gathering at the corners of her eyes.

"You OK, hon?" Cindy asked, rubbing her arm.

Dotty nodded, pasting on a smile. "I'm going to get something to drink," she said, her voice shaking as she stood and dusted off her cutoff shorts. "You girls want anything?" She didn't wait to hear their answer, taking off across the lawn.

Nina turned on the blonde. "You've got to stop making fun of rich people, Cindy."

Cindy gave an apologetic shrug. "Old habits die hard."

DOTTY SAT ON the foot of her bed, her headphones firmly clamped over her ears. She hadn't been able to rejoin the others for the rest of the afternoon, not even for dinner. She needed some alone time, which was spent scanning the recording of her talking to the girls in the attic. She'd listened to it at half-speed. She'd listened to it on fast-forward, making them all sound like chipmunks. And she hadn't heard one single syllable beyond their own conversation. Not an ominous groan. Not a menacing whisper. No guttural *Get out*. Nothing.

As a believer in all things otherworldly, she felt an utter failure. She hadn't heard anything. She hadn't seen anything. She hadn't even smelled the telltale rose water that was supposed to linger in Catherine's rooms. Still, the concrete details she'd learned about Catherine and Gerald so far were disturbing enough. She'd come to accept the idea that Gerald had murdered Catherine, but seeing his motive, laid out in black and white in the diaries, was just awful. She wasn't sure she wanted to know any more. She didn't want to sympathize with Gerald for what he did. She was sorry she'd ever started this project. But she'd be damned if she would be the one to tell Deacon that she wasn't finishing it.

Dotty lay back, switching the headphone jack to her iPod. She closed her eyes. Her meditative bell tracks did their usual trick in relaxing her. Minutes later, she was half-dozing. She felt the foot of her bed dip under unexpected weight. Her eyes snapped open.

Her room was dark. What had happened to her lamp? She propped herself up on her elbows. A dark shape sat hunched at the foot of her bed, shoulders slumped as if the weight of the world was resting on them.

"Deacon?" she whispered. "What are you doing in my room? Are you OK?"

The figure didn't move.

She nudged at the figure's back with her foot.

Her foot met with no resistance.

The figure twisted, turning until the inky shape became a distinct set of shoulders and a head, looking back at Dotty. She screamed, or she would have, but her throat constricted, trapping the sound. It undulated toward her. She tried to scrabble up the mattress, but the weight of the shadow on her bedspread trapped her feet. Dotty flopped onto her back as the shape crawled up her bed, trapping her. She fought against it, kicking and thrashing under the blankets, only to feel her feet go numb under the cold, heavy pressure. The sensation spread up her legs to her hips, and her body was forced still.

What if it didn't stop? What if it settled over her face and smothered her? She whimpered, panicking at the thought of the thick black mass seeping into her nose and choking off her breath.

The head crossed into a beam of moonlight shining through her window. The surface of its skin was constantly shifting, viscous and iridescent as oil, so that the features were indistinct. All she could make out were hollow silver eyes and blinding white teeth against the black, curving up in an exaggerated Cheshire-cat grin that grew wider as it slithered along her body.

It was so *pleased* with itself.

As the weight moved over her covers, Dotty closed her eyes. She wouldn't see this. She'd been so wrong, pouting because she was the only one who hadn't experienced anything paranormal in the house. If this was what the others felt, she wanted no part of it.

Fingers clenched around the blanket, she tried to focus on something besides the fear that kept her paralyzed. Whoever this spirit was, it couldn't hurt her. Not really. The pressure and cold? An illusion. It couldn't hurt her. She wouldn't allow it. She had to find a touchstone. Something positive. She had to think of something else.

Deacon, she thought. Deacon, who loved her so much. Deacon, who shared her blood. Deacon, who would hear her screaming for help, even if she didn't make a sound. *Deacon, Deacon, Deacon, Deacon.*

She felt a hand slide along the sheet over to her throat. Rage and humiliation bubbled up from her belly, replacing the fear and unlocking her throat so she could scream. "DEACON!"

She opened her eyes to see the face hovering just inches over hers, the silver eyes boring into hers as the mouth opened, revealing rows and rows of razor-sharp shark's teeth. *Screw you,* she thought. *Screw you all the way back to hell.*

Before those fangs could sink into her, the overhead light flicked on. The figure whipped its head toward the door and dissipated like smoke. Dotty launched herself out of the bed, throwing off the covers, only to get tangled in them and land on her ass. She flopped back against the bedframe.

"Ow."

"The hell?" Cindy said, blinking blearily into the well-lit room.

Nina, who had flipped the light switch, gawked at where she'd seen the spirit fade away. Lips pressed in a tight white line, she crossed the room in two strides, curling around Dotty, who sank into her friend's embrace.

"You OK?" Nina asked as Dotty rested her head against Nina's lap.

"No," Dotty said, her voice clear but very, very soft. "I am just about as far away from OK as I could possibly be right now."

CINDY TOOK UP vigil on Dotty's other side, awkwardly patting her back. She hadn't had enough experiences with "girlfriends" to know the proper protocol in comforting your friend after the bogeyman makes untoward advances.

"Was this how it was for you?" Dotty asked, shivering against the warmth of Nina's body. "This weird, alien, 'that couldn't have just happened' feeling?"

"Yes," Nina said. "Only I can see how what happened to you would be more scary because it was more of an external thing, rather than being inside someone else's head."

"Deacon, calm down!" they heard Jake yell from the hallway. Deacon came barreling through the door, with Jake stumbling in behind him.

"What happened?" Deacon demanded.

"You heard me yell all the way across the building?" Dotty sat up, wrapping her arms around Deacon's neck.

"I think people heard you in Jersey," Jake told her, leaning against the doorframe.

"Dotty, are you OK?" Deacon asked quietly. "You sounded so scared. I've never heard you— You're never the one who gets scared."

"It was on my bed," Dotty told him, shivering. "I could see it, crawling toward me, on top of me. It was *smiling* at me, like it was enjoying itself."

"What was on your bed?" Deacon asked.

"What the hell do you think, Deacon?" Cindy shouted, advancing on their boss. "A freaking ghost." Cindy grabbed Deacon's *Dinosaurs vs. Aliens* T-shirt by the collar and gave him a hard shake. "You've humored us up to now, looking down your nose at us, grumbling and groaning when Dotty talks about the haunting, because you're just too smart to believe and commit to the idea. Well, guess what, it's real. And this house is getting stronger. It's sending these things after us in our beds. It's scared the absolute shit out of your cousin. And I just realized I am shaking my boss, and I should stop that now. But I can't seem to get my hands to stop moving."

"If we can please move beyond the hysterics!" Dotty exclaimed as Nina pried Cindy off Deacon's neck. Nina pushed him across the room, out of range. The force of her shove looped his arms around her waist, and neither seemed to notice when they remained there. "It was a pretty distinct shadow figure with a very defined head and shoulders. It turned its head toward me, and it was smiling. Like scaring the hell out of me was the most fun it had had in years."

"You keep calling it an it," Jake said. "Wouldn't it be a who?"

Dotty shook her head, her streaked hair falling over her shoulders. "With all of the other 'encounters,' we've known who the people involved were because we *were* them. We don't know who the hell that *thing* was."

"It was Gerald, don't you think?" Cindy suggested. "I mean, who else would it be?"

"But I'm his descendant. Don't you think he would maybe sense that?" she said, rubbing at her arms, desperate to get warm. Cindy draped a spare blanket around her shoulder. "I mean, there are boundaries there that shouldn't crossed, even by the dead."

"But you're Catherine's blood, too," Nina noted. "So maybe some part of Gerald wants to hurt you, because it's like hurting Catherine all over again."

"Well, that is a horrifying explanation that makes more sense than it should," Dotty said, shuddering.

Nina looked up at Deacon. "What are we going to do now?"

Deacon only shook his head. "I have no idea."

Jake adjusted the basketball shorts he wore as pajamas. "Well, I'm wide awake. Being jolted into consciousness by bloodcurdling screams will do that."

Dotty ran her fingers through her hair and gave a forced, cheerful smile. "We're playing Vodka Pursuit!"

Nina asked, "What is Vodka Pursuit?"

"It's like Trivial Pursuit, only with more vodka. It will cheer everybody up, trust me. It will help." Dotty jumped off the bed and went scampering down the hall, yelling for Stolichnaya and pie pieces.

Jake glanced at the clock, which read 12:42. "This is not going to end well."

Temporary Supernatural Reprieves

THEY HAD TO get off the island, even for just a little while.

The fact that Dotty was shaken by what she'd wanted so badly—to finally have some sort of paranormal experience—scared the hell out of Deacon. What she saw must have terrified her. That combined with Cindy and Jake's overblown reactions to each other and Deacon's sudden spiral into full-on, hearts-and-flowers infatuation with Nina had Deacon beginning to suspect something was "off" about the house. Whether it was physiological, psychological, or parapsychological, living at the Crane's Nest was making their emotions go haywire. Everything they felt seemed to intensify tenfold. How else could he explain his initial overblown jealousy of anyone Nina paid attention to?

What worried him was all of his other feelings for

Nina. What if his affection for her was a manipulation? It seemed impossible that any one woman could be sensible, snarky, and sexy all at the same time. Could he be seeing her through lenses colored by isolation and paranormal interference?

It wasn't so much that he wanted to test his feelings for Nina off-island. That would be crass and short-sighted. He just wanted to see how they interacted in the real world. If they were still talking to each other when the Crane's Nest project was over—assuming one of them hadn't been possessed *Exorcist*-style—would they be able to spend time together? Date? Or would they drift apart without the stresses and intrigue of this place to throw them together?

He'd made a few calls and made arrangements with Dotty, and before he knew it, the six of them were gathered in the men's common room, all dressed up with somewhere to go. He'd planned to attend this sure-to-be-dull-as-dirt reception for the charitable boards supported by EyeDee's benevolent foundation by himself. But now he might actually stand a chance of having an interesting conversation at one of these things. Dotty had managed to sneak over to the mainland for appropriate clothes for the others, having snaked one of Deacon's credit cards out of his wallet.

He chose not to think about where his cousin had picked up her lockpicking and pickpocketing abilities.

Besides, despite the questionable "special skills" section of Dotty's résumé, Deacon trusted her shopping judgment. Although she did get distracted by a shiny pair of shoes every once in a while. And then there was that time with the car.

Even if Dotty did suddenly decide to buy a Prius, it would be worth it to hear genuine excitement in Nina's voice for the first time. She was so sincerely and sweetly thrilled by the idea of a night out. Deacon thought he could make out the barely restrained urge to twirl and make the short skirt of her dress bell out. Nina's delicate forest-green dress was a frothy confection of gauzy leaf appliqués frayed at the edges, giving her the illusion of being covered in leaves. She had, however, fought tooth and nail against the matching sky-high platform heels and persuaded Dotty to let her wear her trusty flats. And his suspicions that Cindy had something to do with the intricately twisted hair and unprecedented makeup were confirmed when Nina thanked her for working "fairy godmother" magic on her.

"I don't have to do much to you," Cindy assured her, sliding her hand along her own vaguely pinup-style red dress with draped short sleeves and plunging neckline. "And I still think you should have gone with the red. To heck with your hair clashing."

SMILING TO HERSELF, Nina plucked at the skirt of her dress, swaying so she could watch the hem of the skirt swing back and forth like a church bell. She was usually a homebody. Fancy, crowded, expensive, crowded, tense—and had she mentioned crowded?—parties were not her scene. One of the very few functional aspects of her working relationship with Rick was that he had volunteered for the schmoozing while she focused on her plants. When Deacon announced he was taking them to a "reception" on the mainland, her instinct had been to make some excuse and try to get out of it. But Dotty had gone to such trouble to make sure they were all well-dressed for the evening, and frankly, she hadn't taken the time to make herself this pretty in, oh, maybe ever. So she was going to attend this shindig with a smile on her face and a solemn internal promise that she wouldn't do anything to embarrass Deacon in front of his most likely very rich and/ or very smart friends. Nor would she wear the red dress, because she would never be that brave.

"I don't have the boobs to pull that dress off," Nina said.

"Well, it depends on how you want your night to go." Dotty snickered. Her own dress was a confection of tiered nude lace that was surprisingly demure for a woman who had added extra red and purple curls to her hair only that morning. "And you're right, I picked that dress for Cindy because my friend Robbie told me it is a marvel of modern engineering and will be able to support her straplessly from here until Armageddon."

Dotty actually didn't know much about clothes. She would run around in pajama pants most days if it didn't mean getting funny looks at the grocery store. Robbie was one of Dotty's many former roommates and a buyer for Macy's. He had been happy to give her unclaimed samples according to the sizes Dotty sent over. How Dotty knew their exact sizes Nina didn't want to know. She hadn't had to find anything for Jake, who was his own traveling stylist, or Deacon, who apparently paid someone to pick out his clothes for him.

Now, if Nina didn't have the boat ride to the mainland to dread, this would be a dang fairy tale. She distracted herself by watching Jake's glazed expression as Dotty explained why the matching nude lace booties with the Swarovski crystal skulls embedded in the heels were *very* practical. But soon enough, Deacon announced that their ride had arrived, and Nina started applying seasickness patches behind both ears.

"Um, unless you plan on using those as a fashion statement, I don't think you'll need them," Deacon told her, offering his arm as the group trooped out of the house.

Cindy, Nina noted wryly, seemed intent on keeping as much distance as possible between herself and Jake. As they rounded the corner of the staff quarters, Nina spotted a slightly larger, white version of Deacon's "work" helicopter waiting on the flat section of yard that served as an impromptu helipad.

When Nina's lips pursed, Deacon explained, "Jake said that you get really sick on boats."

"I'm usually an 'oh, you shouldn't have' sort of girl, but this is really sweet. Thank you," Nina told him. "You know, I've never ridden in one of these before."

"Really?" he said. "They're a lot like taxis—cramped, sort of uncomfortable, and you're not sure whether to trust the guy driving."

The flight over the ocean was strangely uncomfortable. While she was very happy not to be on a boat, Nina couldn't help but think of that scene in *Jaws II* when the shark pops up out of the water and eats the helicopter. Fortunately, she was only able to dwell on that cheerful thought briefly. It turned out helicopters went much faster that she'd expected.

Almost an hour later, the group landed at a discreet helipad in a tony area of Boston and took a car service to Deacon's corporate headquarters. It felt very weird to be back "in the world." The lights seemed too bright. The noise of the traffic and the milling crowds was practically deafening. By the time they arrived at the shockingly modest brick building near Dorchester, Nina was considering asking to stop at one of the plentiful corner drugstores for a pair of sunglasses and some earplugs. The building, with its ornate hand-bricked façade and subtle brushed-metal EyeDee logo, looked a bit shabby and aged from the outside, but the moment they stepped through the heavily secured front entrance, Nina's superfuturistic *Star Trek* expectations were met. The walls were a sterile, shiny brushed aluminum, reflecting the delicate gray-blue of the carpet. The desks, on the other hand—while ultrasleek, ergonomic white structures—were covered with various toys and action figures. One particularly impressive employee had constructed a Lego version of Castle Grayskull around his computer, the monitor occupying the skull's open mouth.

Deacon took in Nina's frown as they passed through the main floor to the elevator. "I know, it's a little cluttered. But I've found that people are more productive when they're happy, and having a few things that personalize their desks seems to make my employees happy. Also, I may or may not have instituted Laser Tag Fridays."

Nina giggled.

"What?" he said, chuckling. "Jake won't play with me anymore since I chipped his tooth."

"He hit me in the face with his gun!" Jake called over his shoulder as they got into the elevator.

"How many times do I have to tell you, I didn't see you coming around the corner!" Deacon exclaimed.

"Until I don't have to go to the dentist every six months for a crown inspection," Jake muttered, not even looking toward Cindy as he cradled her elbow, preventing her from bobbling on her high heels as the elevator sprang to life. She raised her eyebrow, as if she didn't quite know what to make of the casual, thoughtful gesture.

Nina laughed. "Actually, I was wondering what sort of toys you have on your desk."

Deacon's fingers slipped on the elevator buttons, making the car stop on the second and third floors before reaching their destination. Nina bit her lip to prevent a smirk. "It's one of those super-revealing Cheetara figurines from *ThunderCats*, isn't it?"

Deacon cleared his throat. "No comment."

Jake flashed him a thumbs-up and mouthed, "Smooth."

Deacon flashed him a rude gesture behind his back.

The doors opened to reveal a spacious rooftop terrace set with about a dozen tables. Long strings of LED-powered bulbs formed a canopy overhead, somehow making the lights of the Boston skyline pop even brighter. Several carefully shaped trees broke up the cement landscape. Two very busy bartenders were working from behind a mobile wet bar to keep the gathering properly lubricated. Jazzed-out instrumental versions of pop songs played softly from speakers hidden under brick and plexiglass benches that flanked the trees.

As soon as Deacon exited the elevator, he was mobbed. While his employees greeted their CEO with casual waves, every one of the other guests, well-dressed, slightly desperate-looking people, suddenly needed to talk to him *right then* about some emerging need in their charity. The press of the crowd darn near sent Nina into a panic, but Deacon slid his arm around her waist, keeping her anchored to his side as he chatted with them. He politely introduced her to each newcomer, but it was clear that their attention was limited to Deacon and his wallet, leaving Nina to distract herself with the decorations until he finally managed to lead her to where his employees had formed a sort of fort out of bar tables. There they would defend their stash of shrimp balls to the death. Nina found she much preferred this side of the roof, where it might have been quiet, but at least the faces were friendly. And they were willing to share their shrimp balls after Deacon mentioned her *Flash Gordon* street cred.

Deacon seemed to relax more around his employees, and soon it actually felt like a party. And Nina . . . Nina felt like his date. Deacon hadn't specifically asked her to come as his date, of course. He'd proposed this as a group outing, but he was orbiting around her like a dedicated moon. He changed his position every time she changed hers, keeping his hand at the small of her back to lead her around the smaller, more welcoming circle and introduce her to his friends. And he actually fetched her a drink, the guy who paid someone to pick out his ties. He used the word *fetch* and everything. And he got her drink order right. She liked her Manhattans to run light on the vermouth, heavy on the cherries.

"The bartender is asking that you be limited to bottled water from here on out," he told her, handing her the cocktail.

"Funny. By the way, are these *silk trees*?" Nina whispered, her tone horrified.

Deacon rubbed his hand along the back of his neck, looking chagrined. "Well, yeah, the staff mostly uses the rooftop for smoking, so we haven't bothered much with landscaping. We rented those for the party. They hide the electrical equipment that's powering the lights and the audio equipment." When he saw her aghast expression, he added, "That was the wrong thing to say. We'll get rid of them tomorrow. We'll send them to a nice farm."

"I will landscape this area for free if you never rent these monstrosities again," she told him in the firmest tone she had used since meeting him.

He nodded. "Yes, ma'am."

Deacon took her hand and rested it in the crook of his arm, escorting her to a long table on the far side of the roof. "Now, can I interest you in dessert, Miss Linden?"

Instead of an elaborate spread of pastries, the table was laid with dozens of small bowls full of graham crackers, Swiss-chocolate squares, peanut-butter cups, peppermint patties, sprinkles, jimmies, crushed toffee, gummy bears, and other sweets. An enormous mountain of oversized marshmallows overflowed from a tureen at the end of the table, next to a small hibachi grill, where guests could use tiny silver sticks to toast their creations.

"Of course, you make gourmet s'mores."

"You mentioned them a few times during our ghost-story sessions," he said. "I thought you would appreciate a chocolate and marshmallow fix."

"I don't know where to begin. Are you sure you can handle 'chocolate-covered espresso bean and marshmallow' Nina?"

"Oh, I think I can handle Nina in all of her forms."

Eyes already widened by the choco-buffet went dinner-plate size. Had Deacon just uttered something overtly suggestive? Without blushing? Nina bit her lip and stepped closer, a movement Deacon echoed, his fingers slipping around hers.

And of course, that was the moment Deacon's assistant and vice president of distance operations, Vi, whose claret hair rivaled Dotty's for color saturation, approached Deacon from behind, much as a shark would sneak up on a baby seal. Nina had instantly liked the young woman, who stood only five-foot-four in her ungodly expensive platform heels but somehow managed to cow Deacon into being socially acceptable. She moved quickly and quietly, her digital tablet clutched to her chest like a shield. "Deacon, you're going to need to say a few words."

Deacon startled. "Damn it, Vi, we've talked about the skulking thing. It's only OK when you aren't using it on me."

"I don't skulk." Vi sniffed. "I move in a stealthy manner. It's not my fault you're too busy making googly eyes to listen for the subtle yet telltale stiletto clacking."

Nina's cheeks flushed a lovely pink, while Deacon shot Vi a death glare. "Viola."

She scowled right back. "OK, OK, no reason to pull out the embarrassing birth names. Anyway, you're going to need to say a few words. We've set up a mic near the fire escape. Here are your notecards with your speech printed on them. You have three minutes to memorize it."

"Three minutes?" Nina marveled.

"She usually gives me two and a half," Deacon muttered, shuffling his cards.

"Well, I'm going soft on you because you've been off-site for a few weeks," Vi said, straightening his tie.

"I'll be right back," Deacon told Nina as Vi brushed invisible lint from his lapels. He turned to his assistant. "Vi, if you spit on a tissue and try to wipe my face, we're going to have words."

"That happened *once*," Vi said as they walked away. "And you had duck sauce on your cheek!"

Nina stared after them, grinning. She would definitely have to spend more time with Vi. Anyone who could wrangle Deacon with such authority would be a fitting mentor for someone who could only control plant life.

Now that she'd adjusted to the sensory overload of the "real world," being off the island, even for just the evening, felt good. Nina felt as if she could think more clearly, more like herself, instead of being influenced by the house, whether that meant its oppressive atmosphere or the direct intervention of ghosts. What had her life become that this was now a normal train of thought? She sighed, sipping her drink.

And as she watched Deacon bickering happily with Vi, she realized that very little about the way she felt about him had changed since they'd left the Crane's Nest. The way they spoke to each other, her appreciation for his thoughtful little gestures, and the goofy grin she couldn't seem to wipe off her face were all the same as they were on the island. It was good to know that whatever else the spirits might be influencing, her feelings for Deacon were very real.

His speech was short and to the point, promising EyeDee's support for all of his guests' causes for the coming year. Nina moved toward the bar to get them both a drink. Deacon would need one when he was done with his comments. His jaw was clenching, and his ears were turning red, which Nina now recognized as his tells for high-stress situations. Throwing caution to the wind, she ordered him a double vodka on the rocks.

Had she not turned her back on the party to watch the bartender measure out the vermouth for her Manhattan she might have sensed Regina sneaking up on her.

"Well, Nora, don't you clean up nicely?" the decorator cooed, smoothing a hand down her skintight black strapless sheath with an intricately beaded black and purple belt at the waist. Nina glanced down at Regina's shoes, which were probably worth more than Nina's car. "And your dress! It's so . . . different."

Nina stretched out her hand in cordial greeting, but Regina failed to take it, wrinkling her nose, as if Nina had dirt caked underneath her fingernails. Pulling back, Nina self-consciously wiped her fingers on her skirt. Before she could respond in a way that *didn't* make her feel like a dowdy high school reject,

Dotty sidled up to Nina and slipped an arm around her shoulders. "Thank you, Regina. I chose it for *Nina* especially."

Regina's dark brows winged up. "Of course, Dotty, you've always had such *interesting* taste."

"And we can always depend on you to wear something barely appropriate for the occasion."

Regina ignored the jibe. "Oh, well, I wouldn't miss one of Deacon's little parties. I know he counts on me to help him make sure everyone is comfortable and entertained. Some people still know how to host, and I'm glad he knows he can trust that to me."

"He has an assistant who makes sure everyone is comfortable and entertained," Dotty retorted. "You're here because he can't figure out how to slough you off like dead skin."

"Charming as always." Regina sniffed. "Actually, Nina, I was hoping I might see you here."

Nina waited for the inevitable punch line.

Regina signaled the bartender, who reached under his station and withdrew a bold purple folder embossed with the logo of her company, Intriguing Interiors. Regina pressed it into Nina's hands. Inside was a neatly typed list of plants and quantities.

"What's this?"

"It's a floral scheme. Mr. Whitney has requested that we 'bring a little life' into the house with some live plants."

Nina's lips twitched, but she managed to hide the smile brewing there. Perhaps she was having more of an effect on Deacon than she'd believed.

"Why would you give her this now?" Dotty asked,

eyes narrowed. "It's not as if the party counts as Nina's office hours."

"Well, it's not as if she thinks she's a guest."

Aaaaand . . . there it was.

At Regina's tinkling laugh, Dotty's hand bunched into a fist. Nina attempted to calm Dotty with a hand on her arm.

"She's here as Deacon's employee, just like the blond cleaning lady," Regina said.

Nina let go of Dotty's arm, because, honestly, Regina had it coming. But Dotty simply ground her teeth and gave Regina the death glare.

Unfortunately, Dotty's restraint meant that Regina was still talking. "I've added several banks of potted plants within the space. Don't bother repotting. I'll choose the containers."

Nina tried to imagine Regina repotting anything except maybe to pass off carryout pasta as her own cooking. Nope. It would endanger innocent plants. She would have to find some way around that. And that wasn't the only problem. Some of the items on Regina's list were downright ridiculous.

The incredulous expression on Nina's face made Regina snap, "What?"

"Well, there are a couple of issues. One, you've got lily and dieffenbachia plants on your list, both of which are poisonous to dogs and small children."

Regina looked completely unimpressed. "So what's point two?"

"The orchids you've selected are problematic," Nina told her. "It's not that bifrenaria aren't perfectly lovely flowers—"

"Yes, I picked them because they're *lovely*. I needed the mix of reds to contrast with the color scheme I selected."

"Well, unless you're planning to display them in Mr. Whitney's shower, you're going to have some very dead, very expensive Portuguese orchids on your hands. Bifrenaria need a constantly circulating humidity cycle."

"Oh, I'm sure it won't be that important."

"They're very delicate flowers," Nina insisted.

"So we'll get silk versions. They're almost more lifelike than the real thing these days."

"I'm sorry, what?"

Regina sneered. "Silk flowers. Surely you've heard of them. They do have silk flowers in the sticks, right?"

"Yes, but asking that I endorse your decorating with faux flowers is a bit of an insult. It would be like me sending you down to IKEA and telling you to use your professional training to pick out a bed-in-a-bag."

Regina smiled sweetly, giving an airy wave to someone across the rooftop. "Oh, don't take it so personally. You're never going to make it as a businesswoman if you're going to be so sensitive."

The dismissive tone, combined with the fact that the woman couldn't even be bothered to look at her, set Nina's teeth on edge.

But Dotty smiled. "And how was it, exactly, that you got the investment capital to open your own firm just after you graduated from a second-tier design school?"

Regina's smile disappeared.

"It was a graduation gift from your parents, as I recall," Dotty added. "And I think my mother mentioned something about your parents claiming your business as a recurring loss on their taxes?"

"I'm sure your mother misunderstood," Regina snapped. "Now, if you'll excuse me, I think Deacon could use a drink."

Before Nina could respond, Regina snatched the double vodka from the bar and slithered across the rooftop. Nina's lip curled back from her teeth in a snarl she didn't know she was capable of. And when Regina pressed the glass into Deacon's hand and ran her fingers along the sleeve of his jacket, she growled, "I think I want to shave her head."

"I thought you weren't interested in Deacon in that way." Dotty kept her eyes wide and innocent.

"The situation changed." Nina's eyes narrowed. "That was then. This is now. And now I kind of want to shave her head."

"That's my girl." Dotty giggled, slipping her arm through Nina's and leading her toward the social train wreck that was Deacon trying to dislodge Regina.

"Nina, it's nice to see you."

Nina froze. The voice made her insides turn to water.

She turned to see Rick Douglas—tall, dark, and sociopathic—standing behind her. He was in his element at this kind of affair, wearing a well-cut black suit and a tailored shirt. If not for the cold cruelty radiating from his dark brown eyes, he might have looked the dashing storybook hero. At one point, she had seen him that way, which may have been the reason she'd let him get away with so much before finally accepting that he was not only a bad business partner but a bad person.

Between the clothes and the meticulously styled

hair, no one would have guessed that this was a man who worked in the outdoors. Of course, technically, he didn't. He left that to his crews. The deep, golden "workman's" tan was accomplished by visiting one of those spray tanning places twice a week.

Over his shoulder, Nina could see Regina shooting her a triumphant smirk. And the mystery of how Rick had snagged an invitation to this party was solved.

As usual, Rick was staring down his nose at her as if Nina embarrassed him just by standing there in her borrowed dress. Dotty's hand slipped away, and Nina was left without a tether. Suddenly, she couldn't draw breath even to speak. There were so many things she wanted to say to Rick or, better yet, heavy objects that she wanted to throw at him. Who did he think he was? What gave him the right to follow her around, terrorizing her? Why couldn't he just leave her alone and move on with his life?

But instead, she was staring at him, silent and practically shaking with rage, giving him the satisfaction of seeing how uncomfortable she was. At the first test of the bravery and peace she'd promised herself she would find on the island, she was failing. She felt so weak and stupid, just standing there clenching and unclenching her freezing-cold hands while the edges of her vision blurred hazy red.

Then Deacon's arm was around her waist, pulling her to his side. Instantly, her nerves settled, and her stomach stopped rolling. Her vision cleared, and she found she could breathe deeply again. Deacon rubbed her arm gently while staring *through* Rick, as if he was a particularly annoying pane of glass.

Nina was finally able to focus on Rick's stupid, smarmy face as he winked at her and said, "Oh, you know me, Nina, I love a good party. And when you run a *thriving* business, it's important to make contacts wherever you go."

Maybe her business would thrive if he would just leave her the hell alone, she thought, as rational thinking bubbled up through the dissipating haze of pissed-off panic. She arranged her lips into what resembled a blithe, pleasant smile, as if she were actually pleased to see Rick and didn't have a care in the world other than sweet-talking the caterer out of more shrimp balls.

Even being a champion bullshitter, Rick couldn't hide the flash of irritation in his eyes or the flexing of his fingers, as if he was itching to smack the smile off Nina's face. With some effort, Rick schooled his features into a more acceptable social mask. He reached out to shake Deacon's hand, but Deacon merely stared, as if he was being offered a dead fish. Rick cleared his throat, clearly caught off-guard by the snub

"Deke, good to see you again."

Nina felt Deacon bristle at the familiarity and the use of the dreaded high school nickname, and she couldn't help but smirk at her former boss's gaffe. Now it was her turn to give Deacon's hand a comforting rub. Rick lacked the sense to pick up on the tension and continued with his *we're just a couple of bros here* spiel.

"Mr. Douglas. I don't remember seeing your name on the guest list."

"Oh, I was lucky enough to be asked as a plus-one," Rick said, glancing in Regina's direction before quickly averting his eyes.

• • •

DEACON WOULD HAVE to have a serious talk with his security team. Invitational charity event or not, they still needed to check IDs before letting people into the building. His sudden urge to place Nina in one of those hyperenforced, suspended Loki chambers for her own protection was overwhelming. Jake could put one together, he was sure of it. But he was sure that Nina would object to being imprisoned like a Marvel Universe supervillain. Also, Dotty and Cindy would just let her out the moment his back was turned.

And unfortunately, during his mental escapade, that douchebag Rick was still talking. "Wonderful place you have here, though the landscaping up here leaves much to be desired. I'd be happy to put together a bid for a rooftop garden. A few ornamental Japanese cherry trees here and there—"

Deacon's smile was just as smarmy. "Actually, Nina has already presented me with a comprehensive plan for the rooftop. I couldn't be more pleased with her ideas."

Nina tried not to let her surprise show through her pleasant mask. She wasn't aware that threatening silk trees was considered a comprehensive plan, but she wasn't about to let Rick see her contradict her boss.

"Well, if that's the way you want to go, that's your choice. By the way, how is our little Nina doing out at your job site?" Rick asked as he sipped his Scotch.

Deacon directed a fond glance at Nina, making her cheeks go pink. "I'm very pleased with her work."

"I'm sure you are," Rick said with barely concealed nastiness. "I mean, you would have to be, to hire a total unknown like her when there were so many other experienced firms bidding. I'm sure she pulled out all of the tricks in her bag to get the job."

"Talent always shines through," Deacon said, his voice glacial.

"Oh, I know all about Nina's *talent*," Rick assured him, his eyes raking down Nina's body.

Nina's jaw dropped, and she surprised even herself when she stepped forward to do some sort of swizzle-stick-related violence against him.

But Deacon pulled her closer to his side, then smiled just as smugly. "I doubt that very much," he said smoothly. "Excuse us. There are some people we need to speak to."

Deacon ignored Rick's sputtering after them as he led Nina through the crowd. It was only then that Nina realized that Jake and Cindy had moved in behind her and Deacon during the conversation and were now preventing Rick from following them by pretending to be interested in his business. Deacon pulled his phone from his pocket, furiously texting with one hand while snagging two glasses of the champagne from a passing tray. He handed them both to Nina.

"Thanks for being the voice of reason," she said between gulps of exquisitely delicate bubbly she barely even tasted. "I would have hated to break up your party when the cops were called. I'm pretty sure stabbing someone with a swizzle stick is a felony."

"It was as much for me as for you. What an asshole!" Deacon exclaimed. "How did you stand working with that douche for two years?"

"He wasn't always that bad," she promised. "He's just

not used to getting one-upped. It's like dealing with a toddler. You don't give him what he wants, and eventually the tantrum becomes less about the thing he wants and more about not wanting to be thwarted."

"Regina invited him. I just texted my security chief. She was the only guest with an unnamed plus-one. I just don't get why she would do it."

"Really? You don't know why Regina would want me to be uncomfortable and socially stressed, maybe make a scene at one of your events and embarrass you? Regina strikes me as the type who likes to sweep the field clear of competition, real or imagined. And if she thought there was a possibility that you would bring me here as your date, she would want to be prepared." When Deacon's eyes widened, she gave a tinkling laugh. "Women are complicated, terrifying creatures."

"You're not kidding." Suddenly, he turned to her. "I can have him ejected from the party, you know. It's one of the perks of hosting these things. I can have people thrown out. And Tasered. Maybe even cavity-searched."

"As much as I appreciate it, that wouldn't do any good." She sighed, reaching out to squeeze his hands. "It would cause a scene, which might make the news, particularly the cavity search. It would make a poor impression on your guests. And Rick would know that he upset me, which I would like to avoid. Better to let him soak up all that free Scotch and make an ass out of himself in front of a bunch of potential clients."

"Weapons of self-destruction, I like it. But seriously, I've waited my whole life to attain the power to kick assholes like that out of my parties. You'd be doing me a favor."

"I'll keep it in mind," she promised.

Behind him, a jazz trio started to play, having waited until after the cocktail hour to begin their set. "Wanna dance?"

"I can't remember the last time I danced," she said, nodding. "A cousin's wedding, maybe, five years ago."

"I can beat that," he said. "Senior prom, sixteen years ago."

"Ouch."

"Dotty was my date."

"Double ouch."

He led her to the dance floor, holding her hand as gently as he would a mint-condition action figure. He slid his other hand around her waist and held her right hand at the proper angle while they swayed in small concentric circles. Dotty was dancing with an older man who was looping her around the floor in wide circles. Cindy had refused all requests for dances but had allowed Jake to get her a few more pastries, which they were planning to enjoy on the fire escape, far from the crowd.

When was that girl going to take pity on him?

Deacon snapped her out of her reverie. "You're actually doing me a favor, you know."

"I am?"

"If the whispering among my staff is any indication, this dance is probably serving as the office pool breaker for 'Is Deacon Whitney asexual?' "

"That's kind of insulting. How is that helping you?"

He shrugged. "I put fifty dollars down on 'not asexual.' "

"They let you bet?"

"Well, I bet under Vi's name."

Nina's laugh came out as more of a cackle, much louder than she intended. And the way she slapped her hand over her mouth to muffle the sound made Deacon guffaw.

While Deacon's employees grumbled among themselves and exchanged bills, another pair of dark eyes watched the couple from the bar. Angry, vicious dark eyes zeroed in on the redheaded dirt-grubber, the pretender sucking up all of the attention and opportunities that belonged to the more deserving.

JAKE PADDED DOWN the hall from the shower room to his bedroom, whistling a little tune under his breath. Thunder rolled outside, making the lights flicker under the strain of the storm. The helicopter had barely dropped them off in time, before the rain started. The sight of Nina, Cindy, and Dotty hustling across the lawn, high-heeled shoes in hand, trying to protect their dresses from the rain, still had him smiling. He wrapped the towel around his neck, squeezing the last drops of water from his thick hair.

"Good night!" he called down the hall, receiving a grunt from Deacon in return. His best friend was currently facedown on his bed, exhausted from the effort of being social all evening. Jake grinned, nudging his bedroom door open. Before he could flick on his light switch, he saw the curvy feminine shape outlined against his bed by the lightning outside. Her back was turned to the door. He grinned, quietly shutting the door behind him.

Cindy.

To say he was surprised to find her waiting for him was a massive understatement. They'd had a very nice time at the party, and he'd taken pains to behave like a gentleman. He hadn't even made any double entendres, and with Deacon's employees' discussions of hard drives, he'd had ample opportunities. He'd walked her to her door, and she'd offered him a sweet, perfunctory kiss on the lips.

But here she was, in his bed, her long blond hair falling in damp waves over his pillow.

He sincerely hoped she hadn't actually meant to crawl into Deacon's room, because that would have been demoralizing.

"Hey, doesn't this break about a dozen of your rules?" he whispered. "Not that I mind, but you were pretty firm about the whole 'no-fly zone' thing."

Jake tried to remember how many drinks she'd had during the party. Surely two or three martinis weren't enough to have her mistaking his room for hers. As much as he wanted her there, he didn't want her to act now and regret it later, undoing all of the trust he'd built with her.

The lightning flashed, and the windows practically rattled with the force of the thunder. Cindy stayed completely still, save for the rise and fall of the blankets as she breathed. Jake wondered if she'd fallen asleep while she was waiting for him. He wouldn't mind that, he supposed. He didn't know if he would be comfortable doing anything besides spooning, with Deacon just a few yards away. He was a man who appreciated his privacy.

Tossing the towel aside, Jake lifted the blankets to

slide in beside her. For a moment, he couldn't comprehend what he was seeing. Or, rather, what he wasn't seeing. There were no legs under his sheets. Trembling, he leaned over the bed, trying to get a better look at her face.

"Cindy?"

The figure rolled toward him, thick wet coils of faded blond hair hanging over a face blued by water and time. She was falling apart, right before his eyes, her skin hanging loose, rotting from bones it wasn't quite connected to anymore. The drooping lips were purple and ragged. Her eyes were white, opaque as milk, and staring up at him, pleading, silently screaming for help. Jake scrambled back, losing his footing on the rug and ramming his back into his dresser. The woman crawled over the sheets toward him, peering over the edge of the mattress while he sprawled on the floor.

"Gerald," the figure whispered, before fading away.

Jake stared at the bed and the sheets left rumpled by what should have been a figment of his imagination. But figments didn't leave behind rumpled sheets. Which meant that there was a ghost in his bed. And given the blond hair and the "recently waterlogged" appearance, it was the ghost of Catherine Whitney.

"What the *hell*?" he yelped.

A few moments later, Deacon came thundering into the room. And Jake suddenly realized there was no way he was going to explain this situation, not with the lightning crashing outside and the wind howling. It was just too creepy, as if verbalizing what he saw would make it more real.

Also, he was going to have to wash those sheets.

"What's going on?" Deacon demanded. "This whole shrieking-in-the-middle-of-the-night thing is getting old really quick."

"Uh, I saw a spider," Jake said. "A big one."

"You saw a spider?" Deacon asked. "That made you scream like a girl and knock your dresser into the wall so hard it knocked over my nightstand?"

Jake held his hands a few inches apart. "Big one."

Deacon frowned down at him.

"Sorry," Jake said. "I think I'll sleep out on the couch."

Deacon scoffed. "What?"

Jake stared at the bed, which he doubted he would ever think of as comfortable again. "I don't know where it went. I'm not sleeping in a room with a big spider."

Deacon objected. "But with the storm—"

"I'll be fine," he insisted. Because there was no way he was going to be able to answer, *I'm pretty sure your great-great-grandmother's ghost just tried to cuddle with me.*

"All right, good night," Deacon called over his shoulder.

"Good night." Jake padded back down the hallway with considerably less pep in his step, clutching his blanket to his chest like a shield.

What had just happened? Sure, he'd had visions in the house. He'd felt strange sensations. But hadn't Dotty said that full apparitions were a rare occurrence? Why would Catherine Whitney appear to him in that water-logged, corpse-like state? In his previous experiences with Catherine, she'd appeared young and beautiful and anatomically intact. Why would she suddenly try to scare him? Were they getting closer to the truth of her murder? Was it that couples in the house seemed to be pairing off and that made her angry or jealous? Was she trying to warn them about something?

He would talk to Dotty about it in the morning. For now, he was just going to sit and stare at the walls until the sun came up.

Unleash the F-Bombs

THE NEXT MORNING, Deacon sat in his office, drumming his fingers on his desk, waiting for Regina to arrive. He loathed the idea of allowing her back onto the island, anywhere near Nina, but he wanted to handle this meeting in person.

Regina's inviting Rick to the charity party was unconscionable. Before, he might have tried to write it off as coincidence. It was possible that they'd met on a work site or even when Rick had bid for the job at Deacon's office. Regina spent a lot of time skulking around his office.

He couldn't take the path of least resistance with Regina anymore. It was far more likely that Regina had looked up Nina's employment history, found out about the harassment reports, and connected with Rick in order to harass Nina even more. His blinders were off, particularly after he (somewhat illegally) accessed

Regina's EyeDee account and saw that she had recently sent an EyeContact request to Rick Douglas. And in a private message, she'd told him, "I think I can help you make sure a 'mutual friend' gets what she deserves. Discuss off of EyeDee," and sent him an e-mail address to contact her. Regina had used Deacon's own software to get at Nina. And he simply couldn't allow that.

His laissez-faire approach in dealing with Regina had emboldened her. Because he didn't react when she pushed a little, she figured he wouldn't do anything to stop her when she pushed a lot. He shouldn't have agreed to the trade-off she'd suggested. He should have just made it a simple no-interest loan. But he hadn't wanted to embarrass Regina. He'd wanted her to feel as if she was earning her money, giving her the sense of accomplishment he got from earning his. His mistake was assuming that she cared about that sort of thing.

He heard the telltale *click-clack* of expensive designer heels long before the knock on his office door. But he made her wait until he was ready to get up from his desk and get this meeting started. He didn't want her to have any sort of impression that she was an eagerly anticipated guest.

"Deacon," Regina purred. "It's been too long."

"It's been a few days," Deacon countered, his tone cold and dismissive. He moved back around his desk and dropped into his chair. He didn't bother offering her a seat. But undeterred by his rudeness, she followed him around the desk and balanced her ass against it.

"Yes, and in all that time, you haven't called me. It's going to be very difficult to complete this project if you don't communicate with me. I want you to be comfortable telling me anything. Any little thing. And just to start this new level of honesty on the right foot, I should tell you that I think your little gardener has designs on you."

Deacon resisted the urge to grin. For some reason, it made him inappropriately smug that Regina had noticed Nina having a reaction to him and vice versa. He wished he could find a way to let Nina know she'd made Regina jealous and insecure without looking like a total jerk. Nina deserved to know that she had that kind of power. "And what if she does?" he asked. "I don't see how that would be any of your business."

"Deacon," Regina wheedled. "There's no reason for us to do this silly dance. We should make our relationship official. We make sense. We're from the same social circles. Our backgrounds are similar. Our lifestyles fit each other."

"That would be awesome, if I were looking for a tennis partner. But I think relationships require a little bit more than that, Regina."

"Oh? Like what?"

Deacon's brain immediately went to Vodka Pursuit and blueberry waffles. He thought of their circle of friends and the clash and complement of personalities. He thought of shy smiles he had to work like hell to get and how they seemed so much sweeter, knowing that he'd earned them. Those insubstantial and yet completely necessary aspects of a life together.

Regina scoffed. "Like love? Love is for children and poor people, Deacon. People like us know what makes for a successful marriage. Marriages that last, that establish successful careers and social standing."

"Would we be having children in this scenario, or would they be raised by their polo coaches?"

"Children would be negotiable," she said. "After a reasonable amount of time."

"Negotiable?"

"I would need some sort of incentive, I think, to bring children into the agreement," she said, hooking her leg over his and sliding into his lap. She fussed with the collar of his button-down, smoothing it over his chest.

Deacon managed not to recoil, but he did enjoy saying, "I think you need to leave. Also, you're fired. Consider your debt paid in full. I don't want to have anything more to do with you."

Regina's expression didn't change, but he suspected that was because of Botox. She unbuttoned his top button. "You're making a mistake. I would hate to leave this job on bad terms, Deacon. The press might get wind of the story. And who knows what sort of details they might print?" She leaned close, as if to kiss him, and he was grateful when she stopped short of touching his lips. "And then lawsuits are filed, pending deals go wobbly, and you might not be able to finish this project without me."

It was Regina's turn to pull back when he flashed an almost feral grin at her. "Details like inappropriate conversations or unwanted sexual advances?"

"I—I wouldn't be able to control what ended up in the news," she stammered, trying to maintain her calm, seductive tone.

"Well, I think *I* probably could, considering I have videotaped you every time you've met with me in this office or my offices in Boston. Oh, including this conversation, which would probably reduce your credibility with pretty much everybody."

And just like that, Deacon parted his legs, letting her drop to the floor on her ass. She scrambled to her feet just in time to see an image of her fall playing on the large-panel screen on Deacon's wall.

"You videotaped me without my knowledge?" she shouted. "That's illegal!"

He shrugged. "Technically, I did it with your knowledge. It was on the fourth page of our employment contract, under 'Confidentiality.' It's not my fault that you don't read what you sign."

She snarled at him, possibly the least ladylike thing he'd ever seen her do.

And he just smiled. He was going to have to show Nina this footage at some point. Much, much later, when they were on steadier terms and the sight of Regina in his lap wouldn't make her nervous.

Regina calmed her expression and straightened her dress. She snagged her briefcase from Deacon's desk and turned on him. "Mr. Whitney, you will be hearing from my lawyers."

"I know your lawyers!" he called after her as she minced down the hallway in her high heels. "And they like me better than you!"

NINA WAS GOING over a checklist with George, her grader, when Regina stormed outside. Cindy turned at the scrape of heels on the stone walkway. Jake and Dotty were also nearby, discussing Dotty's lack of progress on her curse research. But unfortunately for Nina, she was the first person Regina laid eyes on.

"Nice to see you dressed up for work," she snarked as she passed.

Nina glanced down at the stained work shirt, jeans, and muddied rubber boots she was wearing. OK, so it wasn't her most elegant ensemble. But she'd spent most of her morning up to her knees in mulch. And her outfit was a hell of a lot more appropriate than Regina's, which included spike heels that got stuck in the lawn every few steps. But somehow, Nina was left feeling dowdy and grubby.

Well, screw a bunch of that.

Nina pushed the clipboard into George's hands and followed Regina across the lawn. "You know what? Screw you, Regina."

Regina's eyes went wide with shock. "I beg your pardon?"

"You have done nothing but condescend and sneer and prance around in those ridiculous little outfits. News flash, we don't work for you. None of us. We're partners in this, just as much as you are. So the next time you think about telling Cindy to fetch you a coffee or poke at some poor defenseless construction worker's bicep like he's a piece of meat on display, I want you to ask yourself, 'How difficult will it be for me to remove Nina's size-seven garden boot from my ass?' The answer? Very difficult."

Regina drew up to her full height and said in her most dignified voice, "I will *not* stand here and be insulted like that."

"Well, it's a hell of a lot easier than doing jumping jacks while I insult you. Now, run along."

Regina sneered at her but turned on her heel and

walked away. She didn't stop or look back until she made it to the dock.

Deacon came out of the house just in time to hear Nina let loose an F-bomb-laden rant. She did George Carlin proud, using the F-word for *all* the parts of speech.

"I know we're not super-religious, but maybe we shouldn't use the F-word quite so much. Those angry vibes can't be good around the house," Cindy said, wrapping her arm around Nina's shoulders. Nina's head shot up, and she glared at Cindy, who put up her hands in a defensive position. "I'm not saying *no* F-word, just, you know, less."

Dotty watched as Regina got her heel stuck in the planks of the dock, barely avoiding tripping headlong into the bay. Dotty bit her lip and shook her head. "She is not having a good day."

She expected some response from Jake, but hearing nothing, she turned to see that he was far too busy practically dancing with glee. "The only thing better would be if Nina had suddenly demonstrated some heretofore unknown cage-fighting skills and roundhouse-kicked her to the face Chuck Norris–style."

"Not all gingers know karate, Jake," Nina grumbled. "It's a misconception spread by the antiginger media."

"Impossible. Chuck Norris invented the media," Jake protested.

"I want you to block him from Chucknorrisfacts .com right now," Cindy told Deacon. "Or we will be hearing these all day."

"You do realize that I don't control all of the Internet, right, Cindy?"

"I think you can probably pull it off," Cindy retorted, just as Jake quoted one of his favorite facts about Chuck Norris and steak.

Deacon cringed. "Yeah, I'll take care of it."

"Where is Nina going?" Dotty asked, watching as their favorite landscaper made considerable progress across the lawn, toward the beach on the opposite side of the island.

"She probably just needs to blow off a little steam," Jake said. "Having that kind of confrontation, after so many years of holding it in and being polite, it's a shock to the system. She's probably panicking because she was just really rude to someone and she doesn't regret it, and she doesn't know how to process that. She just needs a few minutes."

Cindy was staring at him.

"What?" he demanded.

"That was an insightful and intelligent observation," Cindy told him. "I think I'm a little turned-on right now."

Jake's eyebrows winged up. "Really?"

Dotty kept her eyes on the second-floor windows. "I think I'm going to go . . . elsewhere."

"I'll just go talk to Nina," Deacon said, ducking away while Cindy and Jake stared at each other.

Deacon caught up to her on the beach. The choppy dark blue water rolled across the little inlet east of the house. Nina was sitting on the dunes, with her shoes off and her toes dug into the sand. Her expression was unreadable as she stared across the water. She didn't seem upset, but she certainly wasn't smiling.

Deacon sank into the sand next to her, stripping off his shoes and socks and stretching out his legs.

"So that was a lot of curse words," Deacon said. "An impressive amount of them. A plethora of curse words, if you will."

"Yes, it was," Nina said, nodding. "I would say I'm sorry, but I'm not. I won't even lie about it."

"You shouldn't. Regina had it coming," he agreed. "I appreciate your restraint in not smacking her in the face with a rake."

"Why are you friends with her?" Nina asked.

"I'm not. Really," he swore. "Maybe we were, once, when we were too young to know better. I think I should explain why I'm in a business relationship with her. A strictly business, no-other-past-history-implied relationship."

He heard Nina grumble under her breath.

"About three years ago, right after EyeDee took off and my offices were still in the basement of my ratty old apartment building, Regina came to me. She needed money, a lot of it."

"I thought she already had money."

"Her *family* has money. Regina has an allowance from her parents, but it's pretty limited for a girl of her tastes. She doesn't come into real money until she inherits, and her parents are hale and healthy. Her decorating business is more of a full-time hobby. Her overhead is pretty ridiculous. She keeps an office in a very swanky part of Boston. Nothing but the best furnishings. And despite the crazy prices she charges, she's not making a profit. So she started opening credit cards, a lot of them. When she maxed one out, she would just open another. She'd racked up some pretty hefty debts, and her creditors were getting impatient with her. She could ask her parents for money, but they already give her an annual stipend in addition to her monthly allowance to help her along. She didn't want to admit to them what she'd done with the cards, so she came to me and asked for a no-interest loan. In exchange, she offered to decorate the offices I'd just purchased and any future jobs I might have for her."

"Why are you telling me this?" she asked.

"I just wanted you to know that I never dated Regina. I don't really date anybody, but be certain, I am not, will not, and won't ever date Regina. I just wanted you to know that."

Nina beamed at him, ridiculously pleased. "Not really your type?"

"No, I'm more into the Titian-haired, secretly snarky earth-goddess type. Especially lately."

Nina's face blushed beet-red. "But you don't date?"

"Not in a long time," he told her. "I got hit with three paternity suits last year by women I'd never even met. They thought I would just pay them off to make them go away. A woman walked up and kissed me as I walked out of a Celtics game with Jake, and the next morning, I opened the papers to find out I was having an affair with one of the *Real Housewives of Long Island*."

"Charmaine?" Nina asked, vaguely remembering a news blurb about the EyeDee founder getting hot and heavy with the spray-tanned wannabe starlet.

"She set the whole thing up to try to get more airtime on the show. And what better way to do that than to make your formerly wealthy real-estate-developer husband think you've displaced him with someone who's in the financial papers? So yeah, I don't know what to expect from women anymore. And I don't know what they expect from me. I consider Papa Massimo's pizza and a movie to be a quality first date, but I think they expect foie gras and the symphony."

"Papa Massimo's?" she repeated. "They make this incredible garden-veggie pizza with—"

"Eggplant and broccolini?" He chuckled. "Yeah, it's one of my favorites. Have you tried their white pizza?"

"Are you kidding? That pizza is practically its own food group!" she exclaimed.

"By the way, this is my awkward way of asking you out on a date, just in case you hadn't noticed," he said.

"I wouldn't have to watch one of your crazy sci-fi movies in this scenario, would I?"

"Do you consider Sean Connery running around in red suspendered Speedos and a man-braid a crazy sci-fi movie?" he asked.

"I'm ninety percent sure that I would."

"Eh, we can debate the merits of *Zardoz* versus . . ." He paused and waited for her to name a title.

"Oh, uh, *Legend*."

Deacon frowned. "Really? With the Peter Pan version of Tom Cruise?"

"With the supercool demon version of Tim Curry," she retorted.

He considered it for a moment, then nodded. "I concede. So this weekend? We could actually leave the island. I won't make you ride a boat, if that's a determining factor."

"It's a date," she said, grinning at him.

He smiled right back. "It is."

He settled back on the sand, his hand settling in the space behind her back. She smiled, keeping her eyes on the water as it rolled and pitched before them. A long, lovely, silent moment passed, in which they could enjoy the sound of the sea, away from the noise and chaos of the house.

"I was thinking," Deacon began.

"You always are." She giggled.

"I was thinking that we're not going to have a normal first date. I mean, we've practically lived together for the last few months. It's going to help us get past a lot of the usual first-date awkwardness."

"Surviving the terrors of a haunted house together is a bonding experience every potential couple should go through," Nina agreed.

"I'm going to let the 'haunted' comment slide for the sake of harmony," he said. "But really, the only big first-date hurdle we'll have to get over is the whole awkward first kiss."

"You're assuming I kiss on the first date," Nina said primly.

Deacon groaned and clutched his chest. "Way to snatch a man's hope away, Red."

She laughed. "You will never know if I'm teasing."

"OK, well, assuming there would be a first kiss on our first date, that would be the only potentially weird moment we would have to overcome."

"I'm sensing a scientific hypothesis in the making."

He cleared his throat. "It's more of a proposal." When Nina's eyes went the size of saucers, he added, "Not that kind of proposal! Not before a first date! I'm eccentric, not insane!"

She flopped back onto the sand, cackling.

Deacon carefully eased down on his elbow, aligning his stomach with her side. When she stopped giggling, he said, "I propose that we avoid the awkward first kiss at the end of our date by getting it out of the way now."

"Getting it out of the way?" She poked his ribs with her fingers. "That's a really romantic way of putting it! Also, we've already kissed."

"You know what I mean." He laughed, nudging her right back. "And we haven't had a first-date kiss. Totally different experience from just a regular kiss."

"Spoken like a man who has been negotiating deals with scary international conglomerates for years. Your game needs work, my friend," she said, shielding her eyes from the sun so she could look up at him. She smoothed his wavy hair back from his forehead and considered it.

"Well, maybe you can help me practice," he said, leaning just a bit closer.

She pulled at his collar, guiding him down to the sand with her. Deacon ran his nose along the line of her own and pressed his lips to hers. She kept her eyes open, watching the light play on his tawny eyelashes. He seemed so absorbed by the act of kissing her, totally devoting that giant brain of his to running his tongue along the rim of her bottom lip, teasing her mouth open. Nina moaned as he pulled his mouth away from hers, sliding his lips against her cheek, over her nose, her eyelids.

"I've missed you," he whispered against her forehead. "It's been too long. A man shouldn't have to wait for time alone with the woman he loves. Promise me it won't always be like this. Promise me that one day, it will just be you and me, and we'll have all the time in the world together."

The language was a little flowery for her favorite sensible computer genius. "Deacon?"

Without answering, he crushed his mouth against hers. Images flashed through her mind, crinolines and satin-covered buttons. A beautiful blond woman—Catherine—threading her fingers through dark hair and pressing that head to her breast. She gasped. He kissed her again, increasing his efforts, biting the length of her neck until he reached the sensitive place where her neck and shoulder met. Another image, of Catherine's fingernails scraping down a bare male back, leaving raised red welts.

Nina jerked away from Deacon.

He kissed her forehead, the bridge of her nose, and both of her eyelids and finally pressed firmly against the line of her mouth. "Please."

Pushing her back into the sand, Deacon threw one leg over Nina's hips, pinning her to the ground. She blew out a shaky breath as he rolled his hips, the smooth weight of his erection grinding into her jeans. She clawed at his shirt, tugging it around his shoulders.

"Catherine," he whispered.

Nina stopped cold. Did he really just call her by his dead several-times-great-grandmother's name? He kissed her, rolling his hips again, and Nina felt the pleasant rush of warmth between her thighs. It would be so easy to ignore it, to pretend she hadn't heard. He felt so good against her, and it had been so long for her. Would it really be so wrong to just—

"Catherine," he whispered again.

Damn it.

But before she could push him away, Deacon's hands stole up the line of her shoulders to her neck. His thumbs rubbed along the hollow of her throat, pressing until it was difficult for Nina to breathe. She pulled away, gasping, clawing at his fingers as they tightened around her throat.

Nina shoved Deacon's shoulders until there was space enough for her to sit up. While Deacon's eyes were blank and unfocused, his lip was curled back in concentration, as if he needed every neuron in his brain zeroed in on controlling his hands. Nina grunted, swinging her hand back and smacking the side of Deacon's head.

"Ow!" he yelped.

"Deacon?"

Deacon's eyes were glazed over, and his breathing was heavy.

"Deacon, who are you right now?"

He blinked, still too unfocused to answer. "What?"

"Who are you right now?"

"What are you talking about?"

"You called me Catherine."

Deacon's brow furrowed, and he pushed to his knees. "What?"

"You called me Catherine, and you said a bunch of stuff about missing me, asking me to promise you that we could be together again. And then you started squeezing my throat. Deacon, I don't think it was you. I think someone was speaking for you."

"No." Deacon stood and shook his head, backing away from her. "No, that's not possible. No."

"Deacon, do you think you're being influenced by the house?"

"No."

"Because I think we all are to a certain extent. The important thing is that we choose whether we resist that influence or let it run us over. We still have a choice! We always have a choice!"

"Get back to the house, Nina. Don't stay out here alone!" he yelled as he stumbled back through the grass.

Nina groaned, flinging herself back to the sand. She couldn't believe that Deacon had run off like that. After everything they'd seen, how could he deny that something supernatural had just happened? Who had spoken through Deacon? Was it Jack Donovan? Or Gerald Whitney? Had she and Deacon somehow stumbled onto a meeting spot used by Jack and Catherine during their days on the island? Had they been discovered in this spot where they'd kissed in secret, hiding from the prying eyes of Catherine's husband? Had Gerald found them here on the beach and strangled her?

Poor Catherine. Poor Jack. Both long dead but clearly trapped in the unhappiness that had kept them so preoccupied during their lives.

Had they felt like this? This confused, jumbled mess of emotions that left her unable to think straight? She stared up at the sky, running her fingertips along the lines of her kiss-swollen lips.

She didn't blame Deacon for running, she supposed. If she was confused, she could only imagine what it was like for Deacon, who was far more connected to the Crane's Nest than she. Still, it sort of sucked to have what was a pretty epic kiss interrupted by ghostly possession. Ghosts were so damn rude.

"Well, I'm glad we avoided that first-kiss awkwardness," she muttered.

JAKE HATED TO admit that he actually checked under his bed before he slid between the sheets. It was demoralizing to be frightened of your own bed when you were a grown man.

After an afternoon of publicly berating obnoxious interior decorators and inappropriate eye sex between coworkers, the group had been exhausted. They'd eaten Cindy's clam chowder for dinner and retired early. Honestly, the sheer amount of blushing and head ducking between Nina and Deacon had been enough to make Jake want to call it a night. He had done all he could to avoid bed, spending a few hours sketching in the living room and taking a long, hot shower.

Walking into his room, he could make out the shape of a human figure under his sheets. "N-no, no, no," he stuttered, backing against the door and fumbling for the light switch.

"Jake?" Cindy sat up in his bed, rubbing her eyes. The sheets fell from her shoulders, puddling around her waist, revealing a very sensible pair of pink striped cotton pajamas.

Jake edged forward. It looked like Cindy, and it sounded like Cindy. But what if this was some sort of trick? He picked up a pillow at the end of the bed and tossed it at her, stepping back out of range. The pillow landed against her face with a soft *thwap*.

She shook her head, sputtering. "Is this some sort of payback for the can of polish?"

"Sorry. I thought maybe you were Catherine again."

"I just— I couldn't sleep," she said, toying with the sheet. "I've already had my go-round with the ghostly stuff, but hearing Dotty's story about waking up with— I can't seem to close my eyes. Dotty and Nina drank some sort of stinky herbal tea to help them conk out, but I couldn't stand the taste. I don't want to feel like they have to stay up to babysit me. And I just sort of ended up here."

To Jake's recollection, that was the only time Cindy had ever apologized to him. This must be serious. He lifted the sheets, telling himself that he *wasn't* checking to make sure that she had legs and was a real person. He slid under the sheets and adjusted the pillows beside her, tucking his chin over her shoulder.

"Is it weird, trying to sleep on the wrong side of the dorm?" he asked. "What do you girls even do over there at night?"

"Oh, you know, lounge around in our undies, feed each other grapes. We have tickle fights on Tuesdays."

"I knew the legends were true," Jake grumped into her hair.

She chuckled.

"Want to talk about it?" he asked.

"Decidedly not," she told him. "It's a little humiliating to realize you're a grown woman who's afraid of sleeping in a room by herself. Also that you're smart enough to recognize that you should probably leave an employment situation that is basically insane, but you don't want to do it because you'll lose some of the closest friends you've ever made."

"Really?"

"I don't have a lot of girlfriends," Cindy admitted. "I haven't always had time to maintain those kinds of friendships. Here I don't really have a choice. We're just naturally together, because we're all on the crew. And I'm afraid of what's going to happen when we leave here."

"I'm sure we'll have 'I Survived Renovating the Crane's Nest' reunions every summer," he assured her. "With T-shirts and everything."

"That's not funny," she said, slapping at him. But she was laughing and relaxing into his arms all the same. "And thanks for not making any jokes about finally getting me into bed."

"Hey." He turned her over to face him. "This is not a joke. I'm—I don't want to use the word 'honored,' because you would call bullshit on me, but I'm really happy that you trust me enough to come in here. And I'm not going to do anything to screw that up. I don't want to ever give you reason not to trust me again, Cindy, I mean it. And if that means that we wait until we're off-island before anything serious happens between us, I'll wait with a smile on my face. But I just—I won't waste the second chance you gave me."

She threaded her fingers through his hair, leaning up to kiss him. All of the things that she'd been holding back from him she gave him now. True affection, trust, sincere pleasure, and, if not her love, then the promise that one day soon, they might be headed that way. "You've got a deal. We'll wait." She looked strangely vulnerable, her eyes wide and without guile as she stared up at him.

Wait a minute. Cindy didn't do guileless. "If you're messing with me right now, that's just mean," he told her.

She laughed, pulling him down to the mattress, snuggling her head against his chest. "You'll figure it out eventually."

15

The Ficus:
A Previously Unknown Source of Shame

DEACON SCRUBBED AT his face, the code on his screen morphing into indistinguishable blurs. Sounds from the activity in the house, the constant buzzing of electrical saws, made it through the soundproofing in his office walls no matter what he did. It was frustrating, but then again, it was amazing how much work the crews were able to get done now that Regina's designs weren't hanging over the house like a pall.

After Nina's rather spectacular F-bomb display, Deacon lamented the idea of hiring another decorator. Anthony sheepishly admitted that he hadn't, in fact, ordered any of the specialty flooring or vinyl wallpaper Regina had planned on using, which had held up the renovation process. He just couldn't stomach the idea of the house looking like a strip club. After Deacon stopped laughing,

Jake agreed to take over the decor—with Dotty's help—basing it on the house's original design.

The house, at least the first floor, was finally beginning to look like a home. The entry hall had been returned to its former splendor. The parquet gleamed like caramel under the warm lights of the energy-efficient chandelier. The walls were cleaned and newly painted in a warm cream. It wasn't exactly homey and quaint, but it was warm, and it would be comfortable.

Deacon closed his laptop, folded his arms over it, and smacked his head against his forearms. He didn't even hear Nina walk through the door, using the special code he'd given her. She nudged his arm gently. He started but smiled happily when he saw her face. They hadn't spent much time alone since the kiss on the beach. So far, Nina seemed to be pretending it hadn't happened, which was OK with him. He couldn't quite process the idea that he'd lost control over his body while kissing Nina. He had no idea what he'd said or done. He remembered kissing her—and being very grateful that he was kissing her—and then he "drifted away," as if he'd fallen asleep. There was a blank white space in his memory, and then he woke up to Nina shaking him. The fact that he couldn't remember talking to Nina troubled him. His brain had never failed him. He didn't just blank out for minutes at a time. If he couldn't trust his brain, his increasingly shaky belief in the concrete world that he could see and touch, what could he trust?

Nina.

The girl in question was standing in front of his desk, beaming down at him, practically dancing on the toes of her sensible shoes. He could trust Nina.

"I have something to show you," she said.

Deacon's expression suddenly turned horror-struck. "Don't look!" he exclaimed, throwing himself bodily over his desk.

"What—what are you doing?" She laughed. "If you're going to spend time on that sort of Web site, you should at least lock your office door."

"No, it's nothing like that." Wincing, he stood and revealed a mangled brown bunch of dead plant bits hanging limp from a little plastic pot on his desk.

Her jaw dropped. "How do you kill a ficus? It's like the cockroach of the plant world. They're impossible to kill."

"I don't know!" he cried. "I watered it every day. I gave it plant food. I even talked to the damn thing. Clearly, it was suicidal. It wanted to die. This was a mercy killing."

"This is either the most pathetic thing I've ever seen in my life or the most adorable."

Deacon frowned. When Dotty had told him Nina thought he was "adorkable," he'd been thrilled, but now, it seemed . . . less cool. It sounded as if she thought of him as her goofy little brother.

"I wanted to tell you that it's been all-clear on the Rick front," Deacon said, clearing his throat. "I've been monitoring the security-video feeds. Other than the occasional squirrel or seagull, I haven't seen anything. In fact, he hasn't showed up on any of the security feeds since we arrived."

"Which would suggest a ghost destroyed my greenhouse, which would be so much better." Nina sighed. "Or he could be paying someone on our staff. He could be waiting until the day crews arrive and sneaking into dock on the south side of the island. Don't underestimate him."

"I'm not, believe me. I just don't want you to get stressed about it," he said. "And with that in mind, I want you to take this." He pulled a plain black plastic runner's watch from his front pocket. He wrapped the band around her wrist and snapped the catch.

"I can't take that!" she exclaimed. "For one thing, there's a really good chance I will summon the SWAT team accidentally while climbing into the shower. And two, if I take this one, you won't have a watch that summons the SWAT teams. And since you're a lot more likely to be kidnapped between the two of us, you should probably keep it."

"Actually, I've had this one made for you," he told her, trying to shake the images of her climbing into the shower. He held up his wrist to show her that his watch was still where it always was. "I'm giving the others their watches at dinner."

She lovingly stroked the face of the nondescript watch, making his heart do funny flip-flops. If she was this happy with a stupid plastic watch, how would she react if he presented her with diamonds? For the first time in his life, he wanted to buy a woman lavish, expensive gifts. If it made her smile, he would buy *all* of the diamonds. "Thank you."

But then again, Nina didn't seem the type to get excited over cold rocks. She would want something warm, something alive. A puppy. He would get her a puppy and name it Max.

"So what brings you to witness my secret shame?" he asked.

"Two things," she said, producing a small gift bag from behind her back. She'd picked up the present on a rare trip to the mainland, implementing several seasickness patches in order to go shopping with Dotty.

"What's this?"

"It's one of those digital photo frames," Nina said as he unwrapped it. "Jake helped me set it up. We loaded some old photos from when you were kids, from college, from the early days at your office, and, er, from this summer. I thought you'd like it, since it fits with the whole digital-age theme you have going on. But it gives the room a little personality."

He plugged the frame into a multibranch jack shaped like a tree. The frame immediately came to life, scrolling through various pictures. It stopped on a shot that Dotty had taken of Nina, bent over a flower bed with the sun shining through her hair, a corona of red-gold light forming a halo around her head. Her head was down, her eyes nearly closed, as if she was saying a prayer over newly planted seedlings.

"This is great," he said, placing the frame right next to his laptop. "Really, it's one of the most thoughtful presents I've ever received. Thanks very much."

Nina beamed at him, making his chest ache.

"Now, what was the second thing?"

Her grip around his wrist was unexpected and quite strong. "Well, Deacon, I'm going to lure you out so you can get some fresh air. You've been in here all day, after being in here all day yesterday. It's not healthy."

"That's very sweet, but I have a lot of work to do. My unanswered e-mail count for the day is now in the triple digits."

"Deacon, get out of the chair."

"Did Dotty send you?" he asked, eyes narrowed as she pulled him away from his desk.

"No, human decency and concern for my employer sent me."

"I have work I need to do," he said, even though he didn't resist as she pulled him through the rooms of the house to the back door.

She paused outside of the silver pantry, near the kitchen, where they could hear Anthony's workers installing new appliances and kitchen counters.

"But it's raining," he protested.

She tugged on his hand. "It's misting. The real rain won't settle in until this afternoon." When he groaned, she planted her hands on her hips. "OK, Deacon, I didn't want to resort to this, but I took your cell phone earlier and hid it somewhere on the property."

He gasped, patting his pockets for his phone, which was indeed missing. How had she managed to walk into his office, take his phone *from his pocket*, and walk out without him noticing? Jake was right. He did have tunnel vision when he was working. "You *wouldn't*."

"I would."

"You didn't!"

"I did," she said, completely unrepentant. And darned if she didn't look cute when she was all pleased with herself for phone thievery. "Come on."

"Wait," he said, pulling on her hard enough to make her stumble back into him. He absently patted his shirt and pants pockets, pulling out a mini-tablet, an iPod, an e-reader, and a backup cell phone.

She stared at him, her expression blank.

"Don't start," he warned her. "Lead the way."

She led, but every few seconds, she checked over her shoulder to make sure he was still following. Had she always been so unsure of herself? Or was this some sort of by-product of being stalked and then trapped on Spooky Island? Deacon tried to imagine her as a take-charge, ball-busting type, and it turned his stomach. He wouldn't mind seeing her being more comfortable or even more assertive. But Nina was not made for passive-aggressive snipes or cold stares.

He could see Nina living a quiet life, sleeping late on Sundays, and taking her dog for walks to her favorite coffee shop, because the dog—Max, he was sure the dog would be named Max—and Nina were just so adorable that the baristas didn't care if they loitered at an outside table, nursing a latte for two hours.

OK, when he started naming imaginary dogs, it was time to find something else to think about.

To his surprise, she didn't lead him outside but through the kitchen, down the hall, toward the solarium. She pressed a panel button outside the frosted-glass door, which hissed as it opened, revealing an indoor paradise. Somehow, Nina had brought a tranquil, fragrant garden inside the once-decrepit space. The sweet, delicate scent of lemon blossoms covered the green tang of turned earth and new growth. The walls were lined with several levels of slate-gray volcanic rock, building up to a waterfall that gently fed the sunken koi pond taking up nearly a third of the room. The tiled floor was now covered in sea lavender, with stepping stones that created a path through the greenery and across the pond. Meyer lemon trees blossomed in the corners, sending the occasional white and yellow bloom floating across the room. And in the center of the wall was a bright red button labeled "Ninja Death Squad."

"Now, I didn't go full Asian Modern," she said. "I tried to stay close to the theme of the house, Mediterranean Coastal, while keeping with Catherine's original intention of bringing a bit of the beach into the house. The koi pond is supposed to help you imagine the ocean."

Beyond the white canvas hammock swinging lazily in the corner by the window, the only seating was a double lounge inside an alcove of rock. This was not an entertaining room. This was a retreat, a place where Deacon could hide away. Nina plucked a remote from a side table near the lounge and pushed a few buttons, playing soft flute music. She smiled, almost shy, gesturing around the room with an expectant gesture.

"I thought we were going outside for fresh air," he said, teasing her.

"Technically, the air is fresh," Nina said. "Anthony helped me set up a special reverse-osmosis ventilation system that circulates outside air into the room while regulating temperature and preventing condensation issues, mold, that sort of thing. The whole room is basically a self-contained ecosystem."

"You're trying to appeal to the science nerd in me, aren't you?"

"Shamelessly," she said, winking at him. "And as one final, utterly brazen ploy to capture your inner mad scientist . . ." Nina punched a few more buttons. "Instead of boring old sprinklers, you get simulated rain showers."

Deacon felt the mist before he saw it. He looked up to see the tiny sprayers lining the casement between the ceiling and the windows, blowing out a steady drizzling rain. He chuckled, rubbing his rain-slick fingers together. "Shameless," he told her. "This is beautiful, Nina. Really, it's incredible. I can't believe it's the same room."

"It's what I do," she said. "I just pictured what sort of garden Tony Stark would have wanted and went from there."

"See, that's not fair." He sighed, watching as the tiny droplets clung to her silky red hair, giving it an other-worldly shimmer as she moved. "You can't just drop comic-book references on me like that and expect me to behave in a professional, rational manner."

"I always depend on you to behave in a professional, rational manner," she retorted, stepping back onto the sea grass. Her sneaker slipped on the greenery, and she almost lost her footing.

"Whoa!" he exclaimed, snaking his hands under her elbows and keeping her upright. "This is what happens when you walk around in the rain!"

"Haven't you ever just walked in the rain before?"

"I will not dance in the rain with you like some hip-pie," he said, laughing. "If you want Burning Man dance circles, go see Dot—"

She grabbed his face between her palms and kissed him. "Don't call me a hippie, Whitney."

HIS THUMB TRACED the line of her mouth. The rain-water was cool between her lips. Deacon's slim, elegant hands reached for her; they grasped her upper arms, pulling her close as his lips wandered up her skin.

Nina relaxed against him, shivering as his hands slid over her damp clothes. His mouth tasted like red licorice and some deep, dark flavor that should be added to everything. *Everything.*

"Deac—"

He took advantage of her opening mouth, sliding his tongue past her lips to play with hers. His long, deft fingers plucked at her plain cotton shirt, tweaking her sensitive nipples through her bra. She moaned softly, dragging her hands through his dark, curly hair. His hands slid to her hips, pulling her against him. She could feel the stiff weight of him pressed against her belly. He gently pushed her back, against the wall, where he could hold her between his thighs and the stones.

"Is this us?" she whispered against his lips. "Are you kissing me, or is there someone else there?"

"Please," he whispered, rocking her against his thigh.

She groaned, relishing the opportunity to kiss him again. "We shouldn't," she said, panting. "Not here."

"Why not?" He grinned down at her.

"Grass stains." She giggled, leading him to the partially covered lounge. She pushed a few more buttons, locking the door but not shutting off the indoor rain shower.

The real atmospheric rain was beating out a musical patter on the windowpane as he lowered her to the cushion. She sighed, shimmying out of her wet, uncooperative shorts and tossing the rest of her clothes to the floor. He followed suit, his long, lean limbs twining around her as he rolled her back against the cushion.

Deacon trailed his lips down her collarbone, between

her breasts, ghosting them over her stomach before pressing a light bite to each hip bone. He worked his way back up, teasing her nipples into pale pink peaks.

"This is us," Deacon told her, brushing the damp crimson hair back from her face. "Just Deacon and Nina. No one else."

She nodded. "Just us."

And with that, he pressed inside her, stretching her with a lovely, aching tension that she'd missed in all those months alone. They moved their hips in time, the roll of raindrops spattering against the windowpane providing a pleasant cover for the squeaking frame of the lounge. She smiled against his shoulder, hardly believing her boldness, ending up in bed with her boss on a Tuesday afternoon.

They continued, unaware of the dark, angry figure outside the wall of windows, watching with clenched fists.

RELOCATED, SHOWERED, AND curled against Deacon in her own bed, Nina dreamed. She was in the familiar maids' quarters again. She looked down and saw with relief that she was wearing the distinctive Whitney ring on her finger as she made the bed. She bent over the far corner of the mattress, tucking the sheet tightly. And when she rose up, she felt a large hand slide down the small of her back and give her backside a pinch. She squealed, and the man's other hand clapped around her mouth, pressing her back against his chest.

"Well, look at what I found here," a warm male voice whispered against her ear. "A pretty piece of skirt already bent over the bed."

A thrill of fear rippled up her spine as large, warm hands slipped around her hips and pressed her bum against a solid male frame. Teeth closed gently over her earlobe, tugging insistently.

She sighed as the mouth moved from her ear to her neck. He paused to nibble at the base of her neck, and she turned to face . . .

The scene changed, and she was standing on the roof, on the widow's walk, looking out onto the Atlantic, the setting sun making the waves fire with thousands of golden sparks. She sighed, content, as she leaned against the railing.

"This could be our home."

Deacon was smiling fondly at her, pulling her hands against his chest and kissing her knuckles before pulling her close and planting a much warmer kiss on her mouth. She sighed, turning and relaxing against his hands as they slid over her collarbones and around her neck.

"I built this for you. You don't have the right to leave."

The hands around her neck squeezed tight, and Nina turned to find Rick's sneering face hovering just inches from hers, his mouth twisted into a cruel smirk. He was dressed in an old-fashioned starched collar and vest, a golden pocket-watch chain jangling against his waist. The hands around her neck tightened, his thumbs pressing against the hollow of her throat. She wheezed, fighting for air, while he smiled, his mouth stretching into a parody of a skeletal grin. She clawed at his hands, but his grip didn't relent, squeezing until she thought her lungs would burst.

He laughed as she sank to her knees, dropping a quick

kiss to her forehead as he whispered, "You'll never leave me, Catherine."

Nina bolted up in bed, clawing at her throat. Deacon sat up, wrapping his arms around her as she thrashed. Eventually, she relaxed, sobbing against his shoulder as the last of the dream pressure eased from her throat.

"It's OK," he promised. "It was just a dream. It wasn't real."

He eased her back down against the mattress as her breathing evened out. "Maybe you should get off the island for a while. It might do you some good to rest and relax a bit away from this place," he suggested, his words so softly spoken against her cheek that it took a second for her to register what he had said. She sat up again, glaring at him through the darkness and whipping the pillow out from under his head. He yelped as she brought the pillow down against his face, ruthlessly whacking him again and again until he ripped the squishy weapon out of her hands.

"If you try to send me away for my own good, I will get one of Dotty's Tasers and use it on your . . . hard drive," she growled, glancing down. Deacon's eyes went wide, and he instinctually covered the equipment in question with the sheet.

"OK, OK, I just thought you might be able to sleep better if ghosts weren't giving you nightmares!" he exclaimed.

"Well, it's hardly a romantic gesture."

"I was going to put you at the Four Seasons with a personal chef, a masseuse, and your own facialist."

Nina pursed her lips. "Maybe I spoke too soon . . . No. No! You will not tempt me with presidential suites and shiatsu! I am not leaving. I am not going to leave you here to deal with this alone." She rolled over him, pressing him to the mattress. "I don't know who you've dealt with in the past, but I'm like a persistent little burr that won't go away. You will not be able to get rid of me, do you understand?"

"Do nightmares always make you this assertive?" he asked sleepily.

"No."

He yawned, sweeping her grip off his wrists and gathering her to his chest. He buried his face in her hair and rubbed soothing circles on her back. "Well, that's too bad. I kind of like it."

Circles on her back eventually became circles on her ass and then her hips, until he was plunging those long, talented fingers between her thighs, drawing the wet, aching response from her body into a rippling coil of sensation that had her bucking against him.

He kissed her, swallowing her cries to keep them from waking the others down the hall.

"Deacon," she whimpered against his lips. And he answered by sliding inside her, rolling onto his back, urging her to move over him until she found just the right rhythm. It might have been embarrassing how quickly he could bring her to the edge, but she loved the way she responded to him, the way his eyes lit up when his touch elicited a particularly interesting sound from her lips. Nina wanted him to know how much she enjoyed him. And she did, loudly, giving one last shaky scream as she collapsed against his chest.

Living with the ghosts of thwarted lovers was enough to teach you the value of living in the moment.

• • •

A CLAP OF thunder startled them awake. Deacon was curled on his side, his arms wrapped around Nina's middle. He'd been dozing, his brows furrowing slightly as if he couldn't stop worrying, even in sleep. Smiling fondly, she rubbed her finger between his eyebrows, smoothing out the worry line.

"So what now?" she asked.

"I pray you don't file a sexual-harassment suit?"

She frowned at him. He chuckled, pushing an errant strand of hair out of her face. "This feels like a ridiculous conversation to have as an adult."

"Why don't you go ahead and humor me?"

"I like you. I would like to date you. When we return to the mainland, I would like us to spend time together that doesn't involve possession, my ghostly ancestors, or our annoying roommates. I know that you reacted rather violently to this suggestion before, but really, if you want to leave the island at any time, say the word, and I'll get a helicopter here to take you back."

"Am I fired?"

"No! Why do you always think I'm going to fire you?"

"Do you think I'm too weak to deal with this?"

"No, I just want you to be safe," he protested.

She rubbed the tip of her nose against his. "I am safe. When I'm with you, with the group, I'm always safe."

He stroked her hair back from her face, watching her eyes flutter closed and her face relax into sleep. He wished she was right, that he could protect her from any threat, natural or supernatural. And while admitting that there was, in fact, a supernatural threat was a hell of a paradigm shift, it was nothing compared to the realization that he was madly, terribly, head-over-heels in love with Nina Linden, muddy boots, bad movie preferences, and all.

He already knew that he liked her. A lot. And that he wanted to spend time with her. But as she made him dance in the rain, he knew that he wouldn't be able to live without seeing her every day. He was in love with her. And he had no idea what to do about it.

For now, he would have to settle for security cameras and big, armed, scary people. Dotty would have to handle the supernatural threats. And he definitely wasn't telling his know-it-all cousin that he was in love with her friend. Or that he admitted, if only to himself, to believing in ghosts.

There would be no talking to her after that.

RICK SAT ON the balcony overlooking the greenhouse, grinning. It had been easier to sneak onto the island again than he'd thought it would be. Just a little one-man boat, moored on the far side of the island. The rough trip was worth it to see that bitch squirm. He was being led here, he knew that. He knew he wasn't clever enough to get past all of the security crap on his own. Some invisible force was guiding him, telling him where to dock his boat, where to walk where he couldn't be picked up by the security cameras. The house was guiding him. He belonged here. It belonged to him, no matter whose name was on the island. This place was his. Everything here was his. And the woman, she would pay for her crimes against him. Ignoring him, humiliating him. He would show her who was in charge.

Rick wandered the hall of the long-abandoned nursery wing. The wallpaper hung from the walls in long, tattered strips. But in his head, he saw polished floors and silk-covered walls hung with pictures of his family and his glory days, pitching for his high school's baseball team. This was his home now, his by right. He saw what he wanted, and he took it. That was the way the world worked. People like him knew that.

Now all he had to do to make things perfect was to find that bag. He knew where it was, of course, it was just a matter of . . . Where the hell was it? He needed to listen to the voice. The voice in his head hadn't led him wrong so far. But his head was so fuzzy, and his eyes wouldn't focus on the far end of the hall. He was so very sleepy, and he just wanted to close his eyes for a few minutes.

No.

He needed those jewels. The voice had promised the jewels to him. He needed them; he deserved them after what that bitch had done to undercut him. Now, if he could just focus on what the voice had told him.

In his own bed, on the mainland, Rick snapped awake. He would go back to the island the next day and keep looking.

A Pocket Full of Posies

NINA SNAPPED THE sheet over the mattress, carefully avoiding the urge to press the Deacon-scented linen to her face while it fluttered down.

Deacon walked into her room, buttoning a plaid shirt over his slightly damp "Han Shot First" T-shirt. "You know, you don't have to make your bed every day. I haven't made mine once since I got here."

"If I don't, Cindy will just come in behind me and do it. Her obsessive-compulsive cleaning tendencies don't allow for unmade beds."

He chuckled, nudging her back against the mattress. She pressed her mouth against his. "You taste like roses," he murmured against her lips. "I wanted to say so earlier, but I was afraid it would sound like a line. And a bad line at that."

"It's my lip balm," she said. "Roy's Rose Goo. It's SPF thirty, and being a pale girl, I need all of the help I can get."

"It was more romantic when I just assumed the flowers had been absorbed into your skin by osmosis."

"Osmosis is romantic?"

"Science is the new sexy." With a grin, he eased off of the bed and kissed her palms. "I am going to the house to get some work done. I will see you around lunchtime? Sandwiches, my office?"

"No wasabi," Nina said, nodding.

Deacon whistled a jaunty tune as he walked down the hallway. Nina giggled, forcing herself out of bed and remaking the damage she and Deacon had just done to the pristine sheets.

"Don't think I didn't overhear that happy whistling." Dotty's voice sounded from the doorway. "Finally! I thought you two would explode from unresolved sexual tension."

"Quiet, you!"

But it was too late. Dotty was already doing the victory dance and singing, "You slept with my cousin! We're going to be family! Cindy and I can be bridesmaids! Ah, I can't wait to tell her." She squealed, clapping her hands.

"Dotty, no!"

BUT CINDY HAD already risen for the day, making one last pass at Catherine Whitney's room before Anthony's crews came in to dismantle the furniture and hang new wallpaper. She was more than a little disappointed that her time in the room hadn't yielded Catherine's hidden stash of jewelry or more information about her death. She'd enjoyed being a treasure hunter, but now it was time to move on to more mundane rooms, such as Gerald Whitney's nearly sterile space, which looked more like a cruiser cabin than a bedroom. It was all hard angles and dark colors, nothing like the whimsical grace of this beautiful dryad bed.

Cindy sighed, running her fingers along the rectangular plaques set at head-height in the back of each post. The plaques were ornately carved with rolling leaf patterns. From what Cindy could tell, they would serve as stoppers for the canopy if the maids needed to lower it for cleaning.

Looking closer, Cindy noticed that the central leaf of one of the plaques was shinier than the others. Its sheen reminded her of old banisters, polished by years of hands running down their grains. This particular leaf had been caressed over and over by fingers, the accompanying skin oils leaving it shiny and more preserved than the others. She pressed on the leaf with her thumb and heard a faint click. The carved wooden panel slid upward, revealing an empty compartment about the size of a good Stephen King paperback. Nothing inside but a few bits of tissue paper. It was pleasantly surprising that the door moved so easily, but she wondered whether all of the compartments were empty. She circled the bed and found similar leaves in all of the posts. She pressed each in turn, finding two more empty compartments. On the last post, she pressed the leaf, and the compartment door seemed to stick against something jammed inside. She slid her fingers under the door and pushed the offending object back. The panel popped up, revealing a small leather-bound book, the same size as all of Catherine's other diaries.

Cindy carefully pulled the book from the compartment and checked the inside of the front cover. "June 18, 1900" inscribed in Catherine's careful hand. There was no ending date.

This was it! This was Catherine's last diary. Why had she hidden it in the bedpost? Was she afraid of Gerald finding it? Or had it simply been her habit to keep her current diary nearby?

What had she kept in her other posts? Had those been hiding places for her jewelry? Had the pieces been taken after all?

Every nerve ending in her hands commanded her to open the diary and flip to the very last pages, to read Catherine's last entry and try to get some idea of what she had been thinking in those last few days. But it wasn't her place to read Catherine Whitney's last thoughts. She should take this to Deacon or Dotty. They should see it first.

She ran for the staircase, headed for Deacon's office. She never saw the dark cloud of energy swirling behind her, just inside the bedroom door.

DOTTY CONTINUED DANCING, even as Nina topped her freshly made bed with pillows. Nina rolled her eyes at Dotty's antics but let her indulge. After all, it would be a lot less awkward to date Deacon if Dotty continued to like her. And throwing a lamp at Dotty would definitely reduce her likability.

Nina smoothed the sheet out over the bed, and suddenly, her hands weren't her own. She was wearing the distinctive Whitney ring on her finger. She pushed back from the bed and felt the now-familiar hands at her back.

"Well, look at what I found here," a warm male voice whispered against her ear. "A pretty piece of skirt already bent over the bed."

A thrill of fear rippled up her spine as large, warm hands slipped around her hips and pressed her bum against a solid male frame. Teeth closed gently over her earlobe, tugging insistently. He paused to nibble at the base of her neck. She giggled as she turned to face . . .

Gerald?

Catherine's husband gave her an impish grin as he pulled her into his arms, claiming her mouth with a rough kiss. He turned, yanking her down so that she sat side-saddle on his thighs. "What am I do when such a piece of . . . luck falls right into my lap?" Gerald grumbled against her throat."

"Right here?" Catherine laughed breathily. Gerald wiggled his eyebrows and nodded as his fingers slid over her stocking-covered knees to the apex of her thighs. She rolled her eyes but toyed with the buttons at his throat. "Well, I suppose if you're going to engage in the age-old practice of seduction in the maids' quarters, I should be thankful it's with your wife."

"I'd say it was the best of both worlds, wouldn't you, darling?"

Catherine fussed with her apron as Gerald pressed kisses along her neck. "Do stop congratulating yourself, and help me get out of this dress."

"Ordering your master around?" He chuckled. "You are a naughty housemaid."

Nina sat on the bed, a dazed expression clouding her eyes.

"What did you see?" Dotty demanded. "You had a vision, didn't you?"

"Naughty housemaid. Catherine," Nina wheezed.

Dotty's eyebrows rose. "Catherine and Jack?"

Nina shook her head, struggling for deep breaths. "No. I assumed that's what it was, but Catherine wasn't with Jack. She was with Gerald. And it was . . . not a marital duty. Catherine was having a very good time. A naked good time."

Dotty shuddered. "I'm so glad it was you and not me. I don't think there's enough therapy in the world to fix spiritually reenacting your great-great-grandparents doing the deed."

"What sort of cheating wife has hot, yummy sex with her cuckolded husband?" Nina asked.

"The guilty sort?" Dotty suggested.

Nina shrugged. "I don't know. I mean, I felt what she felt. And she was happy. Really happy. Naked happy."

"'JACK IS BECOMING more and more insistent,'" Cindy read aloud from the latest diary find in Deacon's office, her face red and her voice winded from her dash down the stairs. Deacon sat back in his desk chair, unsure if he wanted to hear Catherine's final thoughts before she died. But Cindy had barged into the office with Jake in tow, insistent that he had to hear the last entry.

He said I won't be able to avoid him forever, and he's right. He keeps finding reasons to stay on the island, extra features and projects to add to the house to extend his tenure here and allow him to be near me. He's got it into his head that I'm going to leave Gerald for him, that the completion of the house is the beginning of a new life together.

"He'll have his house and his children, that's all

he'll want," Jack tells me, no matter how many times I tell him that he's wrong, that I don't feel that way about him. But he says I'm lying to myself, that I'm too fright-ened of Gerald to admit how I really feel. As if I could ever be afraid of the husband I love so much.

There's no arguing with him. No matter how many times I tell him it's not so, he simply tells me I have been fooled. Jack tells me that I've been lied to for so long that I can't tell fiction from truth. He says that I'm too comfortable in the golden cage Gerald has built for me, too frightened to step out into the sun. He wants me to "paint the world with all the colors of my soul," which, of course, means leaving my husband, whom I love, and my children, whom I will not live without, to run off to live a life of shame with a man I have no feelings for beyond ruined friendship. Ruined by his presumption, his insistence that he knows my feelings better than I do.

He's gone too far this time. This afternoon, he showed me a bundle of my jewelry he took from the safe in Ger-ald's closet. He's babbled on and on about an "escape" for the two of us in two weeks' time. He has timed it for my birthday party, Gerald's attempt to make up for the horrid "coming-out" party we had a few months ago. Jack expected me to praise his cleverness, to begin plan-ning along with him. And when I didn't, he acted like a spoiled child, turning red in the face, shoving me into my room, and telling me that I had to "think about the consequences of making the wrong decision."

"Well, it makes sense," Jake said from his perch on Deacon's office couch.

"How does that make sense?" Deacon asked.

Jake shrugged. "Maybe some of the things we've attributed to Gerald have been Jack? The rage he feels toward Catherine? The hostility toward women in general? And what about Dotty's creepy shadow-man experience in bed?"

Cindy suggested, "Maybe it was Jack, looking for another chance to hurt a Whitney."

"Do you smell something?" Jake asked, sniffing. "Do you smell smoke?"

Deacon's chest ached with a sudden surge of disquiet. He wondered what Nina was doing at this moment. Was she alone? Was she safe? Catherine. It all came back to Catherine, Deacon thought. And so far, the only one in the group to have an experience from Catherine's perspective was Nina. He reached for his phone and had just found her spot in his "favorite numbers" list when he heard Anthony scream, "Boss! Fire!"

NINA DIDN'T SMELL smoke. She smelled rose water.

Her feet were moving, toward the nursery wing. The scent grew stronger with every step. How had she gotten here? She had been following Dotty up to the main house to report her latest experience, casting Gerald as a playful, affectionate husband, but then her feet had led her to this part of the house. She didn't even remember climbing the stairs to the third floor.

There were no work crews in the nursery wing yet. She was alone, standing in front of a square panel in the wall. That didn't make any sense. There were no other panels in the wall. Why would Jack Donovan put the panel there? It certainly wasn't there to hide wiring. Why had she been led here?

Biting her lip, she pressed the panel. And with a harsh squeal, it slid to the right, its hinges rusty and dry. The smell of dry rot was overwhelming, overcoming the sweetness of roses. Nina coughed, waving the dust away from her face as it billowed out into the hallway.

Shuddering slightly, she reached into the space and gingerly patted around until her fingers closed around a lump of fabric. Sneezing, she pulled it into the light. It was a mauve silk scarf, tied into a sort of hobo sack around hard, irregular lumps. She set it on a side table and carefully unwound the bundle.

Diamonds. Large, brilliant stones, undimmed by time, arranged in ornate floral settings. A chunky bracelet made from diamond daisies. A choker consisting of two ropes of pearls, centered around a large citrine in a sunburst setting. A golden peacock brooch with emeralds and sapphires set in the tail. A multipaneled Bohemian-style garnet necklace. But what caught her eye was the wedding-band set, two small gold rings connected by small interlocking hinges. The engagement ring was set with a large cushion-cut diamond.

Nina picked up the set, examining the inscription inside the band: "Love always, Gerald."

She could see it. *The ring set was snatched off Catherine's still finger.* The swirls of color in Nina's head made her knees go weak under her. Still gripping the ring, she fell against the wall, sliding down to the floor. *A large male hand ripped the ring from Catherine's finger. The same hand that had wrapped around Catherine's throat, choking the life out of her.*

A series of images sped through Nina's mind and then reversed as if on rewind—a boat turning upright,

Jack sailing it backward toward the shore, Jack pulling the mauve bundle out of the wall, Catherine's dead weight sagging against Jack. The cycle of images raced by until Nina saw Catherine fighting against Jack's grip on her throat, her fingernails digging viciously into his hands.

Nina groaned as she felt the vision shift. *Jack held the Whitney ring up to examine it, then shoved it into the soft silk bundle, huffing in frustration. He shoved the bundle into his jacket pocket, peering dispassionately down the widow's walk steps, where he'd tossed Catherine's body once she'd finally stopped struggling. Over the edge of the roof, he could see the staff forming a bucket brigade to deal with the fire he'd set in the south wing. They were like ants from this height, he mused. Huffing under the weight of Catherine's body, he moved down the widow's walk. Ungrateful bitch, he thought. If she'd just listened to him, if she'd just loved him the way she'd promised, none of this would have happened. He was sure he would mourn eventually, but for right now, he couldn't feel anything but righteous anger over her betrayal.*

He had tried to tell her how it would be. He had tried to explain his plans, that he'd set up a whole other life for them, that they could finally be together. But she'd said no! The ungrateful bitch had told him that he'd misunderstood, that she loved that idiot Gerald. She was going to stay with her husband, whoring herself for a fine house and jewels. And when he'd tried to kiss her, to show her how she really felt, she'd tried to scream! She'd slapped him, scratching his cheek with her little hellcat nails. It was her own fault, really, that his hands had wrapped around her throat. Did she think he would tolerate that from her?

Shifting Catherine's weight on his shoulder, he slid the

panel loose from the wall and dropped the bag inside. He would come back for it. In a few days, after Catherine's body had been found and everyone on the island was too confused to notice that the architect took the time to visit the mourning family. For now, he needed to get off the island before anyone saw him. No one knew he was here. He could get back to the mainland, visit a pub, tell a few jokes so that he was noticed.

He took the back staircase, a route so concealed that none of the distracted staff noticed his escape across the lawn to one of the auxiliary docks. His boat waited for him, and he knew his way around this island. It was no difficulty to find his way, not when he moved so swiftly and quietly through the brush.

He would get away with this, because he was better and smarter than they were, better even than Gerald Whitney, for all his money and power. He was the one who made palaces rise from nothing. Catherine's fate was her own fault for not recognizing his genius. She hadn't waited for him. She hadn't appreciated him. And now she was dead. He might mourn for her someday, but for now, he had to direct his energies into not getting caught. He deserved to move on from this and have the sort of life that others envied. He deserved his vengeance on Gerald and Catherine for their betrayal.

He guided the tiny sailboat out to sea, waiting until the house was no longer in view, and dumped Catherine's body over the side. He watched her sink under the waves, her dress billowing around her like angel's wings. Her own fault, really.

He knew it would take hours to reach the shore at Newport, but it would be worth it. He would be home free. If he was really fortunate, Gerald would take the blame for Catherine's death. It would be a vindication, watching Gerald tried for killing the wife he had stolen from Jack.

Daydreams of Gerald suffering a humiliating trial, possibly even hanging for the crime, distracted Jack, until he was suddenly thrown to the hull of his boat. Springing to his feet, he looked about for what had caused such a tumult. A wake from a frigate. He was far off course. He was in a shipping channel! A churning noise to the north caught his attention. An even larger steamer chugged along in the distance. The wave echoing off the hull was even larger, far taller than his own. The wakes crossed, dipping his hull far below the surface and tipping his boat over. The recoil as the boat righted itself sent him reeling overboard, smacking his crown against the rig. He tumbled into the water, barely conscious, tangling his leg in the anchor line.

His arms flailed, reaching for the line, trying to pull himself back toward the boat. But in the dimming light of deeper water, he could see the end of the anchor line, fluttering after him like a tail. And that was the moment he remembered that he hadn't secured the line to his boat.

The water closed over his head, sweeping into his open mouth. He could feel it flooding his throat, into his lungs. He choked, coughing helplessly, drawing more water in as he sank deeper into the sea's cold embrace.

Even as he died, his mind raged. No! No! This wasn't supposed to be the way it ended. He was supposed to escape! He was supposed to go on to success and notoriety. He was supposed to watch Gerald hang for Catherine's death.

Catherine. Gerald. Everything always came back to them. His brilliance was cut short. The love he deserved was denied him. This was their fault, both of them. With his last heartbeat, he cursed them both to hell, and their children, too. He wished in the deepest, darkest pit of his heart that no Whitney would ever find happiness or wealth. Each generation would be poorer and more desperate than the last. And he would stay right here to watch them collapse.

He wouldn't leave, he promised himself, he would stay in the palace that he had made—that he deserved—and he would watch his curse become real. With that vow, everything faded to black.

Nina fell to her knees and vomited what tasted like seawater onto the carpet. She had known, somewhere in the corners of her brain, that Jack had killed Catherine. But seeing it play out, feeling the pressure close around her throat, was something different altogether.

She wiped at her mouth, then picked the bundle up off the table, rewrapped it, and headed for the stairs. She had to show Deacon; she had to tell him about his great-great-grandparents. She stumbled toward the staircase, only to freeze in her tracks at the sound of a familiar voice.

"Hello, Nina."

Widow's Walk

NINA'S SHOES SKIDDED to a stop as Rick stepped in front of her. Dark purple circles pressed under his eyes, giving the hateful smirk a ghoulish look. His dark eyes were wild and nearly black. She backed against the wall, estimating what it would take to duck around him and dash down the back staircase. But his arms were so very long, and he had all that crazy on his side. Could she whack him over the head with the jewelry pouch? It was pretty heavy, but he would probably see it coming. How was she going to get out of this? She reached for the black plastic watch to set off the SWAT team alarm, but her wrist was bare.

She'd left it on her nightstand that morning, distracted by repeatedly making the bed and by Deacon's rose-scented kisses. Fantastic.

"Rick, get away from me."

"Oh, don't be like that," he crooned. "It hurts my feelings when you look at me like that, like I'm going to hurt you. You don't think I would hurt you, do you?" He scoffed as if it was the most ridiculous idea in the world. "The only thing I've ever tried to do is help you. I gave you a job, didn't I? I gave you a place where you could work and make your ideas come alive. And how did you repay me?"

He growled, his fingers curling into claws.

"You ran off. Without a word, you just left me. What the hell makes you think you have the right? And then you set up your joke of a business, conning people into hiring you with your poor, pitiful, innocent act. Taking jobs that rightfully belong to me. Me. Do you have any idea how that makes me feel?"

"You tried to ruin me," Nina said, her voice shaky.

"You wouldn't even have a reputation if it wasn't for me. I gave you everything, and you left me! You never appreciated anything I did for you."

"Rick, stop this."

"No." He grinned, an unnatural split of his lips over his teeth, and she knew she wasn't dealing with Rick. Or at least, not *just* Rick. Jack was lurking inside her former partner's body like an infection. How long had Jack been hiding inside poor, stupid Rick? Had Jack been the driving force behind the vandalism, the pranks? Perhaps, but Rick certainly wasn't innocent in the situation. She could see the hint of familiar cruelty in those brown eyes.

"I can't stop now," he singsonged. "Not when I've waited so long for this, to see you again, hold you in my arms. You misunderstood before. I didn't explain it so you could see things my way. I deserve that, don't you think? A chance to explain?"

She backed away, nearly toppling over the steps up to the widow's walk.

"Ah-ah-ah." He chuckled, catching her free arm. "Not scampering away, my frightened little kitten. You owe me. You don't get to leave until I say so. You left me before, didn't you?" His lips quirked even higher, making her duck her head. "And we both know how that turned out."

Nina didn't know if Rick was referring to her leaving his company or if Jack was referring to Catherine rejecting him on the roof, but something in the man's smug assurance made her jaw clench. He was enjoying her fear. He was enjoying toying with her. Her head snapped up, staring Rick right in the eyes. "Not this time."

Nina cupped her hands and clapped them as hard as she could over Rick's ears. Roaring, he threw her against the stairwell. Despite the dull pop she heard in her left shoulder, Nina kicked out as hard as she could, aiming for his crotch. His indignant scream echoed after her as she scrambled up to the widow's walk and slammed the door.

She tried to shove one of the large tree planters in front of the door, but it was too heavy. The best she could do was wedge a wrought-iron chair underneath the knob. "Good plan, Nina," she grumbled to herself. "Make the crazy possessed guy angry and then run up to high ground without an escape route. Excellent work."

She ran for the railing, screaming "Help!" and waving her arms frantically. For the first time, she smelled the acrid bitterness of smoke on the air. A billowing gray plume stretched across the sky, hovering over her. She coughed, covering her mouth as the smoke danced around her head. The staff quarters. The staff quarters were on fire and fully engulfed. She could see her friends on the ground, scrambling around with hoses from her gardening shed and trying to extinguish the flames. Deacon was on his phone, apparently calling for his backup security and fire crew.

Rick had set the quarters on fire. Just as Jack had set the children's wing on fire. He was following the same plan that had led to Catherine being strangled and dumped into the ocean.

"Help!" Nina screamed, but no one heard her over the wind and the roar of the fire. Rick's battering at the widow's walk door sent the iron chair scraping against the roof tiles. She ran for the only shelter available as Rick shoved the door open and threw the chair aside with a loud *clang*.

In the far west corner of the widow's walk, she made herself as small as possible behind the ornamental pear tree she'd planted just a few weeks before. Slumping against the cement planter, she snagged an abandoned trowel from the soil. Her shoulder throbbed mercilessly. She clutched the trowel in her good hand, wondering if she could really do any damage with it once he made it to the end of the walk.

"Catherine," he whispered. His voice was too low, roughened by the force of the murderous spirit lurking inside him like an infection. "Why are you hiding from me? I love you. I just want to talk to you, to make you see. Please, Kitty, don't make me beg."

The voice was so familiar, the words so soothing, that she struggled to remember that she wasn't dealing with the man she'd trusted. He was a killer, an insane, possessive monster who had strangled the woman he'd supposedly loved on this very spot.

Nina could hear his footsteps coming closer. No one was coming to help her, she knew that much. The others had run to the servants' quarters to put out the fire. She was cornered and alone, as Catherine had been.

Nina leaned her forehead against the smooth, curved surface of the planter. She was more exasperated with herself than afraid. She should have known this would happen. Her life was not a fairy tale. She wouldn't end up with the prince. She was cannon fodder, the servant girl who got kicked in the head by the knight's horse as he rode away with the fair damsel. She winced as she gripped the trowel, scraping her finger against the sharp bottom edge.

No.

She wasn't that weak, injured woman anymore. She wasn't Catherine.

"Hey." She stood, ignoring the pain in her shoulder as she planted her feet. "If I come out, will you stop the insane chatter?"

He grinned at her, a cocky smile that could have been mistaken for flirtatious. "Catherine."

"No," she said, brandishing the trowel like a blade.

His dark eyes radiated mad glee as he swayed, a cobra hovering in front his prey. "I've missed you." His hands shot up as if to embrace her. Nina swung the trowel upward, nearly catching him across the throat, but he ducked out of the way. As her weight shifted, she threw her good shoulder against his chest. He caught her arms, dragging her down with him and slamming her injured shoulder against the marble tiles. "Really, darling," he sighed, pinning her against the cold, unyielding surface. "Why do you have to make things so difficult for yourself?"

"I'm not Catherine," Nina growled.

"Maybe not," he whispered, trailing cold lips along her cheek. "But you're going to die like her."

With a final kiss at the corner of her mouth, his hands closed around her throat. Nina clawed at his hands, kicking viciously at his shins. She threw her head forward as hard as she could with his hands around her neck, catching his chin between her teeth and sinking them into his flesh until he bled. Rick howled and shoved her away, slamming her head against the marble. Rick's enraged scowl swam before her eyes, and for a second, his features shifted into another face—Jack's face.

She'd wondered what Catherine had thought of in those last moments on the roof, and now she knew. Catherine had thought of Gerald and the children. Because all Nina could think of was Deacon. His face. His smile. His last words to her. She could almost hear his voice.

Oh, wait, that *was* his voice. The pressure around her throat eased just enough that she could focus on the image of Deacon standing over Rick with a shovel in his hands. Rick dropped to Nina's side, gripping his head in both hands as Deacon ordered, "Get your hands off my girl."

It would have been such a resounding badass moment, had Rick not used his position on the ground to knock Deacon's legs out from him and make Deacon whack his head against a planter.

Deacon landed with a *thump* on the tiles. "Ow."

"She was mine first, you know," Rick snarled, his voice weakened by what was no doubt a wicked concussion. His dark eyes drifted lazily, but the angry intelligence inhabiting him kept him talking. "She always belonged to me. No matter what you gave her. She was always mine."

Deacon slowly sat up, wiping at the blood dripping down his face. "I'm not a broken man, haunted by the wife he lost. And I'm not a little boy you can scare anymore. Nice try, setting my house on fire. You think I wouldn't see the pattern? I'm a math nerd. I live for patterns."

Rick's voice changed, doubling, slithering along the ground like fog. "Everything your family built I destroyed. Every failure, every wasted coin, every heartbreak for the last century. I touched it all. I ruined you all through sheer will. Do you really think you can send me away, boy? I will take everything you have. I—"

Rick's tirade was cut short when a tiny mote of light between them grew into a pulsing white star. The light whirled and blurred, taking on a human shape, a woman in a long pale blue dress, her blond hair mussed and falling around her shoulders. She glared down at Rick, whose eyes rolled up into his head as he fell back to the floor. In his place stood the ephemeral form of Jack Donovan, his face twisted into alternating expressions of anger, awe, and feral aggression. It finally settled into a smug grin as he whispered, "Catherine, I've waited for you, for so long. All of these years, you wouldn't let me see you. I've missed you so."

Catherine didn't answer, her face never wavering as she stared through him, as if he were beneath her notice, undeserving of her time. This was the face of the lady of the manor. And Jack Donovan's incorporeal ass was about to get evicted.

Deacon crawled over to Nina, blood dripping down his temple and staining his collar. He scooped her up from the floor, cradling her in his lap. He checked her bruised neck, her eyes, her forehead, kissing each place as he assured himself that she was breathing. She was alive. He wouldn't suffer the fate of his great-great-grandfather, finding that the woman he loved had been murdered in his home. Nina tucked her battered face against the curve of his shoulder. She blinked sleepily at the spectacle before them, unsure whether she was imagining these odd white figures and their ethereal glow.

Catherine hovered protectively between Deacon and Jack, silently staring down the evil spirit.

"Even now, you won't speak to me?" Jack hissed. "After all that I've done for you? After the vengeance I took in your name, destroying the Whitneys' line and their fortunes? I deserve more than this, Catherine. I deserve what you denied us in life. I deserve your love. We can be happy together here, in this house I built for you."

Catherine glanced down at Nina and Deacon, clutched together on the widow's walk floor. She smiled gently at Deacon, threading her fingers through his curly hair, sending a chill down his back. "I couldn't see my Gerald. He'd already moved on," she murmured in a gravelly smoker's tenor, the afterlife result of being strangled, Deacon supposed. She sent Jack a disdainful look. "Why would I want to be trapped here with *him*?"

"Catherine!" Jack howled. "You can't just ignore me. You can't do this to me again!"

Catherine stroked a hand down Nina's bruised cheek, making Nina shudder from the cold touch. "I needed to hold on for my children, for the generations of children to come. I needed you to understand the truth of what happened to me, to my Gerald. I couldn't let them believe that I'd abandoned them. You came from a family rooted in love. Now that you've seen that, I can rest."

Jack shouted, enraged, and flew toward her, arms outstretched. Catherine looked almost bored as she simply raised her palm, stopping him in his ghostly tracks. She drifted closer, and her fingers curled around his near-transparent throat and tightened, reducing his furious growls to a squelched grunt.

Her once bell-like voice came out as a rasping whisper: "You deserve *nothing*."

Jack struggled against Catherine's hold, striking out at her with all of the energy he possessed. But she had waited too long for this moment. Her eyes went completely black with the force of her intention as she concentrated on snuffing out Jack's presence from her home. Jack's fury seemed to drain away as he saw the hatred in his "true love's" face. She despised him. She stared at him, through him, seeing nothing. He was nothing to her.

Catherine kept her grip on his throat, repeating,

"You deserve nothing," over and over as Jack's form faded. It collapsed on itself, condensing into a tiny white star that blipped out like a defective twinkle light.

"You saw that, too, right?" Deacon whispered, staring up at the triumphant, pearlescent form of his ancestor.

Nina's eyes fluttered shut. "We should put that on a T-shirt," she muttered.

Catherine turned toward Deacon, smiling sweetly at him. She tilted her head as she studied her great-great-grandson and the woman he clasped to his chest. Deacon felt as if he should say something, but he wasn't sure what. What exactly did one say to one's deceased great-great-grandmother after solving the mystery of her century-old murder?

He waved awkwardly, carefully shifting Nina's weight. "Hi."

Brilliant.

Nina's eyes snapped open when she heard Dotty shriek, "Deacon!" from downstairs.

Catherine's silence was filled by the thundering footfalls of several people running up the widow's walk steps. Dotty and Jake burst through the stairwell, only to skid to a cartoon halt when they saw the ghostly figure hovering near their friends. Cindy appeared behind them, calling, "Are they OK? Are they O— Oh!"

Catherine's gentle smile broadened to an all-out grin. She floated closer to Dotty, cupping her hands around her great-great-granddaughter's cheeks. Over Catherine's insubstantial shoulder, Jake saw a small light flickering into a solid mass. It grew into a male shape with piercing dark eyes and a lopsided grin. The man was older, wearing a long tailored coat and what Jake was sure were very fashionable sideburns when Gerald Whitney had lived.

"Catherine," he whispered reverently.

Catherine turned to see her long-dead husband, letting out a hoarse, triumphant cry. She moved so quickly to throw herself into his arms that Jake's eyes couldn't track her.

"Can you come home now?" Gerald asked. Catherine laughed, and the light surrounding the two forms grew brighter as their lips connected.

Cindy sighed, wrapping her arms around Jake's waist as the figures turned together across the roof. When they finally broke apart, the spirits turned to the younger people. Gerald gave his great-great-grandchildren and their friends a fond wink, wrapping his arms around his wife and burying his face against her neck. Catherine leaned into his embrace.

The couple's white-hot glow brightened that much more, a blinding supernova of celestial light. Deacon threw his arm over his eyes and shielded Nina from the glare. Jake pushed Dotty and Cindy behind him.

Catherine's paper-thin whisper sounded against the background of the group's labored breathing: "Be happy."

With that, the light winked out as if a switch had been flipped. They all blinked into the sudden darkness. Dotty wiped at her cheeks, tears trailing down her face. Jake surreptitiously wiped his own eyes until a smirking Cindy handed him her blue handkerchief.

For her part, Nina was too exhausted to digest the mind-boggling wonder of what she'd just witnessed. For right now, she wanted a shower and a stiff drink . . . and maybe a CAT scan. She would try to sort through how she felt about watching two souls cross over into the afterlife at another time.

"Tell me you hit that little button on your watch," she said.

"Way ahead of you," Deacon murmured into her hair. "I really love you, woman. But you're never allowed on this roof again, OK?"

"No problem." She sighed. "Love you, too."

"Everybody OK?" Jake asked.

Deacon said, "Nina—" but the patient in question interrupted him.

"I'm concussed," Nina told him, her eyes closed. "A lot."

"Nina's concussed," Deacon said. "And I think my ancestor sent Jack Donovan to hell."

"What about him?" Cindy asked, nudging at the unconscious Rick with her foot.

Deacon winced. "I forgot he was there."

"He's breathing," Cindy said, kneeling over him. "Damn it."

"Some people have all the luck," Nina muttered.

A House Undivided

NINA PLACED A bouquet of lilies and rosemary at the feet of the memorial statue of Catherine Whitney, standing tall, smiling with her hands open and slightly outstretched. A perfect circle of low-slung white begonias surrounded a wide round bed of forget-me-nots. Wide stone benches flanked the little blue flowers. They'd moved the solarium statue of the children outdoors, so that the figure of Catherine seemed to be watching over them as they played.

The artist Deacon had commissioned to carve the stone figure had worked double overtime to finish it. The team gathered around the statue, watching as Deacon and Jake attached a plaque to the base: "In Loving Memory of Catherine Whitney, Cherished Wife of Gerald, Mother of Josephine and Gerald, Jr., Taken from Us Too Soon."

Nina smiled at Deacon as he pushed up from the

ground and slid his arm around her waist. "Having spent some time in Catherine's head, I'm sure she would have loved this," she told him.

"Is it strange that we don't have a statue for Gerald?" Dotty asked.

Jake said, "I think he would be more pleased that Catherine is finally being seen as a loving wife and their marriage is known for the loving union it was."

They stood staring at the newly installed plaque. All in all, they had managed to escape the confrontation with Rick relatively unscathed. Nina had a mild concussion and a dislocated shoulder. Jake had some considerable burns on his hands from fighting the fire in the servants' quarters. And while Anthony had insisted he was fine, Cindy had checked his pulse and found that his poor damaged heart was racing. Deacon had demanded that all of them be checked out at a hospital and had pulled several *I donated a bunch of money* strings to have them assigned to a private suite.

While the staff quarters had suffered considerable damage, the main house remained untouched. The jewelry, save for the wedding set, which had been put aside for Dotty, had been placed in Deacon's safety-deposit box.

Dotty hung out in the hospital room all day, reading over Catherine's last diary and getting some insight into the Whitneys' final days together. For one thing, there was no second lover in the garden on the night of their first disastrous party. Gerald had asked Catherine about her recent distant behavior. She had insisted that they avoid discussing it until after the party. Gerald had told her he didn't give a damn about the party if it kept them in this state of limbo for one more moment. A frazzled Catherine had snapped at him for his lack of interest, and the screaming match had grown from there. The last diary entry showed a resolute, saddened Catherine, heading into what would be her final confrontation with Jack.

I have to explain to Gerald. I have to make him understand that Jack must be removed from us immediately and forever. There is no escaping Jack in this house. He knows it too well. There are too many nooks and hiding places for him to spy from. I won't get a moment's peace. I am going up to the dock, to wait for Gerald and explain. Everything. My part in it. My lies. Everything. I have been a fool. I let myself be fooled, if only for a moment, and let Jack exploit the weaknesses in my character.

I will never again allow my judgment to be clouded. I will do anything to atone. I will make up for my folly. I will prove to my husband that I can be the wife he deserves. I only pray that his love for me has not changed. Wish me luck, diary.

With Deacon hovering over Nina's hospital bed, worrying himself into a froth over whether she was comfortable, sleepy, itchy, or otherwise, Dotty had looked up from the diary and said, "So . . . I don't mean to say I told you so."

Deacon had snorted, fluffing Nina's pillow as she batted his hands away. "Of course, you do."

"At least we know for sure," Dotty had said, squeezing Deacon's free hand. "We know what happened to her now. We know that we came from a couple who loved each other deeply, that their lives together would have turned out very differently if Jack hadn't killed Catherine. They would have been a happy old married couple in a photo album. Of course, Gerald's fortunes might have suffered anyway, and your parents might still have turned out to be tools. But at least we'd have happier ancestors."

"Is that better?" he'd asked.

"It makes me feel better."

"And when Dotty finishes her book—which is awesome, by the way; I've read the rough draft—people will know who was really responsible for Catherine's death and why. Is it wrong that I want to have Rick charged with Catherine's murder, too?" Cindy had asked, pouring Nina a glass of water.

"No, it's natural to want someone to pay," Dotty had told her. "And Rick has been charged with a stunning array of felonies. He'll pay for the trouble he caused Nina, finally, and that restores the whopping karmic imbalance tilting her way."

"I don't know," Nina had hedged. "Part of me feels sorry for him. He wasn't in control of himself when he tried to physically hurt me."

Deacon had pushed her hair back from her face. "When you slapped me out of my strangle mood, didn't you tell me that the choice to resist was what was important?"

"Strangle mood?" Jake had asked. Dotty had shrugged.

"Yes, but we're going to have a problem if you remember every conversation we have in detail," Nina had muttered.

"Rick had a choice," Deacon had said. "Give in to Jack Donovan's influence or be a decent human being. He gave in."

Nina had nudged Deacon with her free arm. "You didn't."

"I love you too much to strangle you."

"Aw, that's so sweet."

NOW DEACON SLUNG his arm around Dotty's shoulders as the early-autumn sun beat down on their shoulders. Jake and Nina discussed the new "nonsubtext, non-Greek" statuary they were planning. Cindy was reorganizing Anthony's borrowed tools, because she couldn't help herself.

"I'm going to miss you, you know," Deacon whispered into Dotty's hair. "I've gotten used to seeing you every day. I know I give you a hard time sometimes, but, Dotty, I want you to know you can come here anytime you want. I promise. You'll always have a place here . . . on the weekends . . . when I'm out of town . . . or maybe out of the hemisphere."

Dotty dug her knuckles into Deacon's side, making him yelp.

"OK, OK, I give," he said. "But since we're talking about spending time here together, what would you think of us unveiling the house on Labor Day? I'd thought about inviting my competitors and the old Newport families for a big open house as sort of a neener-neener. But maybe we should invite my employees and their families instead. We can have one of those old-fashioned lawn parties Catherine had envisioned—plenty of good food, games for the children, and no one being murdered on the roof."

"That sounds great. I'll help plan."

When Deacon snorted, Nina elbowed him in the

gut. "What he means to say is, 'Thank you, Dotty, that would be nice.'"

"And we'll finally be able to tell people the truth about Catherine and Gerald, in the book we have planned, which should go a long way to settling the spirits and clearing up the curse," Dotty said.

"If the curse ever really existed," Cindy teased.

"Skeptical Cindy is skeptical." Dotty sighed, rolling her eyes.

"And I wouldn't have it any other way," Jake said, pulling Cindy into his lap and kissing her neck.

"Is there a chair shortage?" Deacon asked dryly as he took a seat beside Nina and threaded his fingers through hers.

"Yes, it's tragic, really, that a billionaire wouldn't anticipate this sort of seating crisis," Jake said.

"Hey!" Dotty exclaimed. "We've talked about that. No PDA. It's like watching someone make out with your sister."

"You're going to have to live with it," Cindy said. "Because it will be a regular occurrence at family gatherings, holidays, and birthdays."

"Family gatherings?" Deacon said, his voice cracking with discomfort.

"Sure, you think the five of us will be able to spend Thanksgiving with anyone else?" Dotty said. "Who else will want to sit around and talk about that time Jake almost climbed into bed with a waterlogged ghost?"

"I knew I shouldn't have told you about that. *That* has to be the memory we all relive over turkey and stuffing?" Jake asked.

"Yes," the group chorused.

Nina knew this wasn't a pie-crust promise, made in the moment by friends bonded by an extreme experience. They would be close for the rest of their lives. There would be holidays and parties, weddings and children, all together, all looking out for one another. Because who else would understand them?

"Well, since we're talking about scheduling future events." Deacon cleared his throat and knelt in front of her with an elegant silver box. Nina eyed the box—which was too large to hold jewelry—with suspicion. Deacon popped it open to reveal what appeared to be the latest-model cell phone, encrusted in tiny peridots, her birthstone.

Deacon held the phone aloft, ignoring Cindy's hushed "What the hell?"

"I have programmed all of your contacts," he said. "The phone is virtually indestructible, but if you ever break it, I will be the one to take it to the store to get it replaced." Nina lifted an eyebrow. "Of course, I would send Vi out to do it, but you wouldn't have to deal with it. You will never have to do your own tech support. I will take out the garbage, fix broken appliances, go to the post office; basically, any errand you don't want to do, I will do. Or I will pay someone I trust to do it for you."

"Really?"

"I can't bring you flowers," he said, gesturing to the garden. "You seem to be afraid of expensive jewelry. So making your life a little easier is going to be how I show you I love you, all day, every day, for the rest of our lives."

"You're proposing to me with a cell phone?" she said, her eyebrows raised.

"If you think about it, they're both long-term contracts."

"Well, how could a girl resist an offer like that?" she asked, taking the phone out of the box. She turned it on and sighed. "You put a Master Gardener app on here."

"The 'all day, every day' speech didn't get her, but a gardening app did?" Jake whispered as Nina threw her arms around Deacon's neck and kissed him, whispering "Yes, yes" against his lips.

"Everybody has their thing," Cindy told him.

Deacon turned to them. "If the phone thing didn't work, I had a mint-condition Qui-Gon Jinn action figure in my office."

Nina gasped. "You got me a tiny posable Liam Neeson? You really do love me."

Cindy shook her head, glancing at Dotty. "Sweetie, I never thought I'd say this, but out of everybody here, you may be the normal one."

Jake cleared his throat. "With all this talk of long-term commitments, do you think you might want to . . . get a phone contract together . . . someday . . . eventually?"

"Only if you plan on calling me long-distance. If and when you propose, there had better be roses and a string quartet and a clever hiding place for the very tasteful yet expensive ring. And doves."

"Doves?"

"I don't particularly like them, but I want them. So when I say yes, they can be released in a crescendo of romantic fluttering."

Jake's lips twitched at her assurance that she would say yes, but he tamped down his smile quickly. "Seems like an awful lot of trouble for a simple question."

"Well, you did forget that you dated me. A little extra trouble doesn't seem so unreasonable."

Jake slid his hand over his face. "Never going to live that down, am I?"

Cindy shook her head and kissed the tip of his nose. "Nope. But for right now, I am willing to date you anyway."

Nina helped Deacon up from his kneeling position, tucked the phone into her back pocket, and threw her arms around him. Dotty practically tackled them from behind, which turned into a group hug when Cindy joined in, squealing in their excitement over the engagement. Deacon shot Jake a pitiful look over the ladies' heads. "Little help?"

"I don't do group hugs," Jake said, wrinkling his nose.

Cindy's golden head popped up from the huddle. "Yes, you do!"

Rolling his eyes at the cloudless blue sky, Jake huffed, "Fine." He wrapped his arms around Cindy and Dotty. "Yep, this is totally comfortable."

"Have you set a date yet?" Dotty asked.

Deacon frowned down at her. "I asked her to marry me ten seconds ago."

"June 19," Nina said confidently.

"Can we let go now?" Jake asked, pulling Cindy out of the people knot.

Peeling Dotty off of them, Deacon asked, "Why June 19?"

Nina shrugged. "It was Gerald and Catherine's wedding anniversary. I can't think of a more appropriate day for us to get married."

"You want to have the wedding here?" he asked, his face splitting into a wide grin.

Nina made a sweeping gesture toward a set of flower beds she'd just turned. "Right in the middle of the memorial garden I'm planting. I think it would be nice to look out of our window every morning and see where we got married."

"So you're ready to live here, full-time?"

"Well, I think we'll need to spend some time on the mainland for business purposes," Nina said. "But yes, I think we'll be happy here, and I think that would make Catherine and Gerald very happy."

"I think the point is to make the two of us happy."

Nina giggled as he pulled her into his arms and kissed her forehead. "I thought that was a foregone conclusion."

With the laughter of friends echoing from the grounds to the eaves of the enormous rooftop, the Crane's Nest remained peaceful for the night.

Enjoy this sneak peek at Molly Harper's
next Half-Moon Hollow romance

The Dangers of Dating a Rebound Vampire

1

You never get a second chance to make a first exsanguination.

—*The Office After Dark:*
A Guide to Maintaining a Safe, Productive Vampire Workplace

THE SENSIBLE BEIGE pantsuit was mocking me.

It hung there in my closet, all tailored and boring. And beige. *"Yes, wear me to work and let all of your new co-workers know that you have no personality!"* it jeered at me. *"Look at you, all nervous and twitchy. Why don't you just bail on this job and work for the Apple store, you big baby?"*

"You are one judgmental pantsuit." I flopped back on my bed and stared at the ceiling. Ever since I'd received the "you're hired" call during Christmas break, I'd been trying to convince myself that I deserved this job. I was qualified for it. I'd gone through a particularly difficult test of my intelligence and ingenuity to get it. So why was I so nervous about my first day?

"Because, Gigi Scanlon, you are the Queen of All Neurotics," I grumbled, scrubbing my hand over my face. "Long may you reign."

Honestly, I was nervous because this job, programming an in-house search engine of vampires' living descendants for the World Council for the Equal Treatment of the Undead, meant something. If I played my cards right, this would be the only first day of work I would ever go through. The Council was known for offering attractive perks and salaries to hold on to competent human employees, resulting in lifelong appointments. And if I played my cards *wrong,* this would be my last ever first day of work because I would be dead.

"That is not helping," I told my brain, closing my eyes.

OK, if I continued this line of thinking, what would the final outcome be? Not taking the job with the Council. And then I tried to picture my sister Iris's face if I told her that I'd decided not to take the job after all. First there would be elation, and then relief, and then the "I told you sos." I really hated the "I told you sos," which were sometimes accompanied by interpretive dance.

Even after months to adjust, Iris was displeased about my employment—if thunderous expressions and muttered threats when the job was mentioned could be considered "displeased." She didn't trust my supervisor, Ophelia Lambert. She didn't trust the vampires I would be working with. She'd met and didn't trust some of the humans I would be working with. She wanted me to have a nice, safe office job that didn't involve coworkers who might drain my blood. I knew Iris felt guilty for dragging us into the vampire world years ago, and how it may have ruined me for corporate America. But honestly, her worry was getting annoying.

"You can do this. You are more than the post–glory days high school jock. You are more than Iris Scanlon's little sister. You just need to figure out what the hell that is." I launched myself out of bed, slipped into the suit, and pinned my hair into a responsible-looking chignon. I was thankful, at least, that I didn't have to deal with Iris's hair. Her dark curly hair was beautiful—especially now that she had all that vampire makeover mojo on her side and looked like a sexy undead Snow White— but I could barely handle my own heavy, dark hair. I couldn't imagine throwing crazy, sentient curlicues into the mix.

Iris and I shared our mother's cornflower blue eyes and delicate features, though I'd inherited Dad's height. It really irritated Iris when her "little sister" propped her elbow on top of Iris's head. Which meant I did it every chance I got.

Yawning, I picked up my equally practical beige pumps and checked my purse for the third time that afternoon. I'd stayed up all night, then slept through the morning in an attempt to adjust my schedule to my new hours working from two P.M. until two A.M. This was considered the "early bird" shift for vampires, and it was going to take some adjustments for my very human body clock. But at least I would see more of my recently vampirized sister and her equally undead husband.

The house, as expected, was pitch-black, thanks to the heavy-duty sunshades Cal had installed to protect them from sun exposure. Carefully, I clicked a circular button at the end of the hall and waited for the circular tap lights to illuminate the stairs.

I turned the corner into the kitchen and punched my personal security code—3024, the number of a check I bounced for a gym membership I never took advantage of, because Cal and Iris had never let *that* go—into the security pad. Before I could use my clearance to open the downstairs windows, I felt a sudden strike at my neck, the sensation of hands closing around my shoulders. I gasped as my unseen assailant yanked me back against his chest, hissing in my ear. I curled my fingers around the offending hands and dropped into "base," the stable fighting stance taught to me by the jiujitsu instructor Cal had insisted I train with for the past five months. Spreading my arms wide to loosen his grip, I thrust my hips back, knocking him off balance. Dropping to the floor, I stopped my face-to-floor descent with my palms, cupped both hands around his foot and yanked—*hard*. The force of my pull was enough to send him toppling back on his ass.

Springing up, I flicked the lights on to see my beloved brother-in-law sprawled on the floor with a big stupid grin on his face.

"Damn it, Cal!" I yelled, giving him one last kick to the ribs before climbing on one of the barstools. "What is wrong with you?"

"I just wanted to get your blood going with a pre-work reflex test," he said, pushing to his feet. "Well done, you. Your reaction times are much faster."

I threw a banana at his dark head, which of course he caught, because he had superhuman reflexes. Totally unfair. Cal had thrown these little tests at me nearly every day for weeks. Always at a different time, always in a different mode of attack. The fact that Cal had probably downed a half-dozen blood-laced espressos just so he could get up at this hour was somehow very sweet and super irritating all at the same time. I understood that he wanted reassurance that I could defend myself if necessary—and that the insane amount of time and money he spent on my martial arts education wasn't wasted. Seriously, though, I just wanted to make coffee without someone putting me in a choke hold.

But since there were no jiujitsu schools in Half-Moon Hollow, Cal's little tests were probably the most training I would get this summer.

"One of these days, Cal, you're going to sneak up on me, and I'm going to stab you with something wooden and pointy. That's not an idle threat. You've stocked my purse with a scary array of antivampire technology. If Ophelia ever decides to search me, I'll probably be fired just based on the threat my change purse poses to the secretarial pool."

"Which means my evil plan will finally come to fruition." Cal snorted. He had lots of reservations about my working for the Council, so he'd arranged for me to take Brazilian jiujitsu classes, crossbow lessons, and small-blade combat training near my college campus. The good news was I was no longer afraid of walking through the campus parking garage at night. The bad news was that most of the people in my advanced programming classes were now afraid of me, because they'd seen my knife-work gear in my shoulder bag.

"And if you manage to stab me, Gigi, I will deserve whatever pointy revenge you can inflict upon me."

"You're so weird." I sighed, catching my reflection in the glass microwave panel. "Now I'm going to have to go fix my hair again."

"It's not that bad," Cal protested. I ran into the bathroom off the kitchen and ran a spare comb through my mussed hair. Cal leaned his long, rangy form against the doorway, watching me fuss. "Iris would get up and wish you luck, but she hasn't quite worked up to daylight waking hours yet. It's more of an advanced vampire trick."

"There's also the small matter of Iris not wanting me to work at the Council office," I said, leveling him with a frank smile. "It's OK. Cal, you don't have to try to sugarcoat it for me. I know I'm making Iris unhappy."

"I don't know what you're talking about," he said breezily, following me back into the kitchen.

"Aren't you kind of old for blithe denial? Like several thousand years too old?" I asked, ducking when he attempted to ruffle my hair.

"Keep it up and I won't give you this delicious lunch I packed for you," Cal said, digging into the fridge and pulling a small, blue square canvas bag from the top shelf. I opened it to find that Cal had made me a California roll and nigiri with his own two vampire hands. I'd developed a taste for sushi at school and there were no quality Japanese restaurants in the Hollow. So Iris and Cal had watched YouTube videos to figure out how to make it for me, if for no other reason than to save me from truck stop sashimi. This might have seemed like a minor gesture, unless one considered that to vampires, human food smelled like the wrong end of a petting zoo. "You're the only human I know whose comfort food involves raw fish and rice."

"Vampires living in blood bag–shaped houses shouldn't throw stones," I told him. "And this is very sweet. I sort of love you, Cal." I kissed his cheek, something that had taken him years to accept without flinching or making faces.

"You completely love me. Now have a good first day at work. Play nice with your coworkers but don't hesitate to use your pepper spray. If you get into trouble, there's an extra stake sewn into the bottom lining of your purse. Call us before you drive home so we can wait up for you."

"Your employment advice is not like other people's employment advice."

OPHELIA DID NOT deign to visit us on our first day. My fellow recruits and I talked exclusively to Amelia Gibson, the stern vampire head of HR, while sequestered—I mean, seated—in a windowless human resources conference room decorated in "early American prison." In fact, almost everything in the newly renovated Council office was gray: gray walls, gray carpet, gray cement block, and gray laminate office furniture. Cold, impersonal, efficient, it wasn't exactly home away from home.

While the grim-looking security guards processed our security pass photos, we had to sit through the upsetting orientation videos. Most of them involved strategies for not provoking our vampire coworkers into biting us. Since I was pretty familiar with these tips—including "Lunch Break Hazards: Say Goodbye to Garlic" and "Empty Toner Cartridges: Replace Them or Die"—I spent my time studying my coworkers.

It was interesting to me that none of the programmers was older than their midtwenties. The oldest of us, Marty, looked to be about twenty-three or twenty-four. Then again, working at the Council office full-time, we would be exposed to too many of the vampire world's secrets and machinations. We would have access to their leaders. We would figure out how they managed to save enough money to survive on for centuries. That made us a liability as far as the vampires were concerned, and historically, people who were considered liabilities by the vampire community tended to disappear. Maybe sensible adults knew better than to work for vampires. Heck, maybe even vampire programmers were too prudent to work for other vampires, because there were no undead members of our department, either.

I was sort of a mixed bag when it came to vampires and trust issues. I mean, Ophelia was a four-hundred-plus-year-old vampire who looked like a teenager and thought like a Bond villain. So I was going to avoid any situation that would lead to sitting in her office . . . or any enclosed space, really. And sure, I'd been duped and supernaturally hypnotized by a vampire sent by a local supervillain to date me under false pretenses. But thanks to the hypnosis, I'd blanked out most of the unpleasant parts and only remembered dreamy scenes of teen vampire romance.

My mind wandered to the mystery vampire I'd "met" over Christmas break. And "met" was in quotation marks because I hadn't actually introduced myself. Because, well, he hardly stood still long enough for me to see him, much less speak to him. At first I thought he was a ghost. I'd barely been able to make out his facial features the first few times I saw him. And when Mr. Barely Visible finally became Fully Visible (and ho boy, was the visual nice), he'd surprised the ever loving hell out of me by swooping in, kissing me like something out of a Nicholas Sparks movie, and then disappearing.

My imaginary vampire ghost literally just vanished, which was one of the few things pre–Coming Out TV and movies got right about vampires. The undead were stealthy and sneaky and could pop in and out of view in the blink of an eye, and they usually did it when a human was mid-sentence. Which in my opinion is super rude.

The tragedy was that the hot mystery vampire had disappeared, completely and cruelly dropped off the face of the earth after giving me the most world-altering kiss I've ever experienced. It had been months since The Kiss. And despite lip-glossing for months, just in case I ran into him, I hadn't seen so much as a shadow. I was starting to think I'd imagined the whole thing, which would be completely plausible, considering my emotional turmoil over dumping my dependable, solid, and all-too-human boyfriend Ben.

Up close, my vampire had been center-of-the-solar-system hot. He'd looked like every hero in those Jane Austen movies that Iris's friends liked so much, golden hair that sort of curled around his face without being Bieberish, eyes so light brown they appeared gold, high cheekbones, long straight nose, chiseled jawline and a mouth that looked just smirky enough that you could imagine it saying some really filthy things. When I thought about meeting him again, he was always wearing a waistcoat and lounging around a stable full of fluffy, inviting piles of hay.

And that was a big part of why I didn't tell Iris about this, because that's the sort of thing for which she would mock me, mercilessly.

Of course, I didn't know if I would ever meet him again. Considering his five-month absence, I was going to guess not. Why had he even been in the Hollow? He seemed awfully Continental for Kentucky, though that really wasn't an indicator anymore as our little burg seemed to be a magnet for vampires of all origins. Miranda Puckett's boyfriend, Collin, was an excellent example. Tall, smooth, and British, I'm pretty sure that guy *was* an extra in one of those Austen movies Iris's friends liked so much.

But why had my vampire chosen me to pseudo-stalk? It would have been one thing if I'd only seen him the first time at the Christmas tree farm, but he'd seemed to follow me on several occasions. Had he known my schedule or was he just that good at guessing where I'd show up? Maybe that was his special vampiric gift: GPS. A Gigi Positioning System.

That sounded wrong, but fun.

Seeing my new (gray) office, the windowless workroom I would be sharing with my three teammates, did little to improve my concentration. Four modular desks were stuck in four corners with four shelving units. I supposed the vampires considered it "private" since we would be working with our backs to each other.

Still, this was where the perks of working for vampires came in—years of observing human weaknesses gave them enough information to know just how to lure us in. Each of our desks was flanked by a minifridge prestocked with sodas and juice we'd listed on our postinterview preference lists. Our work computers were custom-built from the fastest processors and computers available—as in "available on planet earth," not available at our local Computer Barn. And each of our chairs was the very latest in ergonomically supportive, butt-cradling comfort.

On the far wall, I spotted a console for the latest Orange Door entertainment system, complete with digital jukebox, touch screen, and four wireless headsets.

And in the corner was an enormous aquarium filled with colorful, gliding tropical fish. Ms. Gibson explained that the fish tank was supposed to "accommodate the human need for color and light stimulation without the dangers of a window." I didn't think she intended to make us sound like cats in need of a flashlight to chase, so I let it go. The tank was pretty soothing, after all.

Despite these very nice toys, we still had to pass a four-week probationary period. It was pretty sensible, really, when you considered the reliability of the average college student. It would probably be *more* sensible to give us a much longer probationary period, but we were only going to be working with the Council for a few months before we headed back to school.

Of course, the probationary period was sort of two-fold. Some of us would work freelance for the Council during the school year if we proved ourselves to be competent, trustworthy, and non–vampire provokers. We would be able to keep the cars, the salaries, and the other perks, and then slide right into full-time, post-graduation employment. Sure, it would take some of the angst out my final spring semester, but the dental plan would be worth it.

Beyond the perks, tracing vampire lineage was a challenge. It was a huge mystery waiting to be unraveled and (thanks to a freshman-year switch in majors to computer science) I was one of a very few people who had the skills to do the thread-pulling. More importantly, I would be connecting people to their families, and family was something I'd sorely lacked growing up. Sure, we had a few uncles and cousins who'd been first in line to take "something to remember" Mom and Dad by after they'd died, but disappeared like smoke when Iris and I had needed actual help adjusting to life without parents.

Iris had done her best to give me a solid, happy home life when she was human, but I felt the lack of connection to a larger identity. Of course, I couldn't exactly complain now, with the ever-expanding troop of supernatural creatures that seemed to materialize at our house at the drop of a hat. I deeply appreciated the color and chaos they brought into our lives. And if I could give that to someone else, if I could give them the family they never knew they'd been missing, I would consider it a contribution to the world.

And once the search engine was established, there

would be other opportunities to work on the vampires' secret projects. Who knew what I would see, what I could learn, where they would send me? This was the beginning of an exciting, adult life in which I could establish myself as that elusive "something more" I had yet to figure out.

We were dismissed early, but barely so, after signing a mountain of releases, waivers, and nondisclosure agreements. Most of the paperwork involved agreeing that our estates didn't have the right to sue the Council, no matter what happened. We also signed a single document in which we had to check "yes" or "no" regarding whether we wanted to be turned should we be injured on the job beyond the treatment capabilities of modern medicine. I was surprised to be the only one who actually mulled this signature over. Aaron, Marty, and Jordan all immediately checked yes. Then again, I doubted that those three had any actual vampires in their families. They'd never seen the post-turning adjustment problems, the struggle with bloodthirst, the horrible burnt-popcorn smell that lingered after vampires came into contact with sunlight. They thought it was all nighttime glamour and leather coats.

With a rather redundant warning not to discuss our nondisclosure agreement with our families, Amelia sent us home. At least, she sent Aaron, Marty, and Jordan home. She asked me to stay a few minutes because Ophelia had some papers she needed to send to Iris's business, Beeline. I stood outside Ophelia's office waiting for at least ten minutes, trying not to take it personally that I wasn't invited inside to wait or that when she finally handed the papers out to me, she just shoved an envelope out of her doorway without actually showing her face.

"Thank you," I said as pleasantly as I could, while Ophelia snatched her hand back and slammed the door.

"Company car and a clothing allowance," I reminded myself as I walked out of the employee exit, rummaging around in my purse, affectionately referred to as the Bag of Holding. "A 401(k) and a dental plan."

My keys were, as usual, at the very bottom of my purse. The parking lot was empty, but at least the humans had designated parking right under the streetlight. It was the vampire version of handicapped parking. I would take time to be offended by that once I was safely ensconced in my locked car.

I glanced around the empty lot, once and then a second time, while my heels made a quick clip-clop across the pavement. Just as I passed an unoccupied SUV, two strong hands clamped around my shoulders and yanked me out of my shoes.

I froze. I couldn't move and time stopped and all I could think was, *I'm going to die. Iris is going to deserve such an "I told you so."*

His hand wrapped around my jaw, squeezing it so hard I thought I felt the bone buckle. I pinched the panic button on my keyless remote. In the distance, I could hear my car alarm wail. My feet flopped uselessly two inches above the ground as he—at least, I thought it was a he—dragged me toward the SUV. Given the fact that I was a little over six feet tall, the guy must have been huge.

Fighting back the initial panic, I hoped, somewhere in the back of my mind, that this was another one of

Cal's tests. Calm. I had to stay calm. This was just like getting thrown around the mat by my instructor, Jason. I just had to assess what needed to be done and go through the steps. I threw an elbow back, but missed his ribs, and his grip on my arms tightened. I wrapped my leg around his, hoping to make it harder for him to walk if he planned to carry me off. I threw my head back, hoping to connect with the bridge of his nose. But I missed there, too.

My heart raced. There's no way this could be Cal. My brother-in-law would have cackled like a loon if he'd evaded a head butt. Which mean this was real.

Shit. I was going to die.

My assailant squeezed me tight against his chest and wrapped his hand around my throat, making it almost impossible for me to breathe. But he didn't say anything, which was completely weird. Vampires were notoriously chatty during violence. And he wasn't biting me, which was even weirder.

I was either being attacked by a run-of-the-mill human mugger or a remedial vampire. I wasn't sure which was worse.

I struggled, wiggling my arm loose, and pressed a button on the ugly agate brooch on my lapel, sending a cloud of colloidal silver spray mushrooming around my head. It was harmless to me, but if this guy was a vampire, he'd be allergic to silver in all its forms.

Jackpot! My vampire attacker coughed and spluttered, losing his grip on my arms as the silver did its work. I reached into my purse and grabbed the hairbrush strapped into its special compartment. The ordinary looking purple-plastic brush was another one of

Cal's security contraptions. I gripped the bristles hard enough to make a silver stake pop out of the handle. I rammed the point into my assailant's thigh. It wouldn't kill him, but he certainly wouldn't be chasing after me any time soon.

"AUGH!" he cried, letting go of my arms entirely and dropping me to the pavement like a sack of potatoes.

My knees almost gave under my weight, but I planted my feet. It was a good move, considering that all the guy's weight pitched forward on my back and I was bent in half. The hands gripped at my hair, keeping my head down. I reached back, searching for the hairbrush. I pulled it from his leg with a sizzling hiss, like angry bacon. I raised it to stab the other leg, when he suddenly shoved me aside and leapt toward the street using his completely unfair vampire speed.

"Yeah, you better run," I panted, bending at the waist so I could prop myself against my knees and catch my breath. But the slick material of my suit gave way under my sweat-soaked palms and my hands slid right off. I fell forward and, unable to catch myself, toppled face-first onto the pavement.

Ouch.

Blinking rapidly, I watched the vampire limp away. His blond hair shone almost blue in the sickly light of the streetlamps. He turned back as if he was reconsidering, and I reached into my purse for my final piece of vampire self-defense equipment, a flamethrower the size of a small canister of hairspray. And then my eyes managed to focus on his face.

"Holy crap."

Golden-brown eyes, high cheekbones, long straight nose, chiseled jawline, and a smirky mouth, the same features that had haunted me for the last five months.

Mr. Barely Visible was now fully visible. And he didn't seem to be in the mood for kissing. He was in the mood for attacking me in the parking lot and then running off into the night.

 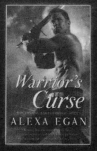